Lisa Dic... OK, FINE, T...

Lisa lives by the Devon seaside, stuffing cream teas in the gobs of anyone who comes to visit, and writing stuff down that she hopes is funny. Her first novel was the copyright-infringing *Sweet Valley Twins: The Twins Holiday Horror*, which she wrote in primary school and gave up on after five pages. Twenty-ish years later Lisa went on to be a *real author* and wrote the Novelicious Debut of the Year, *The Twelve Dates of Christmas*. In summer 2016 out popped *You Had Me at Merlot*. She's now keeping her fingers crossed that everyone will like her third paperback, *Mistletoe on 34th Street*, and that New York City gives her a free apartment near Central Park as a 'well done'.

Follow Lisa online for all her book news and Beyoncé-obsessing:

www.lisadickenson.com
Twitter @LisaWritesStuff
Facebook /LisaWritesStuff
Instagram lisawritesstuff

Mistletoe on 34th Street

Lisa Dickenson

sphere

SPHERE

First published in Great Britain in 2016 by Sphere

1 3 5 7 9 10 8 6 4 2

A CIP catalogue record for this book
is available from the British Library.

ISBN 978-0-7515-6309-2

Printed and bound in Great Britain by
Clays Ltd, St Ives plc

Papers used by Sphere are from well-managed forests
and other responsible sources.

MIX
Paper from
responsible sources
FSC® C104740

Sphere
An imprint of
Little, Brown Book Group
Carmelite House
50 Victoria Embankment
London EC4Y 0DZ

An Hachette UK Company
www.hachette.co.uk

www.littlebrown.co.uk

Dedicated to

New York City
a place that always feels like home,
especially at Christmas

And to Husband Phil,
who proposed there one winter's night

And to *Friends*!
The best TV show in the whole world × a million,
which was also based in New York City.

Part 1

Deck the hall with boughs of holly,
Fa la la la la la la la la
'Tis the season to be jolly,
Fa la la la la la la la la

5 December

2 weeks, 6 days to Christmas

❄

I grasped around, trying to find something to pull my tired body through the water yet again. So cold, so achy, such conflicting feelings as to whether it would be better to escape this hell or just die under the surface of this mud-churned lake.

And I'd *paid* to do this? In *December*? I would give anything to be a chestnut roasting by an open fire right now.

Yes, dying was definitely preferable. Goodbye, world. But then a pair of hands pushed into the squash of my butt cheeks and I was propelled through the sludge, hippo-style.

Then, finally, there was the wooden platform above me. I would live! My thigh muscles remembered they had a job to do and pushed me up out of the mud and into the wintery air, where the noise of a hundred other racers – grunts, groans, people cheering, people laughing, the odd person crying – filled my ears as the brown lake trickled out of them.

I wiped the mud from my eyes with an equally muddy arm, and stretched back to pull Kim out. She broke through the surface like Ariel the mermaid, whooping and pushing her dark curls out of her face. She slung a tiny bronzed arm around my shoulders and we trudged towards the riverbank.

'How fun is this?' she cried, just as I was about to say, 'How awful is this?'

At that point an enormous fairy wing thwacked me in the back and I crumbled down towards the freezing water again. For a second my final ever thought was, I'm going to die … who'll take my place on the stand in New York?, but Kim steadied me. The owner of the wing, a gigantic man who was also clad in a tinsel tutu, a headband and nothing else yelled, 'SORRY, LOVE,' as he picked up speed and ricocheted up the bank and off down the hill.

'Olivia, what's the rule?' Kim warned.

'No grumbling.'

'What happens if you grumble?'

'I have to sit by Jasmine at the Christmas party.' I caught my breath, finally reaching the riverbank. 'I'm not grumbling, I'm fine, this is great, I'm having the time of my life! Thank God Jasmine's not here though. Hey, where's Ian?'

Kim smirked. 'Helping Dee, back at the monkey bars.'

How sweet. 'Of course he is. And Scheana? I feel like I haven't seen her since the start?'

'Me neither.'

I peeped at Kim. 'I do have one grumble. Keep your gym pants on, it's not even really a grumble, think of it as a heartfelt request. Can I come with you to Antigua the week after next? Can I lie on the beach and be so warm I'm almost too warm? I want to feel sweat again. The type of trickly, sun-lotiony sweat that leaves an imprint on a sunlounger.'

We dug our fingertips in the mud-slide that was the riverbank and hauled ourselves up. I'd always fancied trying one of these Tough Muddy Survival events – they looked fun, like a challenge, like a whole day of camaraderie with friends. So when someone at work said they were interested in taking part in one too I leapt in, face-first. What a fantastic way to raise money for the youth centres we work with! I said. What a perfect excuse to up the company's profile in matching running tops! I cried. Relentlessly. And before long I'd cajoled together a team to enter the Fearless Freeze 10k event on December the fifth. December the fifth? The 'Fearless Freeze'? I was a colossal plonker, and now my colleagues were scowling at me every time our muddy paths crossed. But that didn't matter, they'd get over it. The important thing was that the group of teenage girls who were waiting to cheer us across the finish line would see us complete the event in one piece, strong and capable.

I pictured them waiting for us at the end, all orange Girls of the World raincoats and tinsel scarves. They were the best, coming out here to support us at the weekend. Our protégées, they'd grouped together a few months ago to make YouTube videos for us about getting involved in sports even if you don't feel good enough, and they've been big hits, driving a lot of traffic to our website. So I couldn't let them see me acting like my body wasn't capable of sliding through a few more mud patches and surviving a couple more bruises.

Urrrgggghhh, I will not admit defeat, I told myself. No matter how much I secretly wanted to. I missed sitting down.

Kim clawed her way to the top of the riverbank,

shaking her head, and we set off on a slow, tired jog. Just three kilometres and twelve obstacles to go. I was nearly there, ish. On we ran, towards our fate: a thirty-foot tiered wall, which we were expected to scale, that stood atop a hill in the distance. It was covered with people in brightly coloured, mud-soaked running tops, who were charging up and over, pulling up those behind and pushing on the bottoms of those in front. It looked like a scene from *World War Z*.

'Hey.' I slowed. 'We should stop and wait for the others; we need to help them get to the end.'

'I think if we stop now we might turn into ice sculptures. Besides, the finance arseholes have already gone on ahead. And no,' Kim said, trudging onwards and bringing the conversation back around to Antigua, 'you can't come with me; you have to see New York for both of us.'

'But New York is so cold—'

'HEY,' Kim scolded. 'What did we say?'

'No grumbling . . .'

'Besides, New York's always so fun, you're going to have the best time.'

'I will miss you though, and I hate Steve for taking you from me,' I said. 'I'm not grumbling, I'm just saying. And I don't hate Steve really, he's brill.'

'I'll miss you too,' Kim sighed. 'This'll be the first

year since starting at Girls of the World that I won't be doing New York.'

'It won't be the same without you.'

'But I am kind of looking forward to three full weeks off.'

That I could understand. 'This year has just been insane. As soon as I'm back from New York I'm not planning on talking to anyone for the whole of the Christmas break. Just me, TV and jammies.'

Girls of the World was a foundation created to promote women's rights through educating and empowering schoolgirls to be creative, be themselves, and be heard. I was part of a team of six led by the founder, Scheana, a fiercely confident woman with the most appealingly gung-ho attitude. Everyone at the foundation, men and women, wanted to be Scheana when they grew up. I was a Creative Coach, which meant I worked directly with the people we were trying to mentor. We covered everything from the administrative, logistical side of Girls of the World being out there, you know, in the world, to being the faces of the company, and meeting as many people as possible – best of all, the girls themselves.

I couldn't get enough of my job. I got to meet these young women – future CEOs, writers, scientists, artists, inventors, sports people – and learn from them, coach them on how to be who they wanted to be, not just in the future, but now as well. Encourage them, give them an outlet, celebrate them in all their weird and wonderful ways. And it was lucky that I couldn't get enough because we hadn't stopped all year. The company had grown threefold in the past twelve months thanks to sponsorship and lottery funding, and we'd been breaking our backs to keep up and make sure not a single girl, school, society or hope was left behind. Girls of the World began around six years ago, I was there from the start, when it was just a few of us visiting local schools and youth centres in London and Hertfordshire, offering mentoring and skills workshops. Now that we cast the net far wider – nationally, in fact – the resources are much vaster. We'd got apps and contributors and sponsors and now, after years of attending conferences to spread the word about Girls of the World, we were finally hoping to branch out internationally, starting with the USA.

A major, *major*, benefit of working at Girls of the World – aside from knowing without a doubt that you're on an equal pay scale – was the annual conferences where similar organisations from around the world gathered to share thoughts, ideas, seminars and listen to amazing guest speakers. The rumour-mill had been on overdrive about the potential for Emma Watson or Amal Clooney to put in an appearance at this year's New York do, the #IWasHereNYC event.

Kim was an executive in the marketing department and I loved spending conferences with her; she had such energy and enthusiasm. She could waltz into a school and convince a kid on the brink of ditching her biology exam for a smoke with the boy from the upper sixth, to not only take the exam but also to chuck the boy and become such a badass biologist that she would probably end up curing lung cancer. Kim was a miracle worker, our very own Derren Brown.

And now Evil Steve, who was actually really nice, was whisking my Kim away for a romantic Christmas break in the Caribbean. And she chose that over a work trip with me. Sigh.

We reached the wall and I (being the giant in our relationship) crouched so Kim could stand on me and pull herself up to the first ledge.

'Remind me who's going this year?' she called back, reaching her arm down for me. I didn't notice because I was too busy flailing my legs about in the air until some bloke got fed up with being kicked in the knees and helped me up.

'Scheana, of course. Abigail . . . '

'The new girl?' Kim asked.

'Yep, she's pretty nervous. Our fave: Jasmine . . .'

'Oh lord, that'll be fun. How's she being with you now?'

'The same as she always is,' I said, sighing. 'I actually wish she was that cliché of a colleague who was after my job because at least there'd be some healthy competition to it, but she's just a cow for no reason.'

'Is she ever like that with anyone else? I feel like she barely comes across our radar down in marketing.'

'I've seen her throw a strop if she doesn't get her way, and go into a total huff, but I seem to be permanently on the receiving end of her stink-eye. It's like having a third sister.'

'True story.'

Jasmine was a similar level to me at Girls of the World, and had been there nearly as long. We'd just never gelled. Sometimes we'd have an interaction in which I'd think, OK, you're not too bad, today you seem to like me, then the following day it would be back to cursory smiles and under-breath mutters.

Anyway. 'And Dee and Ian are both going too,' I finished.

'Ahh, romantic!'

'I know, I'm really curious if this'll be the year they break and just admit they're seeing each other.'

11

'You never know,' Kim grunted over the next ledge. 'New York is pretty special around Christmas. The temptation of a snog on the Rockefeller ice rink could be just the nudge they need to come clean. Jon will be there to keep you company, won't he?' she asked, all innocent.

'Subtle. Yes, he will be there, but nope, I'm still not in love with him. And as I've said a million times, if I haven't fallen in love with him yet, it's not going to suddenly happen now.'

'Mmm-hmm,' Kim agreed, blatantly disagreeing. 'Have you seen much of him lately?'

'Not since the Amsterdam conference in September.' But I had dropped him an email this week to tell him I couldn't wait for a catch-up, and to find out which flight he was on. And I really couldn't wait – like Kim, Jon was a good friend. Unlike Kim, he had a penis, which meant everyone who knew us both couldn't wrap their head around the 'just friends' part. Jon currently worked on the United Nations' HeForShe campaign, and we met a few years ago on the conference circuit after I saved myself from tripping over a poster stand by smacking his coffee cup from his hand so I could grab it. Selfless. We try to catch up between work events by going for a drink or dinner. One time we even went on the Harry Potter studio tour together, but work has been so crazy this year that I've barely had a minute to myself, so I've been a crap friend and I haven't seen him as much as usual.

We reached the top ledge of the wall (dear God it must be nearly over), and took a breather, gazing back at the obstacles. Dee and Ian's heads bobbed about in the lake, and a couple of other colleagues were reaching the wall below us.

I looked up at the sky, which was heavy with bruised clouds and getting darker by the minute. 'Do you think there's a storm coming?' I asked Kim, who was leaning over the other side of the wall, contemplating the best way down.

'Shit-wise or weather-wise?' she called back.

'Weather-wise.'

'As long as it doesn't stop my flight to Antigua it can be a total white-out this Christmas for all I care.'

And with that, the heavens opened and a blizzard to rival an Arctic snowstorm swirled around us as we ran for our lives.

Just kidding, but it did start to pelt it down with rain. I could see the finish line of this godforsaken race in the distance, and squinting through the drops I could also see the orange raincoats of my girls.

No grumbling, I told myself, for the fortieth time that day.

It was over; we'd made it. We had survived. Kim and I were freezing, but my cheering group of girls made coming across the finish line an unexpected joy.

I made a bit of a show of staggering over the line, holding Kim's hand and making sure the small graze on my elbow was dripping blood impressively. The girls, who ranged between fourteen and sixteen (though we often worked with girls as young as eight in some communities), screamed their heads off when we came through, their orange jackets flapping in the torrential rain.

'You're a superhero!' cried Maya, flinging her arms around my muddy self. At fifteen, she was far taller than me, with a classic basketballer's figure but a heart for athletics. Maya was a girl who'd contacted us a couple of years back because she had a passion for sports but it all felt so out of reach for her. She was painfully shy, and fear held her back from giving her all to her school's limited sports programme – it was all P.E. lessons and netball teams, with a real lack of actually teaching kids new skills. We worked with the school to start up some beginner groups and when Maya's confidence popped its head above water, we helped her pull herself up to the next level. She trained for and then secured a scholarship to a summer sports academy, and now that she'd honed her skills, she coached younger kids there during school holidays.

'I'm a what?' I asked, pretending there was mud in my ear.

'A superhero!' she yelled again, jumping up and down for me.

'Sorry, I didn't quite catch that … ?'

'A *superhero*,' she and the other girls bellowed at me, and I laughed.

The girls were drenched right through, nearly to the same extent as us runners, and so they zoomed home quickly afterwards. I was now thawing out under a heat lamp, cuddling a hot chocolate and wearing a Santa hat (whose Santa hat was this?). I was spending a lovely few moments thinking about how strong and brave I was, when my thoughts were interrupted by the sound of someone calling my name from outside the tent.

'Olivia! Over here. Look down a bit.'

'Scheana, what happened?' I leapt up and hobbled outside the tent, shaking the remaining water from my ears. My manager was lying, damp and bedraggled, on a stretcher. Two paramedics moved aside and tended to a dislocated shoulder while I spoke with her. This place was a warzone. Sort of.

'I think I might have broken my leg,' said Scheana

with a shrug. 'No biggie, but I think I'll be out of action for a while.'

'Bloody hell, where?'

'Lower leg, I think.'

'But where on the course?'

'On one of the big log things.'

'Does it hurt?' I asked.

'Yep, loads, but I wanted to talk to you about work.'

'Now?' I shifted my weight and I'm sure I heard either my sodden T-shirt or my rib crack. Was I starting to freeze?

'Just a quick thing. Well done on completing, by the way, you did brilliantly, I'm so proud of you all.' Scheana reached out and squeezed my hand like a person on their deathbed. 'Urgh, you're glacial. I'll keep this quick. New York is ten days today, and I'm not going to be able to go.'

I must still have had a lot of water in my ears, because I couldn't be hearing this right. 'You're not going to what?'

'I'm not going to go. To New York. My leg won't be better in time. So I need someone to take over as head of Girls of the World. Temporarily. That person needs to represent the company in New York, and try to push us forward. They'll need to be quick-thinking and a good problem solver, even with few resources. You have no idea how many little tasks befall a manager in the lead-up to a trip like this.'

'I'LL DO IT!' I yelled. 'Let me do it, I won't let you down. Can I do it?' This was the break I'd been waiting for, for so long now. I wasn't pleased that Scheana had broken her leg, and I wasn't trying to squeeze her out, but with Girls of the World growing and expanding so quickly, I wanted to be part of it. One day I wanted to be a director in this company.

'Are you sure? It's a big responsibility. I'm not talking about you opening up our first US office or anything, but that's where we want to be heading. I'd want you to get some balls rolling; it's not just about publicity this year. I want Girls of the World to have its foot wedged in the door of Manhattan by the time I go out in the Spring.'

'Consider me your go-to girl for wedging!'

Scheana hesitated 'You've had a busy year. You aren't feeling too burnt out?'

'No.' Yes.

'Because you don't know busy until you've been in charge of something like this.'

'I can do it. I've been to New York four years in a row and I want to be more involved. You focus on your recovery and I'll look after everything. I promise.' Ohmygod, could I do this? Yes, of course I could. I had to now, thanks, big gob.

'Good, I was hoping you'd say that. In that case, from now until the new year, you're the boss.'

And with that, the paramedics returned and wheeled Scheana away. I stood motionless for a moment, partly because I was now an ice sculpture, partly because I had a million thoughts whizzing around my head. I was in charge of New York. Like Godzilla! Completing the Fearless Freeze had made me feel pretty invincible, like a poster girl for Nike, so I could definitely conquer running the New York trip. This was going to be easy.

❄

I returned to the tent and squeezed my bum back onto the bench under the heat lamp, in between a snoring woman and a man who looked close to throwing up.

I was the boss . . .

Dee appeared, her long frame pink all over from the severest of workouts. 'Um, did I just see Scheana on a stretcher?'

I nodded. 'She thinks she's broken her leg. She's OK though, she's gone off in an ambulance.' I knew Scheana wouldn't want her injury to overshadow our achievement so I added, 'She says well done to everyone. Look what we just did! That was hard work but we slayed those muddy hills and slippery bloody monkey bars.'

'What about those dangling electric wires?' said Ian, staggering over to us and putting his hand on Dee's back before quickly removing it. 'I nearly gave up at that point.'

'I welcomed that,' I said, like I was some kind of Kray twin. Like a *boss*. 'The electric shocks warmed me up.'

Dee and Ian had been into each other for so long it was sometimes hard to remember that they weren't 'public'. Ever since Ian joined marketing at Girls of the World several years ago they'd been close, but despite the lingering looks, the obvious chemistry and co-workers spotting them out together at least once a month, they'd never come clean about their relationship. They clearly wanted privacy, for whatever reason, so it was an unwritten Girls of the World rule that we all respected that.

'Right, folks,' Kim said, walking into the tent with a leaflet clutched in her hand. 'It says the tear gas used under that polythene obstacle wasn't real tear gas and it was totally safe. So you're not going to go blind. Olivia.'

I blinked a few times to make sure. 'OK thanks. All right.' I took a deep breath. 'So I have something to tell you guys about Scheana and New York . . .'

9 December

2 weeks, 2 days to Christmas

❄️

I scrolled through the music on my iPhone – surely I had at least one Christmas track on here? Ah-ha! 'Let It Go' from *Frozen*; that counted. I stuck it on repeat and put my phone in the speaker dock just as my doorbell rang.

'Shit me, it's *freezing* out!' burst Kim, as I opened my front door to the sight of my friend – all pink nose and frostbitten fingers – peering out from a mummification of long woollen scarves.

She pushed me aside and unpeeled the layers down to a moderate covering of two woollen jumper dresses, tights, snow boots and a hot water bottle. Kim was always cold, even in the summer, so December in the UK was her Everest.

'I'm not even sorry about choosing Antigua over you any more,' said Kim, shaking out her curls. 'It's definitely true what they're saying; winter is coming.'

'Let it Jon Snow . . .' I muttered with a smirk, leading Kim to the living room. She stopped short.

'I thought we were having a Christmas party?' she demanded. 'Where are your decorations?'

'It's only you and me.'

'I don't care! It's our annual Christmas get-together, you insisted that we have it at your house, and you don't even have a tree. I'm sorry, are we homeless? Christmas isn't Christmas without a muthaflippin' Christmas tree.'

'You'll be in Antigua over Christmas – good luck finding a Christmas tree there!' I looked around my sparse maisonette. 'Besides, there are decorations.' I wafted an arm past a tea light on a side plate, and a bottle of Baileys.

'*Argh*.' Kim started furiously wrapping herself back up in her four-hundred-foot scarf. 'First of all, Antigua will have a lot of Christmas trees, and second of all, we have to go and get *you* a Christmas tree. Now.'

'But . . . but . . .' I looked around. 'We can't go out now, the pizza's in the . . . freezer.'

Kim wasn't listening. She was already nose-deep in

my hall cupboard. She emerged and lobbed an armful of coats my way. 'Dress warm, come on.'

'You're so hardy since we did the Fearless Freeze,' I muttered.

'I'm so hardy, Tom Hardy called and wants his name back.'

'You're so tough, you should marry Hilary Duff.'

'You're so weird, you should grow a beard.'

We stepped outside and the cold air hit me like a dry-ice bucket challenge. The dark street twinkled as wet pavements reflected the strings of Christmas lights between lamp-posts. I stamped my feet and blew into one clenched fist while I locked my door. 'Where exactly does one buy a Christmas tree at seven p.m. in the middle of London?'

'No idea,' said Kim, marching off down the street before whizzing around. 'Actually, of course I do. How do you feel about artificial trees?'

I shrugged, unsure what the right answer was.

'Shrug? That's all you give me? Your mother taught you better than that, lady. Always have an opinion, am I right? And *everyone* has an opinion on real versus fake. Do you like them full, real and nice-smelling, or perfect, symmetrical and low-maintenance?'

'Are we still talking about trees?'

'Of course.'

'I think I prefer fake. Because I kill things.'

A passing teenage boy darted a shocked look at me, clutched his phone tightly and ran away.

'Plants, I kill plants,' I clarified loudly. 'And therefore probably trees.'

'Then answer me this,' said Kim, a big smile creeping onto her half-hidden face. 'What do you think of when I say "Christmas shopping"?'

'Oh!' I knew this. 'The scene in *Love Actually* with Rowan Atkinson and the necklace and the dried flowers and the cellophane.'

'Nope.'

'*Serendipity*? You know, when they meet over the last pair of gloves?'

'No, something not from a Christmas movie.'

'January sales?'

'What is wrong with you? John Lewis, of course!' We reached the tube station and within minutes were squeezed among commuters and tourists, roasting like turkeys under all our layers.

Kim was still rabbiting. 'The snowman . . . ? The bear and the hare . . . ? The penguin . . . ? The man on the moon . . . ? Liv, you're killing me.'

'Oh, I remember the penguin advert! He wanted a girlfriend or something, right? But I don't recall the other three.'

'Well, congratulations on being the most cold-hearted person in Britain. Have fun on your throne of stone.'

Just as I was beginning to really dislike the feeling of another passenger's roll of wrapping paper jabbing me in the eye, it was time to untangle from the tubers and spill out onto soggy Oxford Street. It was still heaving at this time in the evening, with a mash-up of every Christmas song from *Now That's What I Call Christmas* booming from open shopfronts.

Kim marched us both up the street, weaving expertly like a Dickensian street urchin through the crowds while I bumped my way past the other shoppers and generally made everyone hate me. We stopped in front of John Lewis.

'Merry Christmas! Get in,' Kim commanded.

❄

I'll admit it; John Lewis is lovely at Christmas. Immediately I wanted to buy the entire Scandinavian winter lodge-style fake living room just inside the entrance, from the faux-fur blankets to the log tea light-holders, to the snow-sprinkled reindeer ornaments. I was just reaching for a miniature frosted tree in a pot when Kim slapped my hand away.

'Nope. You need to think bigger. A Christmas tree

is going to light up your whole apartment; nay – your life.'

Off we trotted, accepting some of the most wonderful swag of the year from smiling sales assistants en route: a mini mince pie, a shot glass of Prosecco, and a spritz of the latest Philosophy festive scent. By the time we reached the wonderland that was the Christmas department, I was humming along to 'Something Stupid' like I was Nicole Kidman herself. 'How about this one?' I stopped at the first tree, an all-white creation whose spray-painted branches glistened with glittery faux-snow. I liked it.

Kim scrutinised. 'It's a bit ... blank.'

'I like it; it would go really well in my apartment.'

Kim gave me a pointed look that I ignored. 'You know it's only up for about a month, right? We're not shopping for one to coordinate with your curtains.'

'Nope, I like this one.' I fingered the branches, willing myself to feel Christmassy. I squeezed my eyes shut for a moment, trying to tug back memories from my past of twinkling, traditional ... no. I fell short at the recollection of a Santa in board shorts passing out slices of watermelon. I opened my eyes and focused on the tree, which *was* pretty. 'I like the glitter, I like the fake snow, and I like the thought of buying those three-for-two baubles in red and covering it with them.'

'Like blood spatter on a white wall.'

'Oh. I'll get the gold ones then.'

'If that's what you want . . .' Kim caressed the fluffy branch of a gigantic fake-fir that could have been lopped down from beside Santa's house in Lapland.

'I want the white one; you don't own me.' My strange affinity with this blank, emotionless tree was something I could mull over with my therapist, Squidgy Rabbit the stuffed toy, sometime. But for now I smiled at my friend, who succumbed to my will, and helped me pull the box out of the rack, giant-Jenga style.

Kim looked up at me halfway through the task. 'You will make time for Rockefeller, won't you?'

'Well . . .'

'That's one Christmas tree you aren't allowed to not care about.'

I pictured the towering tree in my mind, an icon of New York at Christmas, and Kim's favourite place in the world. 'I don't know, I'm sure I'll go past it . . .'

'Liv, you have to go, it's our place.'

'But you won't be there, so it won't be the same anyway. And I don't know if I'll really have time—'

'*Make* time. Please. I know you're one pair of fingerless gloves away from Ebenezer Scrooge but we've been on the New York trip together every year, and

26

every year we go and see the Rockefeller Christmas tree together. This year you have to go for both of us.'

I looked down at my fingerless gloves. Was Kim right? Was I a Scrooge at Christmas? No, I had nothing against Christmas. I liked Christmas, it's just that I didn't really … care about it. I'd watch a Christmas movie if it was on TV, and drink Baileys if it was on offer, and exchange a couple of presents with my family sometime around the big day, depending on when they were all free to get together. But when you grew up in a family who escaped for two weeks of winter sun every Christmas, and were now spread out around the world, traditions and 'proper Christmases' were a bit off the radar.

Christmas to me was a very lovely, very welcome break from work, from my team and the pressures that come with any job. It was a time to catch up on sleep, and it was the milestone between September and March where I gave my legs a shave.

'I'll go to Rockefeller,' I said. 'I'll send you a photo. If I have time.'

'You're the boss this year, you'll have time.' Kim heaved the box out and, satisfied, trotted off towards the counter while I armed myself with gold baubles (and one box of the red) and a red reindeer to go on the top, because I'm not keen on fairies and the stars looked too prickly.

All of a sudden I felt weighed down, not with Christmas decorations but with responsibility. There was no getting away from it – I *was* the boss this year. The past few days had zoomed by, a speeding train of note-taking, decision-making, list-creating and what felt like endless phone calls with Scheana. I'd boarded the train without really thinking: was I ready for this? Could I handle it? It was beyond exciting, but one niggling thought had been popping up ever since the day of the race ... was I out of my depth?

❄

On the tube ride home, I trumped that passenger with the awkward rolls of wrapping paper from the previous journey, by forcing everyone to angle themselves around my Christmas tree box as if it were Baby Jesus himself.

'I love my Christmas tree,' I sighed, hugging the box. I'd show Kim who was Ebenezer Scrooge.

'Praise the lord!' Kim said, embracing me with one arm. 'And you promise you'll go and see Rockefeller?'

'Sure. This is my first ever Christmas tree, you know.'

Several eavesdropping passengers side-eyed me like I was mad.

'No way.'

'Seriously. We've never had a family Christmas at home, and I've never had one in my flat before.'

'Not even with Kevin?'

'Nope.' I looked away, the best I could, without staring straight into a stranger's set of boobies. It still smarted to think of him, even after all these years. 'We always had Christmas separately, and we never decorated because all the spare money went towards ...'

'... the house fund,' Kim finished for me, putting a much-needed end to that little conversation. Kim thought for a moment, whilst sucking on a complimentary John Lewis candy cane. 'I think New York is going to be really good for you. This year, especially. You've never been the one making the decisions about the schedule and planning the itinerary. You've always been told you have to do this at this time, and be there at that time, and have dinner at Ristorante el Blandezvous while making small talk with delegates.'

'This isn't going to be any different – I still have to make sure everyone does the same job.'

'But *you're* in *charge*. You want to have a business meeting over hot chocolates at the top of the Empire State, you can do it. You want to hold a feminist rally on the Central Park ice rink: just book it, honey pie.'

I gulped. All I heard was 'business meeting', and suddenly the fear of everything being On Me hit me again.

I had to make sure Girls of the World's presence at the #IWasHereNYC conference was a success. I looked at my new tree: Christmas would have to wait.

❄

Back at the flat we decorated my tree, Kim dancing along to a particularly festive episode of *Strictly Come Dancing* I'd recorded (she'd declared my one Christmas song as 'crap') while I found myself thinking about not wanting to think about Kevin.

Trickles of regret ran through me as I hung the gold and red baubles. I shouldn't have spent this much on a fake tree. A little part of me bitterly thought that Kevin wouldn't be worrying about spending money on his Christmas tree. Well, he didn't need to save up again from scratch, did he? A part of me broke loose to wonder about him and where he was now. Did he find the big house in the country after all? Was he with someone else? Had he grown up enough to treat her better than he had me?

I looked at my flat. It wasn't even *my* flat; getting out of rented accommodation seemed like such a faraway dream.

Luckily Kim trod on my toe at that point while cha-cha-cha-ing backwards. 'What are you standing still for?

It's Christmas, you're going to New York next week, *Strictly*'s on!' She saw my face and stopped. 'Are you OK?'

I stood back and observed the tree. It did look nice. 'I'm not sure I should have spent money on this tree.'

'Don't start that again.'

'But—'

'Nope. You're in a good job; you're well behaved, like, *all* the time with your money. You can treat yourself once in a while; it's hardly going to make an inch of difference.'

'I'm not well behaved all the time. I like living wild. I ate a muffin for breakfast the other day, and it wasn't even the breakfast kind.'

'What kind was it?'

'Blueberry. They were reduced in Sainsbury's.'

'That's still the breakfast kind.'

I shrugged. 'Fine. Maybe I'll just move in with you and Steve. I'll be the spinster in your basement, the bitter old Miss Havisham in your granny flat. The fly in your ointment.'

'That's the Christmas spirit I was after,' Kim said, and twerked against me (I think she was trying to jive) until I snapped out of my bad mood and started twerk-jiving with her.

11 December

2 weeks to Christmas

I swung back and forth on my desk chair staring into the darkness outside, the phone glued to my ear. It was only five p.m., but the bleak midwinter had me straining my eyes to see anything other than the blur of office lights in the building opposite.

It was the day of our office Christmas party, and my last day in work before I left for New York on Monday. There was Christmas music playing through the receiver in one ear, and Christmas music playing from someone's computer in the other ear. All around me my co-workers were opening sneaky bottles of wine, unplugging printers to make room for their straighteners and tottering to and from the loos to put make-up on. The entire scene was like something from a Boots advert, and I couldn't help but smile. Especially at the mismatch between those who had gone for all-out sparkle and those who'd opted for grotesque Christmas jumpers instead.

Dee wandered over, her lipstick a little smudged. She motioned elaborately to see if I wanted a glass of wine but I shook my head. I still had a million things to organise and alcohol would wash them all straight out of my head.

'We're all leaving soon,' she stage-whispered. 'Shall we wait for you?'

'You guys go for it. I'm on hold with the conference venue in New York; I might be a while.'

'Is there anything we can do?'

'No, no, you go and have fun. Have a drink for me.'

Ian appeared through the door, and Dee said, 'OK, see you there,' and scarpered.

I watched her walk past Ian, their eyes meeting. They smiled tenderly at each other and he nodded his head in low-key approval of her sparkling outfit.

Still on hold, I went back to my to-do list. Now that I was in charge, this year my list was much longer than it had been in previous years. I still had to print out everybody's tickets, insurance details, conference information and other paperwork, in duplicate. I had to confirm the rooms and the flights, for everyone. I had to collect up all the promotional material that was currently in piles around me. I was waiting on the venue to confirm they'd received the material Kim, Ian and the rest of the marketing department had sent over. And there was more, so much more.

Suddenly Kim materialised in front of me, a vision in sequinned black shorts, black tights, and the ugliest Christmas jumper I'd ever seen. She snatched up my to-do list. 'You're still on hold?'

'Yep.' I nodded. 'New York is busy today.'

'Hang up and come to the party with meeeeeeeee.'

'I can't. I want to but I can't. I have a million things to finish.'

'You look tired,' she said, emptying the remnants of a box of Quality Street on to my desk.

'Thanks. I am a bit. There's just ... lots to think about.'

'But you're going to New York on Monday, yaaaaaay!' she said, attempting to inject me with a Kim-boost.

'And then I get to come home and sleep, yaaaaaay!' I answered and immediately felt ungrateful. One of the many things I loved about my job was the travel, so it was unfair of me to act like it was such a nuisance. I shook myself out of it. 'It's fine, I'm fine. You go and enjoy the party for me. Make sure someone snogs somebody on the dance floor, OK?'

'You don't think you'll even make it later?'

'I promise I'll try. And if I don't I'll catch you at some point over the weekend.'

She gave me a look that said she knew full well she wouldn't be seeing me tonight, and then started dancing backwards towards the door. 'All work and no play makes Olivia a right old pissflap,' she warned, before disappearing into the night.

Pissflap I may be, but this pissflap had things to do.

Damn it, I was still on hold and now I needed to piss.

❄

Nearly two hours later I wearily entered my flat, my eyes squeezed shut and a giant yawn on my face. My arms were full to the brim with stuff I needed to take to New York. I dumped everything, along with my handbag, shoes, coat and bra, in a heap in the hallway.

I just need a ten-minute rest, I thought, and then I'll go back into town for the party. Just ten minutes ...

I noticed that there was a light on in my living room; I could see it under the door. I didn't leave a light on this morning, I know I didn't. But ... did I? Maybe I did. I'd been so preoccupied lately.

I opened the door super-slowly, and saw a person crouched in the corner of my living room. I sucked in a silent lungful of angry air. The grubby little Artful Dodger! Their hands were fiddling about with all my stuff and pocketing all my worldly goods, I bet!

Affronted, and before I could think better of it, I reached out, thwacked the first thing my hand touched with all my might, and sent an object catapulting across the room towards my intruder. It turned out to be a Christmas bauble, which did nothing more harmful than bounce off their back. In comparison my white Christmas tree toppled and crashed by my feet, branches falling everywhere and the rest of the baubles springing to safety and rolling across the floor.

The intruder looked up and pulled off their baseball cap. Underneath was a late-teenage girl with a pouty mouth, dark, thick eyebrows (the kind I think you'd call 'on fleek') and eyes identical to mine. My little sister Lucy blinked at me.

'What. The actual. F—'

'What the actual *indeed*, and don't you swear at me!' I pointed a Christmas tree branch at her.

'I swear *all* the time.'

'What are you doing back, and in my house? What's happening?' The branch was still outstretched. Was I overtired or was she really here? I felt tears tickle the backs of my eyes – I wasn't used to having an emotional reaction to seeing my family members, but she was back and safe and . . .

Lucy reached me and, taking the branch from my hand and throwing it on the floor, wrapped her arms around my neck. I laughed and hugged her back, broken out of my confused state. 'When did you get back from Peru?'

'This morning,' she yawned, stepping back. 'I tried to call your office but your phone was engaged all day and the receptionist was getting pissed at me.'

'Why didn't you call my mobile?'

'I lost my phone somewhere around Machu Picchu.'

'Lucy . . .'

'Relax, whatever. I'm here now and we're together again.' She came in for another 'shut-up' hug. 'I'm so glad you're finally home; can you make me some food?'

❄

Needless to say I had no real intentions of heading back in for the Christmas party, and Lucy turning up provided the perfect excuse. The truth was that once I'd stepped in through the door the thought of going back out to see work people, the same people I'd be spending four whole days and nights with next week, instantly lost any appeal. Instead, I whipped up a quick spag bol while Lucy told me about her latest three-month backpacking adventure around South America.

'I brought you something back.' She reached into her bag and pulled out some bright, stripy Peruvian cotton trousers.

I put down my wooden spoon and reached for the trousers, holding them up in the air. They would fit Barbie better than they would fit me. 'Lucky these look the perfect size for you and your Cara Delevingne body; maybe you should keep them. Also, they smell of weed.'

'Well I don't know how that happened, but I guess I'll hang on to them then.' She took them back with a smile and watched me return to cooking.

'What?' I asked, feeling her eyes scrutinising my back.

'Why don't you travel more?'

'I travel all the time; I'm going to New York on Monday.'

'Yeah but those are work trips. I'm talking about fun trips.'

That tiny bubble of bitterness appeared deep inside me. I didn't want to get into this now. 'I can't, I have to save up.'

'Ah yes, for the house in the country. You know, you

really don't seem like someone who would want to have a house in the country.'

'Of course I do.' I chucked some seasoning into the sauce and steered us back to safer ground. 'But anyway – my work *is* fun!'

'Are you seriously telling me you'd rather be going to New York for work than with friends, or on your own?'

I hesitated.

'You hesitated.'

'OK, this *one time* I would rather be going on my own, but only because it's been hard work organising it this year, and I'm kind of exhausted, and Kim's not going. The pressure is really on me to do a good job, and I want to show that I can. So, I'm excited, but I'm looking forward to it being over. I'm looking forward to coming home. Jon'll be there though, which'll be good – he's my friend who works—'

'Yes, I know who your friend Jon is; you talk about him all the time.'

'I hardly ever see you!'

'He's the dude in that photo you keep in your bed-side drawer, isn't he? For when you're lonely at night?' Lucy sniggered and dodged out of the way of a piece of spaghetti I lobbed at her.

'That photo is only in there because people kept making comments when I had it out on the table. It was a fun day, I like the memory.' The photo was taken by Kim the first year I knew Jon. We were on bikes in Amsterdam and she captured the exact moment *after* we'd been smiling at the camera: a lorry had trundled past us on the narrow cobbley streets and came within a whisker of the front of Jon's wheel. His face is contorted in surprise and panic, and even though my bike was behind his and completely out of the way, I had screamed and promptly fallen off. The camera had caught me mid-fall.

I served up dinner and we walked back to the living room, where Lucy took the best sofa spot.

'So what's with the Christmas tree? You're into Christmas now?' she asked.

'I'm just . . . experimenting.'

'That's what all the girls say,' Lucy cooed, kicking a few baubles out of her way and into the corner of the room.

I looked around at the mess, wanting to move the conversation on, and a thought reoccurred to me. 'How did you get into my flat?'

'You don't need to know.'

'But—'

'Great pasta. I haven't had pasta for yonks. Thanks, sis.'

My sister is a sneaky mofo. 'And what were you doing

huddled in the corner when I first came in? I thought you were a burglar.'

'A burglar? Stealing what, your paperbacks? I was using your laptop but I couldn't be bothered to get up off the floor. I'm tired. What do you think about Thailand for Christmas?'

'For who?'

'Me.'

'Just you?'

'It might be just me initially but I'll meet people in the hostels.'

'*This* Christmas?' She was leaving again? I felt that overtired, weepy feeling creeping back in, which is so unlike me – so unlike any of my family.

'Yes.'

'But you just got back,' I whined. 'Christmas is like, two weeks away. When would you leave?'

'I don't know, I'll stay around in this country for a few days, I need to do some laundry. Maybe middle of next week?'

'How long would you be gone for?'

Lucy pondered this for a moment. This was clearly another whim; she rarely actually sits down and plans anything. 'Just four weeks or so, I'd be back for the family get-together. So? Thailand?'

I sighed, thinking. 'Is it safe?'

'Is anywhere in the world safe any more? What's the point in worrying about it? But yes, I'm not dumb, I would stay safe. It's sunny, and that's the main thing.'

My family and sunshine. It was like they were allergic to December in the UK.

'Why don't you go to Miami and visit Anne?' I said. My other, older, sister Anne was living in the States as an hotelier and it felt like ages since any of us had seen her. 'Miami has lots of sunshine. And the women wear those teeny-weeny bikinis ...'

Lucy nodded. 'I do like that. But why would I visit Anne? She's coming home in January. Why would I waste a flight on going over there?'

'Maybe you'd want to spend Christmas with her?'

Lucy chuckled and stuffed in some more spag bol.

'Or you could go to Lanzarote with Mum and Dad? Or is it Tenerife? Where are they going this year ...?'

'Yeah, that's going to happen,' scoffed my sister.

'How do you even have any money left?' I wished in that moment I didn't always bring things back to money.

'I work in the hostels when I'm out there – cleaning, doing whatever. It's only really the flights I need to cough up much for, but I usually save up a small amount between each trip. I think I can just about afford these

Thailand flights. Yes. I'll book it tonight.' She nodded. I had to give my sister props – she was decisive.

'Don't you think it would be good to save up just a little bit for the future?'

'Nope.'

'Right then.'

She saw my face and knew to tread a bit carefully. 'I'm alive now, aren't I? Why should I only think about Future Lucy? Present Lucy just a-wanna have fun. Future Lucy can kiss my ass.'

It was time for me to snap out of this mood and feel happy for her. My money troubles weren't her money troubles and vice versa, and the thing I've always loved the most about Lucy is her wanderlust. 'Thailand does sound nice. I bet they have amazing cultural shows, and those beaches where it's just you and the turquoise sea and the white sand. You could do yoga. A yoga retreat!'

'Oh my god, why are you the most boring person in the world? Yoga? Cultural shows? I'm nineteen, not fifty-nine.'

'One: being in your fifties is not old. Do you think Nigella Lawson or Michelle Obama are too old? And two: I'm not boring, you're boring. Why don't you stretch yourself while you're there?'

'No, no, no, I'm not doing a yoga retreat.'

'Not that kind of stretching. I mean, creatively.

Enrich your life. You should write poetry! Or write those inspirational quotes that go on beautiful pictures that everybody loves.' Maybe *I* should go to Thailand? One day.

'You are literally the last person in the world to still love those.'

'No I'm not. Or you could do *volunteer work*!'

'Or I could just hang out and enjoy the place I'm in. Travelling is enriching in itself – you told me that. I am literally being a Girl of the World.'

She had me there. 'Well, OK. But when you're back I want to hear all about it. And just promise me you won't do anything you don't want to do out there.'

'As if I would!' My sister started fist-pumping and chanting, 'Screw the system, screw the man!' so I rolled my eyes at her and went back to gobbling my pasta.

12 December

1 week, 6 days to Christmas

❄

'I know you've told me a hundred times, but which island are you and Dad going to be on this year?' I shouted towards the living room from my bedroom, as I entangled myself in a bright red polo-neck jumper before finally tossing it aside. I was packing for New York, or throwing my entire wardrobe onto the floor, whichever way you wanted to look at it.

'Tenerife, with the Gladstones and the Coyhamptons in Maggie's beach hut,' my mum said, coming into the room and stepping over a pair of discarded knee-high boots with holes in the soles. She and Dad were visiting from Bradford on Avon for the day. She handed me a mince pie and I raised my eyebrows. 'I didn't bake them, but since this is our only pre-Christmas get-together I thought I'd better pick something up from M&S.'

Lucy was sitting on my floor picking through my discarded clothes for anything she might want to pinch to take to Thailand, then discarding the poor things for a second time. A loud snore came from the other room, which meant Dad was merrily fast asleep, clearly enjoying watching the old Western he'd found on TV.

My dad, Roland, a pharmacist, is one of those very serious men with a neat beard and a straight moustache that made hipster facial hair want to try harder at school. Despite spending every winter in the sun he most certainly will be wearing a shirt, thank you very much, but if you're very lucky it might be short-sleeved and then you could have a tantalising glance at his crinkled elbows. He thinks his own jokes are hilarious, but he just doesn't quite get anyone else's, but it's forgivable when he does unexpectedly brilliant things like chop his own hair into a wonky disaster in camaraderie with me when I did the same and couldn't stop crying. (This was in my mid-twenties.)

The lady of the house – my mother, Gina – is all muumuus and paintbrushes, though it's part of her character even more than her lifestyle. An artist, she paints constantly and likes to look the part of boho earth goddess, but then shops in Waitrose because she can't be bothered to grow her own veg. She can't bear cooking but loves eating, and joins every single human rights march she can make it to.

I had no idea who Maggie or the Coyhamptons were, but the Gladstones were family friends who only started winter-sunning with a vengeance when my sisters and I stopped going on holidays with our parents. 'Does Tenerife have black sand?'

'Yes, I'm going to create some wonderfully dark abstract paintings.'

'Mum, you're on holiday, not demonstrating oppression. Give yourself the week off.'

'That's what your father said. He can't wait to – and I quote – "not have to see those incompetent knobjockeys for ten whole days" but what you all don't understand is that if you have colleagues like mine you don't want to be apart from them. You love them, like family.'

'Your paintbrushes are not your family, Mum,' Lucy said from the floor, trying to unpick the squirrel embroidered on the front of one of my jumpers.

'Well at least they want to spend Christmas with me,' she teased, lightly. 'Sure you girls don't want to come along this year? I think there's space on the plane. There's certainly space in the beach hut – it has nine bedrooms, plus a snug, plus a grotto pool modelled on the Playboy mansion, apparently.'

'Gross, no thanks,' said Lucy.

Mum tinkled with loud laughter, which woke Dad up with a snort, and I cringed, and put a miniskirt back in the wardrobe. 'What kind of a beach hut has those things?' I asked. 'Aren't beach huts just sheds with pastel paintwork?'

'Come with us.'

'I can't.'

'We'll pay.'

My heart sank a little. 'It's not just about the money ...' It was a lot about the money. I still had a long way to go to build up that house deposit I'd lost. Not *lost*; that I'd had taken away from me, by my husband-to-be, Kevin. And I wouldn't get back my New York expenses until the new year. *And* I'd just spend forty-five quid on a fake bloody Christmas tree (which, now rebuilt, looked really nice again and I'd named it 'Mary Christmas', not that I'd told Lucy). But on top of that I just needed to be on my own for a couple of weeks. I needed a break. From everything. From everyone. And from trying to right the world. Maybe I'd finally try that yoga video by

Jennifer Aniston's instructor. Or maybe I wouldn't, let's be honest. 'My New York flight gets back only a day or two before you leave, it'll just be too much of a rush.'

'We don't leave until Christmas Eve. If you change your mind, just say the word.'

I hesitated, holding a black dress up against myself and looking at my reflection.

'Don't take that,' Mum said.

'Why?' I asked, surprised. It was hardly risqué – this dress was practically Amish.

'What is it you always say? If you have to think about something it's not meant to be?'

I went back to studying my reflection, thinking about how wise I was.

'Come here,' Mum said. 'We've got you something.'

'Did you get me something?' Lucy was suddenly alert.

I lolloped close behind as she walked out of my room. 'You got me something? Like a Christmas present?'

'Of course like a Christmas present, and no, Lucy, I didn't get you anything yet because up until all of five minutes ago I wasn't aware you were even back in the country. Roland, wake up.' She slapped his legs and he opened his eyes and glared at us and then glared at the Western movie, and then glared at us again. But it was

OK, he wasn't cross with us; some people have resting-bitch face, my dad has resting-glare face.

'I got you something too,' I said, panicking. My eyes flickering around my flat until they settled on an un-burned candle.

'It's not "Love" again, is it?' Mum asked.

'What's wrong with love? Everyone likes love ... OK fine, I'm a bit late with shopping this year, but I was going to pick you out some things in New York and give them to you in January when Anne visits. Sorry. I have a tree.' I showed them Mary Christmas again.

'The problem with Christmas trees—' My dad started to launch into one of his long-winded stories but Mum stopped him with a Look.

'Here you go.' Mum handed me a small box.

'What is this?' I asked, lifting the lid. Nestled inside the box was a ring with diamonds and emeralds encrusted all the way around. 'Mum, are you asking me to marry you?'

'This is my engagement ring.'

'WHAT. THE ACTUAL. F—'

'*Lucy!*'

Memories flooded back of being a little girl and holding Mum's hand for what seemed like hours, twist-ing the ring around over and over again, watching the stones catch the light and glint under the conservatory

lights. Mum hadn't worn this in years. I'd almost forgotten it.

'When I started painting it kept getting so mucky
that I decided to put it away and keep it safe, and
stick with my sturdy old wedding ring instead,' Mum
explained. 'It's been sitting in this box for far too long
now. It could do with a clean but I just didn't have time
to take it anywhere.'

Dad smiled at me, then closed his eyes again.

'It's yours now,' Mum continued firmly. 'To do whatever you like with. It came from Tiffany's so it might
be worth a bit now, if you wanted to sell it—'

'No!' I jumped in, snapping the box shut and clutching it. 'No way!'

'Now, I'm just saying, if you decide that you want
mon—'

'Nope, nope, nope, I am not selling your engagement
ring. I'm going to look after it so much. Thank you.'

A look of relief washed over Mum's face. She reached
over and reopened the box, which was still in my hand.
'Good. But if you're keeping it don't keep it hidden
away in this box for another twenty years. Wear it.'

'On my ring finger?'

'If you want. Your ring finger isn't the property of
some future boyfriend. Wear it on whatever finger you
like.'

In fact, when I tried it on, it was loose on my ring finger, but it looked nice on the middle one next to it. I held it up to the light, watching it twinkle.

'It looks lovely on you,' said Mum, and Dad let out a grunt of agreement without opening his eyes.

'I'm going to take such good care of it. I won't take it to New York.' I started pulling it off my finger.

'Oh, do take it to New York, she'd love to go home.'

'She?'

'A diamond ring should be a she, don't you think?'

'It's not something I've ever thought about, actually.' I paused, something just occurring to me. 'Wait, so it's a Tiffany ring from New York?'

'That's where we got engaged.'

I felt awful for having forgotten all of this. I really needed to pay more attention to my parents' stories – this was their history, *my* history. 'Tell me the story again?' I asked.

Mum settled onto the arm of the sofa and put a hand on my dad's shoulder, who reached up and rested his own hand on hers, still half asleep. I remembered how Kevin always used to reach for me in his sleep and I felt fondness at the memory. But, as usual, it was iced with the tang of resentment that I just couldn't scrape off.

'It was the height of summer and we were on a road trip with the Gladstones,' Mum began. 'Well, with Bette

Gladstone, who was called Bette Archer at the time and her spotty boyfriend whose name I don't remember. She'd split up with Bill for the summer to sow some wild oats, but realised a couple of weeks in that this new boyfriend was about as wild as a field of mud and her oats were better off back on Bill's pastures.'

Mum paused to shuffle in closer to Dad. 'I digress. So we'd driven down that morning from Rhode Island to Manhattan and it was such a hairy drive into the city that we all went for a drink at the Rainbow Room as soon as we had checked into the hotel. One drink turned into several Long Island Iced Teas and before we knew it your father had taken me up Fifth Avenue, into Tiffany's, and proposed right there in the middle of the shop!'

I laughed. 'Did you get a round of applause?'

'More than that, we got the VIP treatment – a glass of champers which I refused because I suddenly felt like I needed a really strong coffee.' Mum reached for my hand and studied the ring on my finger, a smile on her face. 'I couldn't take my eyes off that ring. I just kept peeking at it every moment I got. It is lovely, isn't it?'

'It's beautiful . . . are you sure you don't want to wear it again?'

'Oh lord no, it's been off too long, it won't fit my big mummy hands now. And it looks lovely on you. You wear it from now on, if you want to, then it will be like we're spending Christmas together,' she teased.

'Since when did you get all sentimental about Christmas?' I asked. 'I thought we were having Christmas in January, when Anne's home. Isn't that still the plan?'

'It is, my love, I was just kidding.' Mum stood up and Dad flopped down sideways onto the sofa and woke himself up with a start. 'If you don't want to spend December the twenty-fifth getting a bikini wax with Marge Coyhampton and me, that's your loss, but I don't really blame you.'

'Anne is going to be so angry I got your ring.' I smiled. 'Lucy seems to be over it.'

Lucy was back in front of my laptop looking at pictures of full moon parties in Thailand. 'If I wore jewellery like that it would be lost within, like, a day,' she declared.

Mum nodded. 'And Anne has already said that she's getting, in her own words, "our cold dead corpses to hand over to that Body Worlds exhibition she's obsessed with", so the least I can give you is my jewellery before I'm turned into a mannequin. Now, who wants another tea?'

I squeezed in next to Dad, New York packing forgotten, and nudged him playfully with my shoulder. 'I love that you bought a Tiffany ring for Mum and proposed on a total whim.'

He yawned. 'It wasn't a whim,' he said seriously, quietly. 'It just took a bit of Dutch courage. I would have proposed to your mum anywhere in the world from the day I met her, and I still would.' And with that he shut his eyes again and went back to sleep.

Mum beamed, I twisted the ring on my finger, and even Lucy smiled to herself.

❄

Later that night I was forcing Lucy to watch *Miracle on 34th Street* with me. I was wondering if I, too, just needed to *believe*.

Halfway through, shortly after Lucy had got bored and left to meet up with some friends at the pub, I gasped, stopped the film and called Kim. 'I am The Worst.'

'Pardon?' she asked, pots and pans clanging in the background.

'Have you seen *Miracle on 34th Street*?'

'Of course, I'm not dead inside. Let me guess, you haven't?'

'I'm watching it now.'

'The old one or the new one?'

'The old one. I think. The one with David Attenborough.'

'Richard Attenborough, and that's the new one. The old one's in black and white.'

'Oh. Anyway, I'm watching it and I'm noticing a theme with these Christmas movies: *A Christmas Carol*, *Scrooged*, this. There's always a grumpster who doesn't like Christmas. Am I the grumpster in our lives over the festive period? Am I the villain? Am I the Alan Rickman?' I gasped. 'Am I the secretary?!'

Kim's laugh tinkled down the phone then I heard her tell Steve everything I'd just said. 'She reckons she's the Grinch,' she tittered before coming back to me. 'Firstly, bravo on the *Love Actually* reference, I was beginning to suspect you'd never seen that all the way through either. Secondly, *A Christmas Carol* and *Scrooged* both focus around the same grumpster, and thirdly no, you aren't a grumpster, you're just ... misunderstood.'

Hmm. I'm not sure that's what I was going for.

'Look,' continued Kim, 'you are perfect just as you are, you don't need to celebrate Christmas or even like Christmas, you just need to enjoy it however you can, because if the only thing you're looking forward to about Christmas is the break from work, you're basing your life too much around work.'

I thought about this for so long that I heard her

put the phone down on the side and start dishing out dinner.

'So I'm not ruining Christmas for everyone around me?' I eventually called down the receiver.

Kim came back on the line. 'Nope, you haven't ruined Christmas. Remind me when you fly?'

'The day after tomorrow. Monday. You?'

'Tomorrow, midday.'

'So soon! Call me from the airport?'

'Of course. Night-night, Jack Skellington.'

'Who?'

'Never mind.'

We hung up and I checked my clock. It was nearly seven thirty in the evening and I still had Kim's Christmas present here. I was usually so organised but my life felt chaotic at the moment, so I hadn't taken it over. It was a small, festive travel kit – Santa-patterned flight socks, a tartan sleep mask, a cosy soft grey wrap and some special edition Christmas jelly babies. As a last-minute addition I plucked a small white branch from my Christmas tree, and tucked it under the ribbon.

Leaving my house I walked straight into the lightest of snowfalls. Tiny, snow-bunny-soft flakes drifted down and floated about in the breeze for a while before settling onto the pavement and melting.

It was about a twenty-minute walk to Kim and Steve's house from mine, and as I trudged along, past window after window with Christmas trees glittering behind them, I found myself counting down again. Two more sleeps, then four nights in New York, then back here and I was off until January the fourth. I yawned. I couldn't wait to get home.

I reached Kim's and for a moment thought about peering through their window, watching a happy scene and singing 'The Christmas Song' in my head, pretending I was in a Christmas movie, but decided not to be creepy.

I put the present down on the doorstep and cracked open the letter box. Kim lived in an actual house – not even a flat – like a proper grown-up. She had a *letter box*; I know, right?

'*God rest ye merry gentlemen let something blah blah blaaaaahhh!*' I bellowed towards her living room.

'Bloody hell, what was that?' I heard Steve yelp.

'That's my little rehabilitated Grinch!' said Kim, thundering to the door, which she flung open and we hugged each other as if we were lovers about to be torn apart by war.

'Don't leave me for Antigua, I'm not rehabilitated yet,' I grumbled into her dressing gown.

'I don't want to go to the Caribbean with a stupid

58

boy, I want to go to New York with you and get married at the top of the Empire State Building.'

'Hey ...' called Steve from inside.

I pulled back. 'Don't you dare get married on a beach in Antigua. *Don't you dare.* As maid of honour I forbid it!'

'Are you mad? I would never. Come in, it's freezing out there and this rain is making my dressing gown soggy.'

'It's not rain ...'

'Is it snowing? STEVE, GET OUT HERE IT'S SNOWING!' She padded out in her slippers and looked up. 'It's a Christmas miracle.'

Steve appeared at the door and greeted me bashfully, aware that he was partly responsible for swiping Kim away from me this Christmas.

'You see this, Steve?' I waved my hand about. 'Snow. Maybe it'll stop your flight and you can't take my beloved away from me.'

'I think even British airports can handle more than this little lot; it's not even settling. Sorry ...'

I moved over to hug him. 'I'm just kidding, Stevey-boy, have a marvellous time, and a very Merry Christmas. And take a lot of care of Kimberley, remember she's a bit of a scaredy-cat on flights.'

Kim thwacked me with her little fists. 'Lies! I'm not

scared of anything. Anyway, booze is free so I'm just going to go into a Jack Daniel's coma and wake up on the beach. Are you coming in—'

'Nope, I just wanted to drop this off and leave you to it.' I handed my gift to Kim and then squashed it between us in another hug. 'Don't get eaten by a shark or sliced in half by a jet ski because I love you so much.'

'OK, don't you fall off the Empire State or burn your tongue on all that diner coffee. Say hi to the Rockefeller tree for me. And I'll bring you back your Christmas pressie from Antigua – sarongs and rum, as requested. Love you heaps.'

I left them both on the doorstep, Kim clutching her gift in her dressing gown like a grown-up Orphan Annie.

It felt nice to give people gifts at Christmas, in the snow, and tell them you love them. There was no denying it. I felt warm and a little bit holly-jolly. Though as I looked up at the sky and those fat snowflakes I couldn't help that strangely cynical side of me from wondering, if it wasn't December, if it wasn't Christmas at all, wouldn't I still feel exactly the same way?

13 December

1 week, 5 days to Christmas

❄

I woke up and thought: New York tomorrow. Tomorrow! Despite the organising, the hard work, the worries and anxiety and desperation for it all to be over, excitement popped in my chest. I love cities, and (after London) New York took the crown. I couldn't wait to see it again. I loved the ridiculously tall skyscrapers, the steam that pouffed out from vents on the street, the glittery pretzel carts, the food. One day I'd visit it properly and do all the tourist things, but even just being there – walking to and from the conference centre, using the subway, seeing the skyline – was enough to make me feel part of Manhattan.

And I wasn't the only one excited.

Bundled in PJs, slipper socks, slippers, a sweatshirt and a dressing gown, I wandered across my flat to open the curtains and looked at my phone. A message had come through at six a.m. from Jon.

Can't wait to finally see you again tomorrow!
Best Christmas present ever ☺

He was so sweet.

Opening the curtains I saw that a small amount of the snow from the night before had settled, like someone had dusted icing sugar on the Victoria sponge that was London. The sky was full of thick white clouds and on the street below people were slip-sliding about on the frosty paths, their laughter drifting up to my ears.

I did a yawn at the window and padded back into the warmth, making a coffee, and pulling out my to-do list.

My eyes were soon drawn back to the window. The main thing on my list, the thing that really mattered, was getting everyone to New York, and getting them home again before Christmas (and not letting Girls of the World collapse on my watch). So if the UK was going to choose this year, out of all the years, to have a white Christmas, I could only hope nobody would let it snow until we were home.

14 December

1 week, 4 days to Christmas

❄

My bags had been packed and waiting at the door for twenty minutes, but still I had a final zoom around to check everything was in order. Passport packed, plug sockets switched off, Sky+ set to record the *Strictly* final, Kevin McCallister not still upstairs asleep ... No no, that's just in *Home Alone*.

I threw a final pining look at my sofa and then turned to leave. Five days, then you're all mine. I'd been spending so much time at the office lately, I was a little homesick before I'd even left for the airport.

Gloves on, I stepped outside and locked my door, my

breath puffing out in front of me. The air was cold – really bloody cold – but my big sensible parka made me feel like Smug of the Century as I passed a group of teens in trendy, thin leather jackets. I dragged my suitcase carefully over the pavements, which felt hostile and icy under my boots, pulling it around a discarded bottle of Prosecco covered in frost.

I'd be in New York soon. Would I drink Prosecco? Would I make a good impression, and be as charming and confident and strong as everyone needed me to be? So much could come out of being the one in charge on this trip. It could be the cold, or it could be the adrenalin, the excitement, that made my hands shake.

Stopping outside the tube station to rifle through my paperwork for the fortieth time – yes, all booking confirmations for all team members were present, as expected – I was interrupted by my phone jangling with a text message. It was my sister, Anne.

> Hey! Mum says you're flying to the US today. Let me know when you get here – you should come to Florida! Much warmer than NYC. Are you getting the parents Christmas presents?

That was pretty typical Anne. I'd sent her several emails, texts and Facebook messages about flying over today, but things go in one ear and out the other with her. Anne has lived in Miami for seven years and is as independent as they come. And even though she infuriates me sometimes with lack of organisation, I couldn't wait to see her when she visited in January; it had been too long.

When was the last time our family was all together? Maybe last January? No, Mum was away at a painting retreat last time Anne was home, and Dad didn't come on our trip to Miami the summer before. So it had been a couple of years since we'd all been together, I realised with a shock.

No time to think about that, or reply to Anne's message now, though; I had an airport full of fuckwits waiting for me. Sorry, I mean *colleagues*.

❄

In the days that had passed since the Fearless Freeze, everyone's bruises had faded and their aches and pains were all but forgotten. The only sufferings now were hangovers from the Christmas party, which just wouldn't shift, and Jasmine's chronic face-like-a-slapped-arse. I'd done my manager duties for the time being, getting them all through check-in and security successfully, explaining to them *one more time* about the rules surrounding expenses, and now we were at the gate killing time.

I looked around the huge terminal at Heathrow. Holidaymakers were getting into the Christmas spirit thanks to the free-taster spirits in the Duty Free, an oddly relaxing panpipe carols medley played on repeat across the speaker system, sleepy children clutching reindeer slippers and carefully wrapped gifts stared out of the windows at the aeroplanes, and couples, full of festive cheer, loitered, giggling, outside the window of the Tiffany's store.

I had my nose stuck inside a paper cup, breathing in the aroma of my spiced hot chocolate. I looked up at the large HSBC black and white panorama of the New York skyline. See ya soon, sis, I thought. Although in reality, I'd barely be any closer to Anne once I was across the Atlantic than I am now. But being on the same continent felt nice. I wondered what she'd be doing right now, and over Christmas Day this year.

'Jingle bells, Batman smells ...' a familiar, deep voice sang softly behind me.

I pulled my gaze from the skyline and turned to face one of my favourite people in the world, a huge smile on my face. Hello, my friend, I thought.

Jon stood there, tall and lean and familiar in every way, dressed in faded jeans, a teal jumper and a large coat that looked toasty warm. His brown hair was a bit longer than when I last saw him, and just thick enough that it all shifted direction if he ran a hand through it, or tucked his fingers in like a comb like he did when he was thinking. His face was open and warm, like a cartoon bear, with big brown eyes, moo-cow eyelashes, and two different smiles depending on what he was smiling about. Smile one was large, wide and showed all his teeth. It crinkled his eyes and he looked delighted, like he was on the brink of laughter. Smile two he used when he was listening, or thinking, and his lips would curl in, giving him soft, round cheeks.

He greeted me with his delighted smile, and pulled me towards him into a bear hug. I breathed in the smell of his woodsmoke-scented wool coat. 'Please tell me you're on my flight,' he begged.

'BA0173, the one fifty-five.' I pulled back, pointing at my gate, and he groaned.

'Damn you, BA! I'm on the one that leaves at five past one. Can't you just switch with Carl? Come on – airlines aren't very strict about things like people getting on the right plane.' Carl worked with Jon, and was a notoriously awful travelling companion. If he wasn't snoring or throwing up, he was talking about bus timetables.

'Actually, you know what I could do?' I leaned in

conspiratorially. Jon listened intently, eyes sparkling. 'I could run at the woman on the boarding gate and knock all her boarding passes in the air, then just point to someone up ahead and tell her it's my dad—'

'—and she'll let you right on the flight! Yes, that works, I saw it on a documentary sometime about some kid who got lost in New York?'

'Exactly. Now if I could just find my Talkboy . . .'

Jon laughed and pulled me into another big bear hug. He was very touchy-feely today and it felt so cosy that I squirrelled in closer to him. He looked around the rows of seats, scanning the faces of the families, the business people, the weary travellers. 'Wait . . . no Kim?'

'No,' I sighed over-dramatically, unintentionally flashing a glum look at my colleagues. 'She's on stupid holiday in stupid Antigua with her stupid fiancé.'

'Is he really stupid?'

'No, he's lovely, I'm just bitter because I'm stuck with this lot, without her here to keep me sane.'

'Hey, you're stuck with me too, remember.'

'That's true. And I'm not being fair, these people are fine. Pretty much.'

Jon followed my gaze. 'So who's with you this year, boss?'

Boss. It still sounded very odd to my ears. 'How did you know?'

'I heard it on the grapevine. Congratulations. So you're in charge this trip? I like it.'

'It's only temporary . . .'

'Hey, if one of your girls got woman of the match, or won a writing competition, would you tell her to play it down because her glory might only be temporary?'

'You're right, I wouldn't. OK fine. I'm the boss, bitches.' Hmm, it still sounded a bit alien coming from my mouth. I tried a 'boss' stance like Beyoncé does when she stands on stage, hand on hip, but this parka was just not letting me feel it. 'Anyway, this year I have, as part of my entourage, Ian and Dee—'

'Have they . . . ?'

'Of course not!' I laughed. 'And that girl there on the phone is Abigail, she's new. And she is all the emotions – I honestly can't tell if there are more tears of excitement about seeing New York for the first time or tears of sadness at leaving her boyfriend behind. And finally . . . *Jasmine*.' I sneered instinctively upon saying her name.

Jon's eyes opened wide. 'You let her come? That's very Good Samaritan of you. Or bonkers.'

'Sometimes, just sometimes, I put the personal development of my team members before my own personal feelings. Plus she was already booked on when I took over from Scheana, so I didn't have much choice.'

Jon sniggered. 'You'll be pushing her off Trump Tower within three days, development shnevelopment. So which one is she?'

'The sour-faced one, texting.'

'Oh her! She's pretty.' Jon looked down at me, amused.

I gasped at his betrayal. 'Oh she's pretty, huh?'

'Yeah, maybe I'll get to know her.'

'You know what, you should. She's a peach. I think she could make you really happy, assuming you didn't want to keep your balls. In fact, I'll set you up.'

'Thanks, buddy, that would be great.'

'You'd be perfect together.'

'I know.'

'Why don't you get married and have her babies?' Despite myself, I was starting to get annoyed.

'I *should* have her babies; imagine how adorable they'd be.'

'I'll see you at the wedding.'

'Ohhh, actually, you're not invited . . . '

'No?'

'No . . . she doesn't like you.'

'*Judas!*'

Jon laughed and turned his back on Jasmine, gazing on me once again. 'Which one of them are you sat with for the flight?'

'None of them. I booked the seats myself and just happened to not be able to squeeze us all in together.'

'Clever! So just you, hey? Billy-no-mates?'

'I have my favourite kind of friends with me, present company excluded, of course.'

'Ahh, the books. What have you brought this time around?'

I opened my handbag to reveal three paperbacks, a mix of genres, all based in New York. I'm a bit of a bookworm, and reading was one of the things I was looking forward to catching up on during my weeks off when we got back from the Big Apple. My only condition for travel reading was that the books have to be set in the place I'm visiting.

Jon peered inside, his breath tickling my hair. '*The Interpretation of Murder, Sex and the City, Catcher in the Rye* – good choices. Which are you going to start with?'

'I'm thinking the *Murder* one. It might give me some good ideas in case my team prove too much to handle on this trip.'

Suddenly, I became aware of conversation around us dulling. People were staring at the TV screens set up around the departure lounge, showing BBC News 24. We looked up to see a weather woman standing in front of a map of the UK that was covered in dark cloud and snowflake icons.

'... *Strong winds and freezing temperatures could well bring a white Christmas a little earlier than Santa would have planned. We now join Bethany Weatherstorm at Heathrow airport.*'

Everyone seemed to move at once as hundreds of commuters abandoned their bags, just like all the posters around the airport tell them to (not!), and pressed themselves against the windows. Of course, the glass looked out over the runways, and the newscaster was standing among taxis outside the entrance to the T5 departures entrance, but that didn't stop anyone.

I raised my eyebrows at Jon and we tittered about how ridiculous people were being, before rushing over to join them. Outside, the sky had darkened so that it appeared to be almost the evening rather than the middle of the day. To my left I spotted Abigail staring at the bruised clouds with worry, twiddling with her necklace.

'Back in a mo,' I said to Jon and edged my way through the crowd, over a coat and a teddy bear and a fallen carry-on suitcase. 'Hey,' I said when I reached Abigail. 'How are you doing?'

She turned to me, a forced smile on her face. 'I'm fine, just, you know, hoping we're not going to die.'

'We're not going to die. Get down from there.'

'From where?'

'That ledge you're on. There's no point in climbing up there and waiting for the worst when everyone's saying to stay inside.'

She pointed at the sky. 'But we do have to go outside. Into that.'

'Good point. But let's just listen to the TV for a moment and find out what's going on.'

We turned to the screen, where newscaster Bethany's hair was blowing about in the wind. '... *and officials are saying that while there are no disruptions to service yet, overnight conditions could worsen, and travellers are advised to arrive at the airport in plenty of time.*'

'There you go, see!' I said to Abigail, jovially. 'We'll be in the big NYC by the time any of this is a problem.'

Abigail nodded and stared and nodded and stared. 'I have to go and call my boyfriend.' And off she zoomed.

I walked back to Jon.

'Everything OK?' he asked.

'Just making sure that if they weren't nervous enough already, my team are now terrified of the weather reports.'

'The weather's nothing to worry about – I just asked some of the ground staff and they said flying conditions were fine at the moment.'

'I don't think it helped that I basically said, "Hey,

74

don't worry, it's not like we have to go outside! Oh, wait ... '"

Jon laughed and we looked back at the TV, where the news had moved on to a different story involving politicians and underwear. I zoned out. What if there was a problem in the air? What if the plane had to be diverted to Quebec? What if everyone in my team died? Except me, and then I had to tell all their families? And what if they then all blamed me, because I was in charge, and I didn't stop them getting on the flight? Oh, I was the worst manager ever!

A soft flick on the top of my head startled me out of my panic. 'Hey!' I laughed, turning to Jon.

'I said your name at least three times, but you seemed to be spiralling into some inner monologue. Are you wishing the flight had been cancelled?'

'No, no, no ... well yes.'

'You can do this, you're a natural.'

'I know I can really, I think I'm just a bit burnt out, it's making my brain all floppy.'

He gave me a knowing smile, one that calmed me instantly. 'I've got just the cure. Do you have snacks for the flight?'

At that moment, an announcement came over the tannoy. 'Ladies and gentleman, we will shortly begin boarding British Airways flight 0177 to New York's John

F. Kennedy airport. Would passengers in rows forty to fifty-five please come forward with your passports and boarding cards ready.'

'That's me, I've got to go,' Jon said regretfully, slinging his holdall over his shoulder. 'I cannot get the window seat again and climb over Carl. Here, take half.' He pulled a giant crunchy almond Toblerone from his duty-free bag.

Toblerone! 'I couldn't possibly, you're a growing boy.'

'You have to, take it.' He heaved and puffed and shredded the wrapping. '*Gah, Toblerone*, why do you have to show me up for the weakling that I am?' Eventually the bar snapped in half, and Jon thrust it into my hand and with a swift kiss on the cheek and a 'see you on the other side', he headed towards the gate.

I watched him fling the other half of the chocolate into his bag and rush towards Carl and a few other familiar faces from the HeForShe office. Carl grinned widely at Jon, his flight buddy, and I watched as Jon put aside his grumbles and returned Carl's smile with a welcoming one of his own. He turned his head and grinned at me one last time, mouthing a goodbye, and I mouthed one back.

I held my half a Toblerone close (*no sharing*) and went back to my mishmash of colleagues, who had all, bar Abigail, returned to their seats and were looking so bored you'd think they'd been waiting for four years.

Jasmine looked up from her nails, briefly, with raised eyebrows. 'Who was that weirdo?'

I bristled. 'He's not a weirdo, he's Jon. He works on the HeForShe campaign, and we've been friends for years.'

'He looked needy as hell to me.'

What's that supposed to mean? I thought. 'He's not needy at all.'

Jasmine gave a *yeah, right* look that made my blood boil. Hold it together, Olivia. Let's not chin her one in the middle of the terminal.

I rolled my neck around. More coffee. That was what I needed – a big, frothy, creamy latte. And I had just about enough time to grab one and catch fifteen minutes of peace and quiet before our flight was likely to begin boarding. Even the thought made me feel more zen.

I got up and fished my wallet out of my carry-on bag, asking Dee to keep an eye on the rest of my things, and was about to head to the Starbucks kiosk when I spotted Abigail back by the windows again.

I looked at the espresso machine, puffing out plumes of steam like an inviting little train willing me to come on board. And I looked at Abigail. Coffee, or colleague?

Myself, or others? Being kind, or not giving a flying fudge? One more sniff of the air in the direction of Starbucks and I turned and made my way to Abigail, suppressing a sigh.

'Still not feeling this weather?' I asked, gently.

'You're going to think I'm so ungrateful,' she said in a low voice. 'I really am excited about seeing New York, and going to the conference, I just ...'

'You know, once I was trying on a swimming costume in Next, and it didn't fit *at all* – one of those ones with cut-out side bits that basically drew circles of shame around my muffin top – and I was at a critical point in the trying-on process. Tucking my granny pants up under the costume to see what my booty looked like. So I'm leaning forward, hand shoving excess fabric basically up my bum, flesh *everywhere*, and some kid yanks open the curtain. And he laughed. He shouted "Big fat bum!" like a warning alarm to the rest of the store, and before I could get my hand out of the back of the costume and close the curtains I felt like I had a hundred shoppers' eyes on me.'

Abigail blinked.

'My point,' I continued quickly, 'is that bad things can happen anywhere, anytime, when you least expect them. So there's no point in worrying in advance.'

'Oh.'

Perhaps I'd overshared. Hmm. Perhaps it was time to reel it back in and try another angle. 'The first time I went to one of these conferences on my own, I was so convinced the plane was going to crash and I would die alone that I took a Tamagotchi with me for company. And it wasn't even the nineties; it was like, five years ago.'

'What's a Tamagotchi?'

'Oh, never mind. The point of that story was not to worry about going on your own, because you're *not* on your own. You're with us. And you're sitting with Dee. And nothing bad is going to happen, mainly because we're talking about it, and bad things can't happen if you've already spoken about them because people aren't psychic.'

'But I bet all the people—'

'Let's not worry too much about the science behind that theory. Are you just nervous about the flight, or is it anything else?'

Abigail was silent.

'Coffee for your thoughts?'

'Huh?'

I pointed towards Starbucks. 'I'll buy you a coffee if you tell me what's bothering you. Maybe I'll be able to help, rather than just tell stories that I'm not sure are quite hitting the mark.'

Abigail followed me to the counter and selected a hot chocolate while I went for that latte, because a latte with a friend in need is still better than no latte (even if it's not as good as a latte alone). I took a sip. *Mmm*, I love you a latte.

We strolled slowly back to the window with our drinks, me waiting for Abigail to open up. A few slurps of chocolate in and she did.

'It's not so much that I'm nervous about travelling on my own. I mean, I am. I've never been on a flight on my own before. But it's more about ... about ...'

'About your boyfriend?'

'Yes.' She blushed. 'Am I being really obvious? It's just that he and I haven't spent a night apart in a really long time, and I think I'm going to miss him a lot. I'm worried I'll be all jealous and paranoid about what he's getting up to.'

'Does he give you a reason to feel like that? Has he done anything shifty before? Do you want me to kill him? Because I'm in my thirties which means I'm very wise and I *think* we're allowed to kill twenty-something punks once we women are in our thirties.'

Abigail laughed, wetness balancing on the window ledge of her lower lid. 'I'm not sure that's true.'

'No? How sure?'

'Pretty sure. But no, he's basically the perfect

boyfriend, I don't think he'd cheat on me in a million years, I'm just worried that I'll turn into a crazy monster. Urgh, you must think I'm such a fifties housewife.' She surreptitiously wiped her eyes, which I pretended not to notice.

'Of course I don't. Everyone's entitled to their emotions and feelings. Being in love doesn't stop you being a feminist. It's a good thing actually – you obviously have the same respect for him as a man as he does for you as a woman. It's all about equality.'

I was beginning to think I should have my own talk show. One where I help and motivate people. We could have a Girls of the World TV channel. I could be Oprah! Moreover, this coffee was nice.

'Also,' she continued; so I hadn't quite solved the issue yet, 'also, I feel a little bit bad, because we always said we'd go to New York for our honeymoon.'

'You're engaged?' I spat. She was only twenty-three!

'No, I'm only twenty-three! But, don't tell anyone this ...' She leant a bit closer, as if any of the other passengers would have given two hoots. 'If he asked me I'd say yes, and I have this teeny-tiny feeling he might ask me this Christmas.'

'When do you turn twenty-four?' I asked. 'I mean: yay! So you really are looking forward to getting back to him.'

'Yep.' She nodded.

'Then just think of this as a research expedition. Scoping out all the places you want to go with him in the future. Would you like me to make sure you have a rubbish time on this trip?'

'No.' Abigail smiled. 'Thanks though. Are you married, Liv?'

'Nope.'

'Do you have a boyfriend? Or girlfriend?'

'Nope and nope.'

A blush stained Abi's cheeks. 'I'm sorry, that was really rude, and nosy. I didn't mean to pry.'

I downed the rest of my coffee. 'It wasn't rude, unless you were implying there's something wrong with not having a partner?'

'Not at all!'

'Then it's not rude, it's just a question. Like, "Do you watch *Orange is the New Black*?" or, "How many lamps do you have in your house?" I'm not keen on relationships.'

'No? No. Me neither . . .' Abigail was still blushing, lost for words.

'Liar.' I smiled. 'And by the way, I do watch *Orange is the New Black*, and I have five lamps in my flat, FYI, which is a bit ridiculous really because it's only got three rooms and I try and save electricity by only using two of them.'

'Two rooms or two lamps?'

'Two lamps.' Awkward silence. 'How many lamps do you have?'

The tannoy crackled at that moment and up leapt seventy per cent of the waiting passengers, lobbing laptops in bags and coats over shoulders. Toddlers were grabbed by the ankles and boyfriends were laden frantically with a million travel pillows. The stampede towards the gate was Anglophiled by speed-walking as opposed to running, and silent determination instead of shouting.

Being the Most Well Behaved Girl in the Airport, I hung back, scolding (silently) these people – they all had reserved seats! There was no need for this madness!

'Ladies and gentlemen, thank you for your patience. We'll shortly begin boarding British Airways flight 0173 from London Heathrow to John F. Kennedy airport in New York City, and today we'll be calling you to the gate by your row number. Please take a seat until your row number is called. If your row number has not been called and you approach the gate I'm afraid you will have to wait. Please only come to the gate when your row number is called. *Row number.*'

About three people left the hoard while the rest

stood stoically, celebrating themselves for their selective hearing.

'So are you feeling OK about the flight?' I said to Abigail as we walked back to the others. 'SIT,' I ordered, a little gruffer than intended, to Jasmine who was leaving the group to join the crowd.

'Yep, I'm OK. Thank you,' Abigail replied.

'Sorry about the swimming costume story. Not a nice mental image for you there.'

'No problem. I'd all but forgotten . . .'

We edged away from each other. I think enough had been said.

'What time do we get to New York?' Dee asked, as if it wasn't written on the boarding pass in her hand.

'Twenty-five past five, New York time,' I said.

'So what's that UK time?' asked Ian.

'That would be nearly ten thirty.'

'How long is the flight?' Jasmine said, looking towards the plane as if it was as boring as a number ninety-three bus.

'Seven and a half hours.' Un-grit, you naughty teeth . . .

'Do you think we get a meal on the plane?' asked one of them, as they merged into one big FAQ page on the BA website.

'Yep.'

'What meals?'

'Probably lunch.'

'Will there be chicken?'

'There usually is.'

'I don't like chicken.'

'Then have the pasta.'

'Hmm.'

'We'll now be boarding rows forty to fifty. If you're sitting in rows forty to fifty, please approach the gate now. If not, please bugger the buggering hell out of the way.'*

*I paraphrase.

'That's us,' said Abigail to Dee.

'Me too,' added Ian. And Jasmine turned to follow them. Her version of a big smile and a 'me too!'

'Are you not sitting with us, Olivia?' Abigail turned back.

I put on my best pained look. 'No, unfortunately I couldn't get five seats near each other, so I'm right up in row twenty-one. Don't have too much fun without me! See you on the plane! Byeeeee!'

I sat back down and inhaled. *Ahhhhhhhh.* Peace at last. I tapped my carry-on bag, feeling my thick books inside. Books are the best. They have nice covers and loads of words, and they don't ask anything from you other than your enjoyment. Soon, my pretties.

Ten minutes later I was on board, shoehorning my bottom into my window seat on row twenty-one, far far away from my colleagues. Now I don't know if you're aware of the science behind aircraft, but I believe I'm correct in saying that when airborne you are 'without time zone', and it is officially legal to eat, drink and sleep at whatever time of day it happened to be. Ten a.m. flight? Have a wine, whydontcha. Just eaten din-dins at the airport and boarded an eleven p.m. aeroplane? Sure, why wouldn't I have dinner number two and start a movie now? And just because you just left the UK at lunchtime doesn't mean it isn't the *perfect* time to get out your blanket and pillow and have a snooze.

Midday-shmidday. I ripped into my plastic-coated pillow and blanket, and plopped my ginormous Jed Rubenfeld book on my lap before the plane had even left the ground, because I am in fact ninety-two years old, in spirit.

I opened my tome and curled myself into the uncomfortable pillow-against-window set-up. But then I felt a tap on my shoulder. A shoulder tap this early on was unlikely to be a complimentary glass of merlot, but I lifted my head anyway, only to see Jasmine looking down at me, eyes of ice.

'Nobody told me I'd be sitting in the middle seat.'

I bristled. Perhaps it's a skill, something that would be useful if she ever took a career as a barrister or something, how everything Jasmine said sounded ever so accusatory – something to make the listener feel stupid, or like they'd missed doing something important. She was a toughie, because she was a frosty, stroppy cow who went against everything Girls of the World stood for.

'If you'd checked in online yesterday you may have been able to pick your own seat. I did say that in the email.'

'I didn't see the email.' She sighed. 'It's fine, it just would have been nice if someone had mentioned it, that's all.' She stared sulkily at my window seat. 'I get quite vommy in the middle seat.'

'Me too. Here, have my sick bag.' Oh hell to the NO, lady, there was no way I was about to give up my seat for her.

'I might need more than one,' she fumed, so I punched her in the face.

OK, I didn't, instead I said as pleasantly as I could manage, 'That's all I have, I'm afraid.'

Without another word she stropped off and I was just about to open my book's cover again when Dee slid into the seat next to me.

'Oh, Dee, I think someone's sitting there, he's just finding somewhere for his bag ...' I pointed at a middle-aged man who seemed to be getting further and further away as he searched for some space in the overhead lockers.

'I just wanted to check something with you about the schedule,' she said in hushed tones. 'Did you say we were going to be busy every evening?'

'We don't have any plans for tonight, but we arrive around five thirty New York time, which will feel like ten thirty p.m. to us. So by the time we're out of the airport and at the hotel, I think most people will just want to hit the sack. Tomorrow there are day-one drinks and the cultural performance at the end of the conference and I thought we could all go out to dinner after. The second day we have the networking and the movie screening, and then the last day we have the gala dinner. Then we fly home the day after. So we do have plans every evening, but there'll be a bit of free time here and there, and I don't think the gala dinner on the last night will go on too late because some people will be heading home that evening.'

Dee was nodding, her mind whirring. 'OK, OK, I hear you,' she chirped. 'So we'll make the most of things – you know, of New York, while we can. Gotcha, thanks, Olivia, forget I was even here.' And with that, off she flew.

It was also Dee's birthday the day after tomorrow. I hadn't forgotten.

By now, my seat-mate was back and after a few polite exchanges about the weather and the in-flight movie choice, we settled back ready to ignore each other for the next seven and a half hours.

The take-off was surprisingly smooth and before long we'd ascended up and through the thick, watery clouds. Above us the sun shone in all its glory amid a bright blue sky, and the clouds became a blanket of fluffy snow beneath. My mind turned to imagining spending a 'traditional' Christmas, snowbound in a log cabin, stockings hung above a fireplace, Wham! wandering about throwing snowballs at each other and then shaking it out of their mullets . . .

I tapped my fingers on my book. I bet Jon's Christmas would be just like that. He was a Christmas jumper-and-carols type of man. Staring out of the window I wondered how ahead of us his plane was. What was he doing right now? Was Carl bothering him? Was he watching a Christmas movie on his seat-back entertainment? Would he be my New York bestie without Kim here? Because as much as I wanted to be on my own, I did feel a tiny bit lonely.

Elf. I bet Jon was watching *Elf*, which was one of the on-demand options. Taking a deep breath I put down my book, signalled for a beer, and decided to give Christmas spirit a try . . .

❄

Two hours into the flight I woke up with a snort, just as the end credits were rolling. Dammit. My mouth was dry and the man next to me raised his eyebrows just a fraction which suggested I was the worst person to sit next to in the world. I both wanted a drink, and wanted to pee, which was very conflicting.

Standing up and apologising profusely for my basic human functions, I edged out of my seat and wandered towards the loos between business and premium economy, past rows of travellers, headphones in, staring at the backs of the seats in front. One lady was watching *Magic Mike XXL* and fanning herself. I came to a stop behind the drinks trolley where I hovered nonchalantly for a while as if this was just where I wanted to hang out, thank you very much, before the air steward gave me an apologetic smile and edged the trolley closer towards me.

'Oh, sorry,' I flustered. 'I thought you were going the other way.' I tried to flatten myself against the nearby seats, very aware that my bottom was blocking half of Channing Tatum's bottom on fanning lady's screen.

'Would you mind just . . .' the flight attendant said.

'How about I just . . .'

'Perhaps I could go back a bit.'

'No, no.' I backed away, embarrassed. 'I'll use the loo at the other end.' And with that I ran away to the toilets in the middle of the plane. Where the queue was incredibly long.

Edging through the aisle to the back of the queue, my bladder ached. Now I was upright all that coffee and beer was ready to come out of me, and I danced and jiggled about in the aisle, waiting. Who the hell was in there?

The people in the queue in front of me were tutting and stretching, and they kept filtering off to the cubicle on the other side at the first chance they got. Eventually I was at the front, thank God, because I was this close to having to whack on some Tena Lady.

Come onnnnnnnnnn, I willed the person in the cubicle. Had they taken a magazine in there with them or something? I was about to knock on the door when I heard the faintest of giggles inside. You had to be kidding me. So I leant in closer, obviously.

'I'll give you a merry little Christmas,' a man's voice

purred quietly behind the door and I snapped my head back in shock. Oh *God*! Urgh, I actually really hoped he wasn't in there on his own.

'*Mmm*, show me your Christmas baubles,' murmured a woman, and I nearly passed out, but my bladder, curiosity and human instinct for wanting to perv meant nothing was dragging me away, so as nonchalantly as I could manage I leant in closer and listened.

'I am going to do this to you every day on this trip,' he growled and I looked around to see if anyone else was aware. You guys, I wanted to scream, *mile-high club going on right here, now! Like in the movies!!*

Wait. Where was Dee? She wasn't next to Abigail (who was downing a mini bottle of wine and clutching at her necklace). Where was Ian? He wasn't in the seat behind.

No. They couldn't be. They were always so discreet at work – it was the worst-kept secret in London that they were together but they'd never be this careless, surely? Dee in particular would be mortified if their workmates caught them so much as holding hands.

Beside me the toilet door thumped and shuddered and a quiet guttural moan that could have belonged to either of them could be heard, though apparently only by me. In the same way dogs are the only ones that can hear certain high-pitched noises, it would seem I was the only one who could hear two wiry office workers climaxing.

I didn't know what to do. I wanted to leave and go back to my seat, but I didn't want them to risk running into anyone else when they came out. What if Jasmine or Abigail saw them? What if this was illegal and the cabin crew called for an emergency landing in Greenland to get them off the plane? I really needed them at the conference ... And should I say anything? Was this against office ethics, something I should discipline them about? But nobody needed a telling-off right after sex. What if it Pavlov's-dogged them and conditioned them to never want to shake their tail feathers again for fear of being reprimanded? I hated myself, I was such a matron. Also, *I really had to pee.*

I was still thinking about this when I looked up and saw the she-devil climbing huffily out of her seat and over her neighbour.

'Hi!' I yelled out when Jasmine began heading this way, still a good ten rows from me.

She looked up and furrowed her brow at me. 'Hi?'

'What are you up to?'

'Just going to the Ladies. That OK?'

'Sure, bit of a wait with this one though, you might want to try the back.' I pointed, hoping she'd follow my gaze, but she didn't, and behind me I heard the tap turn on in the cubicle. They'd be coming out any minute.

A woman stepped into the aisle in front of Jasmine, who audibly sighed with impatience. The woman noticed, smiled at her and took her time getting her book from her bag up in the locker. I could have snogged this woman for buying me some time, but there were enough inappropriate shenanigans going on already.

Buying Dee and Ian time, I should say. What were they doing in there? *Get out, get out, get out.* They'd better not be going a second round; this wasn't *Sex and the City*.

The tap switched off and I heard Dee whisper, 'Got everything?'

Book lady sat back down.

Jasmine stepped closer towards me.

The cubicle door unlocked.

And a very minor jerk of turbulence saved the day.

As the plane rocked I did the first thing that came to my head and hurled myself forward, tumbling into the aisle at Jasmine's feet, wailing as I went down. She stared down at me, utterly perplexed, while the two people on the aisle seats next to me leapt up and without realising they were creating a human screen, blocked the view of the toilet cubicle behind them.

'Ouch, owwwww, the turbulence . . . ' I wailed.

'It really wasn't a big deal,' said Jasmine, still doing nothing to help other than scowl. 'They haven't even switched on the seatbelt sign.'

Dee's face appeared between the two other passengers and looked down at me, flushed pink. 'Liv? Are you OK?'

I looked her in the eye. *That's right. I know.* 'Are you?' I muttered, pulling myself up. Disaster averted. Their modesty would remain intact for now but I knew I'd never think about Christmas baubles in the same way again. 'Thanks, everyone, I'm fine, I think I'll be OK now, I'm just going to . . . ' I edged back and into the toilet cubicle, snapping the lock shut behind me. Then my skin crawled because all I could think of was Ian's naked bottom and what he and his shlongadong had been up to in here moments before.

I peed – *praise the lord* – without any part of me touching any part of the bathroom, and then exited the toilet cubicle without another word to Jasmine who was waiting impatiently outside. Before turning back to my seat I looked over and caught Dee's eye again, and she blushed furiously and pressed her nose into the sky mall catalogue.

❄

The remainder of the flight brought very little drama, unless you count Ian panicking that he hadn't completed his ESTA visa waiver form, and then remembering half an hour later that, in fact, he had completed it after all.

Eventually we landed in a clear-skied New York, safe and sound, with all thoughts of snow and storms behind us. Passport control took so long we all stopped making polite conversation and stood in weary silence, and by the time we blurred our way into baggage claim getting to the hotel was the only thing on anyone's mind. Even Abigail had run out of interesting things to text to her boyfriend.

One by one our bags came out, each of them enough of a distance from each other that it was one long nail-biting fest to see whose luggage had accidently been diverted to Kathmandu. I had five things to collect altogether: my bag, a giant poster tube, a big flat thing containing a cardboard cut-out of some cheery-looking youths, an extra case filled with paperwork, and a bubble-wrapped bag stuffed with giveaway knick-knacks that was supposed to be delivered straight to New York along with our other stuff, but turned up at our office just after everyone else had left for the Christmas party.

Miraculously, everything arrived, so I herded my

team and all their baggage out of the airport and onto a bus, yawning.

The sky was inky black, but as the shuttle neared Manhattan – what seemed like hours after it left the airport – we all perked up. Christmas lights and room lights from a thousand skyscraper windows blanketed the city and I leant forward with excitement as the Empire State Building finally came into view. Despite all my stresses and strains, I did love this place – the women were powerful and respected, the architecture was jaw-dropping, and the youth were inspired to learn and help and be leaders. And with the low sounds of Nat King Cole playing on the bus's radio, a small flame of Christmas spirit unwittingly ignited in my belly.

I peeped over at Abigail, who was pressed against the window, her phone screen being held up next to her. Abigail saw me looking and whispered, 'I want my boyfriend to see this with me for the first time, so we're FaceTiming.'

We drove through the Lincoln Tunnel and stop-started our way through the traffic in inner Manhattan. The bus was toasty warm but outside I watched locals wrapped to the nines, fingers curled around their hot coffees and feet bouncing up and down on the frosty pavements. Despite the cold there was merriment in the air, and as the bus trundled round the corner onto the magnificent Fifth Avenue I whipped my head back and forth like I was at a tennis match, trying to focus on the stunning, extravagant window displays we passed.

Dee and Ian sat in the seat in front of me, and you'd never know they had a thang going on, other than the way they glanced at each other warmly as we passed Tiffany's.

'We're here,' I said into the darkness, when the shuttle came to a stop. My team flopped sleepily out onto the pavement in front of the Hotel Vue. Dee and Ian, Abigail, and of course Jasmine, all hung back while I pointed out our bags and boxes and tubes to the driver and sorted the tip and the thank yous, but this time, I didn't even care that I was in charge of everything. I was in New York, and it felt good. I felt . . . home.

'We're here,' I breathed.

'Yippeeeee!' cried Dee, but her cheer merged into a yawn. Abigail was just staring up at the nearest skyscraper in awe. Or she was asleep.

'Come on then, let's get inside.'

The hotel lobby was warm and welcoming. A Christmas tree stood in the corner and the smiling doorman helped us with our bags. An enormous wreath hung above the reception, and the smell of hazelnut coffee emanated from a help-yourself urn by the lift, with Hotel Vue mugs stacked at the side.

'Coffee,' I declared, pointing. 'We should coffee up, we can't go to sleep yet or we'll be up at two a.m.' It was seven thirty p.m. New York time, which meant it was twelve thirty a.m. in the UK. 'Does anybody want dinner?'

I received a noncommittal noise from them all in reply as they stroked their bellies, full of rubbery plane pasta and Toblerones.

'Excuse me, ma'am,' said a beautiful concierge in his twenties with dark skin I just wanted to lick. 'We're serving complimentary wine and cheese in our lounge until eight thirty, if your party just wanted to snack. You'll also find fruit, crackers, cookies … it's pretty tasty.'

Suddenly everyone's bellies weren't so full and we agreed to dump our bags and meet back down in the lounge in ten minutes – any longer and I thought we'd lose people to their vast American beds. And eight minutes later, I was already there, sinking down into a cream leather sofa by a window that overlooked Madison Avenue, Christmas radio tinkling in the background. I took a long sip of Prosecco with a *Mmmmmmm*.

Maybe I should live in New York. In this hotel. They have wine and cheese and little crackers in the shape of fish. I could blow the small house deposit I'd been building back up; I could forget work and responsibilities, and just live here. My sisters did it (minus the hotel) so why couldn't I?

Jasmine appeared and sat down opposite me with a sigh. Abigail perched beside me like I was some medieval king and she was my concubine.

'Everything OK, Jasmine?' I chirped. Just try to find something to complain about.

Jasmine looked up at me, then at her surroundings, thoughtfully. Before she could answer Ian appeared with a plate bursting with cheeses.

'Best. Hotel. Ever,' he declared, and Jasmine sank back in her chair and stared out the window. 'So what's the plan tomorrow, boss? Do we need to be up and hailing cabs by the crack of dawn?'

'Not really. The conference opens at ten, so we should be there for nine. I might go a little earlier than that just to figure everything out. You have the address and all the contact details in the conference pack I gave you, so if we don't travel together feel free to jump in a cab to take you there in the morning. We'll probably subway-it the other days though, to save a bit of money.'

I took a yawn break and noticed Jasmine becoming visibly more slumped at the thought of having to use the subway.

'Does anyone want to have a walk outside for a while?

Try and stretch out the time before we go to sleep? We're right by Fifth Avenue so I bet the Christmas shopping would be good . . . ?'

That was met with nothing more than a fat load of yawns, and I thought, well screw you guys – I don't want to hang out with you either. So I polished off my cheese, grabbed a takeaway cup full of hazelnut coffee and left the alluring cosiness of the hotel for the night air of New York City, on my own.

One thing that never fails to amaze me about New York is how the whole place looks like a studio set. The brownstones really do have steps leading up to them that people sit on, people like Carrie Bradshaw. There really are basement-level bars on side streets like in *How I Met Your Mother*. Steam really does plume out of pipes poking from under ground in the middle of streets, like in all movies and all music videos ever. Being somewhere so familiar in so many ways made one feel very welcome, very at home.

Fifth Avenue was amazing. The buildings a hundred storeys high, with elaborate Christmas lights climbing up the outside. Enormous festive window displays lured in the happy Christmas crowds, still thick and jolly even at eight o'clock at night.

My legs were slowly turning to mush and I knew my sleepy self couldn't walk far. Perhaps if I could speak to someone I'd last a little longer, because you don't just fall asleep mid-conversation.

I tried Anne, but there was no reply, just a thousand rings. Instead, I went into the first store I came to: a gigantic Hollister crammed full of shoppers and beautiful sales people pretending to fold clothes. However, I'd forgotten my head-torch, and if you've ever been into a Hollister you'll know it's the worst possible place to be if you need to stay awake because it's so dimly lit you could probably nap on a stack of skinny jeans and would only wake when a frantic buyer nudged you out the way to find their size. So I left Hollister, crossed the street, and went a couple of doors down, to where the skyscrapers briefly halted to bow down to the ornate St Patrick's Cathedral.

I stood outside and gazed at it for a while. It was both a funny and humbling sight in the middle of an avenue full of towering glass and extreme wealth. The cathedral takes up a whole city block, its twin marble, Gothic spires rising over a hundred feet into the air. At this time of night it was lit up against the dark with gentle amber spotlights, and understated Christmas wreaths hung above the entrance and upon the two spires.

Inside I could hear the soft sounds of carols being sung and an organ spilling melodies that rose up and out of the stained glass windows into the night air. I breathed it in, my tired body and brain relaxing into this feeling.

My mind tried to wander to its familiar place of deep thoughts, worries and plans for tomorrow, but it didn't have the strength. I'd been awake long enough. I looked up at the cathedral one last time, and then succumbed. It was time for bed. Goodnight, New York.

15 December

1 week, 3 days to Christmas

❄

I woke from a deep sleep to a world that was still pitch black. My eyelids fluttered open and it took me a moment to process where I was – the tight sheets, the blinking red light on the TV opposite the bed, the shrill ringing of my mobile.

Urgh, hadn't I *just* got to sleep? Goddamn you, jetlag, you arsehole.

I sat up and tried to loosen my muscles. I was in the buff and my mouth tasted of yesterday's blue cheese. My extreme-knackeredness the night before meant I'd stripped off my flight clothes and fallen face-first in the bed without even bothering to open my suitcase and retrieve my toothbrush. *Hawt*.

'Hello?' I croaked, stepping out of bed, pulling the whole duvet with me and moving across the carpet to the window.

'Good morning! Are you here yet?' Jon's chirpy voice seeped into my ear.

'No, isn't it like, three a.m.?' I pulled back the heavy hotel curtain to see that it wasn't pitch black – it was more fireplace-ash-grey, and yellow cabs were already zooming past the hotel on the street below like they couldn't believe their luck at the lack of gridlocked traffic.

'It's seven thirty – did I wake you?'

'Seven thirty?! No, no, you didn't wake me. I am up and raring to go.' I scratched my boob and stifled a yawn. 'Good morning to you too.'

'HeForShe had to get here first thing to help set up for the keynote speaker – I'm such a moron it didn't even occur to me you wouldn't be here until later.'

'Actually, you've provided the perfect wake-up call; I should get there a little early to find our stand, and name badges, and . . . ' There was so much to do, it was a little overwhelming.

But I could do it.

'Do you need a coffee?' I asked. One thing at a time.

'I'd love a tea.'

'I don't know if I can get that for you here, but I'll see what I can do. I'll be there in about half an hour. Forty-five minutes. An hour tops.'

I jumped in the shower, turning on the TV for some company, and stood under the hot water to let the plane journey and the shuttle bus and the groggy head slide off me and down the plughole, along with all the nutmeg-scented hotel toiletries I dumped upon myself. I ran through a mental to-do list for the day: get coffee, get team to conference, find stand, get everything set up, hope I don't cock anything up, try not to trip over and pull stand down with me, get benefactors and interesting people to come on board with Girls of the World, enjoy self. But mainly don't cock anything up.

Stepping sleepily from the shower, I allowed a short moment to observe myself in the bathroom mirror, and wondered if I'd feel more boss-like if I had arms like Michelle Obama. Probably not – it was a fear of saying something so idiotic that Girls of the World became an internet-meme laughing stock and crumbled to the ground, all because of me, rather than my physical appearance. But even so, thank God I had my Hillary Clinton-inspired business woman outfit with me for day one of the conference. Though *I* had voted for matching conference T-shirts, like we usually had, but damn democracy got in the way and it was vetoed by the others who 'just this once wanted to look like stylish New Yorkers'.

I padded towards my suitcase, one eye on E! News – what had Bieber done now? – and unzipped its thick black lid.

Where was my power suit?

Where were my clothes?

Why was my suitcase full of humongous men's Y-fronts?

No, no, no, this couldn't be happening. I closed the lid with a bang and checked the luggage label.

WHO THE HELL WAS TIMOTHY TAM?

I couldn't have picked up the wrong bag at baggage claim. I can't have *not* checked the label. I can't only have yesterday's smelly, crumpled clothes to wear to represent my company – to represent all the youth and the next generation of Girls of the World everywhere in New York City.

Oh God, was there anything I could fashion out of a pair of Y-fronts?

I called the airport with shaking hands.

'John F. Kennedy airport, how may I help you?'

'Help – I mean hello, help. I've come home with the wrong bag, I—'

'Let me transfer you to baggage claim.'

I waited, suddenly feeling very exposed in my hotel dressing gown. Maybe I could wear this, and claim kimonos were totes all the rage in London. Why hadn't I checked the suitcase last night? That would teach me for being too sleepy to bother to get out my toothbrush. I deserved Y-fronts and tooth decay. I glared at the suitcase with resentment.

'John F. Kennedy airport baggage claim, how may we help you?'

'Oh um, hello.' Why did I always put on an ultra-British phone voice when abroad, like I was Judi Dench's protégée? 'I was on BA flight 0173 yesterday from London Heathrow and I picked up the wrong bag, and this one belongs to a man and I don't have my clothes and he has no underwear. Except for mine!' Oh, what if he was wearing my underwear right now?

'What does your bag look like, ma'am?'

'It's black, and square, and quite big, I guess.'

'Are there any distinguishing features?'

'No, not really . . . ' For shame. If I shared luggage taste with Mr Tam, Y-fronts King, maybe it was time to invest in something a bit more stylish.

'All right. Could you confirm your name and address for me, as written on your luggage tag?'

'It's just got my name and email address on it, because I read somewhere that if you put your address down and someone steals your bag, they'll also know where you live and that you're not home, so it's better not to put those things.'

'All right. Could you confirm your name and email?'

I reeled it off, spelling it all out carefully.

'All right. Could you tell me something in your bag? Describe some clothing to me, for example?'

'Yes, I've got ...' My mind went blank. What pyjamas did I bring? What outfits did I bring? What shampoo did I bring? *Anything?* 'Oh! I have a jumper in there with a squirrel on. A sweater. With an embroidered squirrel, that looks like it's been picked at.'

'Is this a child's sweater, ma'am?' asked the woman, confused.

'Nope, it's mine. It's cashmere, if that helps ... make me sound more normal.'

'All right. We've got your bag, ma'am.'

'You've got it?' I whooped at the poor woman. 'Can you send it to me at the Hotel Vue on Fifty-Fourth Street, or will I have to come and pick it up from JFK?'

'We'll put it on the next shuttle to your hotel, ma'am, and we'll pick up the gentleman's case also if you leave it with your concierge. It'll be with you later on this morning.'

'Oh thank God, I love you.'

'All right, thank you, ma'am.'

OK ... but what now? I looked at the case of underpants.

※

Dressed in my hotel robe and slippers I knocked lightly on the door of Dee's room, because this chick owed me. I looked up and down the deserted corridor in case Emma Watson herself suddenly strode by.

There was no answer. I knocked a little louder. This time I heard the sound of a scurry of movement before Dee opened the door without removing the chain.

'Hello, OLIVIA, yes, work, right ...' Dee panted, wrapped in a duvet, half her hair standing upright.

Are you kidding me? Bonking again? Where did this woman's energy come from? 'Nope, not quite yet. Actually, I was wondering if you could do me a massive favour and lend me something to wear – my bag got switched at the airport and all I have is—'

'Nope, soz, I can't let you in, I'm afraid,' said Dee with wide eyes. 'Could you try Abigail?'

'She's about twenty sizes smaller than me unfortunately,' I laughed, trying to peer into the darkened room. 'Maybe you could drop something over to my room when you're, um, dressed?'

'Sorry,' Dee said through an ever-decreasing gap in

the doorway. 'I'm just not sure I'll have time, and I've left the shower running, try Jasmine, she'll have loads of stuff, bye then, bye.'

The door closed. Are you *kidding* me? I'd laid down on an aeroplane aisle for her, beside discarded flight socks and dropped mini-pretzels, and she couldn't even throw me a jumper? Don't these people know I've had sleepless nights recently just to make sure they're all set for this trip and that nothing goes wrong? I've carried the bulk of the heavy marketing material to and from the office, to and from the train stations and the airports, just so they don't have to worry about it. And now I've messed up and I need their help and . . .

I took a breath. This inner rant wasn't helping. Dee wasn't doing this intentionally, and no, she probably hadn't thought about or realised all the things I'd been stressing over. She was just trying to enjoy a bit of time away with her man outside working hours.

I turned to face the room of the one person I didn't want to have to ask for help. I wished Kim was here. I'd never fit in her clothes but at least I could bribe her to ask Jasmine on my behalf.

Smoothing my hair and tilting up my chin, I rapped on Jasmine's door.

Jasmine swung open the door instantly and looked me up and down. I wish wish wished I wasn't barefoot at the time (other than hotel slippers), because Jasmine towered over me in chunky-heeled thigh-high boots, worn over smart leggings and a cashmere jumper, a look that I would have surely looked like a chilly hooker in, but Jasmine carried off as winter business chic. She looked so New York it was infuriating.

'Morning,' I said pleasantly.

'You might want to get dressed,' she answered, clearly thinking I was a total thicko.

'This is why I'm here. I wondered if you could do me a favour ...'

She raised an eyebrow and waited for me to continue.

'My luggage got switched at JFK, and I'm not going to get my bag until later today. My travel clothes are gross, so I wondered if I could borrow something of yours?' *Urrrrrrrrrrrrrgggggggghhhhhh*. 'Please?'

'I don't know if I have anything that'll fit,' she sighed, walking into her room and I followed. My room had a better view than hers. Haha.

Jasmine stared at her array of clothes, neatly arranged in little clusters in her closet. 'I don't have much, I planned all my outfits before I came so I don't have a lot of spare pieces ...' She thumbed reluctantly through her wardrobe.

'Really, anything will be fine,' I said.

'You might fit into this.' She flung a green pencil skirt

at me. 'Just be careful with it. And this is the only top I can lend you.' She gave me a thin vest top which is the kind of thing I'd wear under a top rather than *as* a top.

'You don't have a shirt or anything?'

'Nope. Not without leaving myself with nothing to wear while we're here.'

... 'Right, OK, well thanks ever so much, you're a lifesaver. Did you want to head down to the conference together?'

'No thanks, I'll see you there. We don't need to be there until nine, right?'

'Yep. OK.' *Fine. Good.* 'Thanks again, see you later.'

Back in my room I squeezed myself into Jasmine's clothes. It wasn't that I looked *bad*, I just resembled a fourth, lumpy Kardashian sister. The skirt hugged me and my thighs tightly, and the vest top – which no doubt skimmed Jasmine's frame modestly, was instead pulled, *dragged*, over my size-or-two-up torso, to the point that my cleavage was Jessica Rabbit-like and the fabric was bordering on see-through. Hello, ladies. What kind of a first impression was this going to make?

I sniffed the jumper that I'd flown in. It smelt of sweat and plane food; this was going to have to stay here. I pulled on my coat, perhaps I could just keep this on all day?

Sighing at myself in the mirror, I gave a small prayer

that there would be merchandise stalls at the conference selling T-shirts. I had to go.

❄

You know those dreams where you're naked, and at work, and you're like, I know I'm naked but I really have to go into this meeting so I hope nobody laughs at my vag? Well, even under my vast coat, that's how I felt walking into the conference venue that first morning. I built it up so much in my head that I could barely look any of the early starters in the eye and instead legged it to Jon's HeForShe stall.

I squeezed behind the curtain and into his booth and dumped the coffee cups on to the table. Thankfully, he was the only one around. He greeted me with a big smile and leant over to kiss my cheek but I stopped him. 'Wait, I need you to be honest with me.'

'Good morning!'

'Good morning. Tell me the truth; what's the first thing you think when you see this?' I flung open my duffel coat to reveal my outfit.

'Aroooga!' Jon said, a small blush creeping onto his face. I whipped the coat back closed again. 'Hey, no, you look great. I just need to take a minute to remind myself of the HeForShe code of ethics, excuse me.'

'It's too much though, isn't it? Could you see my bra?' I peeked inside my coat. There was definite bra outline.

'Well, um, just a little bit.'

'This is a disaster . . . this is a disaster! My first time paving the way for Girls of the World and I march in, nipple first. I'm not promoting women's rights, I'm just promoting women! She did this deliberately, you know. She knew it wouldn't fit.'

'Um . . . what?'

'Jasmine! She had shirts; I saw the shirts, but *noooo*.'

'Why are you wearing Jasmine's clothes?'

'I took the wrong suitcase at JFK and mine won't be delivered to the hotel until later today. It was Jasmine's spare clothes or yesterday's very un-fresh woolly leggings and flight socks. What am I going to do? I can't represent Girls of the World in this, I'm like a fifties secretary.' I hugged my coat around me, sadly. 'Thank you though, for saying I looked nice.'

Jon picked up one of the coffees and handed it to me and then put his heavy hand on my shoulder. 'You want to borrow a shirt?' he asked kindly.

I love him. 'You have a spare shirt with you? Here at the conference?'

'Yep, Mr Prepared. Always take a spare shirt in case you sweat, or meet a damsel in distress. Or in no dress – haha.'

'A shirt would be perfection!' I literally could have snogged his face off and had his babies in that moment, as he rifled through his bag.

He pulled out a neatly folded forest green shirt and held it up to me. It matched the skirt perfectly, which wasn't a good thing. 'No, you can't wear this; you'll look like a Christmas tree. Take my shirt and I'll switch into this.'

'No I couldn't possibly . . .' but Jon was already unbuttoning his black shirt.

'This isn't a peep show, pervert, turn around,' he teased.

I smiled and we turned away from each other in the small space, and as he removed the shirt I took off the vest, so pleased to no longer be squeezed into that corset of a top.

'Are you still looking?' he asked.

'No!' I turned my head just as he did and met his eye.

'You are!'

'I was just checking you weren't looking, which you were.'

'You are so into me.' He handed me the shirt and I handed the green one to him. Our eyes met again briefly, both making a point of not looking south, before we turned from each other again. I shook my head, not allowing my gaze to slide to his bare back. As I slipped on the warm black shirt, which was soft and comfort-able, and smelled of Jon, our arms bumped and his warmth was like sitting close to a log fire.

I tucked the shirt into the pencil skirt, and when I turned back Jon was in the green shirt, sleeves rolled up, perched on the edge of the table and smiling. 'Much more respectable. You look nice.'

I looked down. 'Thank you. I'm sure it's a bit baggy on me but at least I can breathe. Jon, you're my hero.'

'Flirt,' he teased, not taking his eyes off me. He stood and stretched. 'Who would have thought that less than twenty-four hours into the trip I'd have the one and only Olivia Forest wearing my shirt and bringing me breakfast.'

'Knock knock,' a female voice called, and a smiling American woman poked her head around the curtain. Jon turned and beamed.

'Dani!'

'Hey, Jon, good to see you!'

They hugged and I watched them. Mainly her. She was very lovely-looking, and her lob haircut was the kind you see on Pinterest all the time, all golden and wavy. When she let go of Jon and looked at me, keeping her hand warmly on his arm, I felt myself blush a little.

'Hi,' she said, with a huge smile and perfect teeth and enviable pink lipstick.

'Oh, I'm sorry,' said Jon. 'This is Olivia, she's fronting the Girls of the World stall this year, we've known each other for years now, and Liv, this is Dani, one of my HeForShe US colleagues.'

'I don't get to travel to all the conferences, only the US ones,' Dani explained, shaking my hand. 'So I haven't seen this dude for like, a year.' Jon *was* a dude. He was smiling at her as she continued. 'I've heard of Girls of the World though, I'm sure. You inspire young women, right? Creatively?'

'Yes, exactly! That's exciting that you know us! Come and visit the stand later?'

'I'd love to! All right, I'll leave you kids to it, *so* good to see you again, Jon, you wanna get together some time while you're here? Catch up?' She flashed another show-stopping grin and went to leave, but for some reason I felt the need to stop her and explain my presence.

'I had a wardrobe, um, malfunction this morning so Jon was being a total hero and giving me his shirt.'

Jon, clearly amused by my need to justify my presence, nodded. 'It looks better on you than me.'

'No it doesn't.' Yeah it did. 'I ended up taking the wrong suitcase to the hotel, and my only option for a top was this tiny see-through vest thing of my colleagues. There was just fat bulging everywhere.' *Why* do we women always feel we need to justify our presence by putting ourselves down? I willed my gob to shut up.

Dani just chuckled. 'Honey, there's not an inch of fat on you, I bet you looked amazing, but good job on being the hero, Jon. Remember that time you saved me when I spilt wine on my dress at last year's gala and you gave me your jacket?'

'I do. What can I say; I guess my clothes just suit women more than they suit me.'

With that, Dani waved goodbye, and I turned back to Jon. 'Thank you again, I owe you one. If you ever want to borrow a top off me, help yourself. I'd better go.'

'You're welcome. Good luck out there.'

'And to you.' I inhaled, nervous. 'Yes, and to me.'

❄

I went off to find our Girls of the World booth, safe in the knowledge that my boobs were no longer hanging out. The booth was in a nice spot between a coffee stand and a book stall, so obviously I was in heaven. We weren't in a prime position – those were reserved for the bigger foundations, those that sponsored the conference, worked directly with the keynote speakers, or were high profile companies that everyone wanted to be involved with (such as HeForShe). But it was a decent size with a great view of everyone else, and as I remembered how much I loved the industry I was in, my nerves started to slip away.

I set to work setting up our booth, opening the boxes and tubes to reveal all of our promotional material, our posters, our banners. We were there to raise awareness of our company and hopefully to get some interest from American investors with the aim to expand across the pond, but we had a secondary aim of increasing awareness of our existence within the general public. We wanted the women – and men – that visited the conference to feel happy and inspired at our booth.

I was just placing some stacks of Tina Fey's *Bossypants* and Amy Poehler's *Yes Please* books on the table, next to a basket full of orange Girls of the World activity books, pencils and badges, when the rest of my team trundled in, coffees in hand, yawning. Jasmine's face fell when she saw that I looked halfway presentable.

'Hello, sleepyheads! How's everyone feeling?'

'Great!' – Dee.

'A little tired but feeling pretty good.' – Ian (gross, no wonder you're tired, you dirty bugger).

'Nervous . . . ' – Abigail.

'Fine.' – Jasmine.

'Right then,' I continued. 'We are t-minus fifty

minutes, so Ian and Jasmine, you're on banner- and poster-hanging duty; Abigail, can you set up the Talking Point booth at the back with Dee; I'm going to finish the table and set up the laptop. When you're done, have a little walk around so you know where the loos, the snack stands, the exits are, and meet back here at ten to ten. All right? Go!'

I quite liked telling people what to do.

❄

All companies with stands at #IWasHereNYC were gathered at one end of the conference venue for a short opening speech from the president of the foundation. 'OK, ladies and gentlemen, thank you so much for coming, for all your hard work and dedication to spreading the word and making the world a happier place for women to be in, and for gathering here today. The doors open to our public in five minutes, so good luck, enjoy the conference, and I hope to meet as many of you as possible at our seminars and talks over the next three days. And don't forget the delegate drinks party tonight with the amazing cultural show that's being put on for us by some of the talented students of Juilliard. Tomorrow is movie night with some great networking opportunities, and then we have the end-of-conference gala on Thursday, which is always a highlight. I can't wait to meet y'all!'

The microphone was switched off and a hum of excitement buzzed through the conference centre.

I turned to my team and whispered, 'Five minutes!'

They nodded. Every year there was always a feeling of slight trepidation before a conference started – we loved what we did but we were still on show, still answering questions and trying to sell ourselves, asking people to buy into Girls of the World by giving us their support, be that through funding, contacts, including us in their youth programmes, booking us for talks and seminars and workshops. America was a big pit of possibility, and I was sure we could do well partnering with their summer camps and their extra-curricular activities. But even so. It would still be easier to hide in the back of the booth and not to talk to anyone.

This lot needed a pep talk, and this was on me now.

'Who wants to go home?' I asked. They blinked at me. 'Who wants to run out of here, grab their bags from the hotel, leg it to the airport and go home?'

'We just got here,' Abigail said, slowly. If anyone was going to jump at that chance to go home, I thought it would be her.

'But do you want to be here?' This time they nodded, unsure what I was getting at. 'Because it's nearly time, there are going to be potential investors, companies we could partner with, and most importantly a shit-load of women are going to come through that door any minute now, and I need you guys to help me make this our best conference presence yet.'

Oops, I'd tipped the scale the wrong way and now they were beginning to look afraid. I was putting too much pressure on them. 'We can do it,' I continued. 'Um . . . ' I glanced around me and in the distance I saw Dani and her big grin as she chatted away easily, now wearing a pink HeForShe T-shirt. She looked like the perfect cheerleader. I turned back to my team. 'Let's start again. We're in America, right? Well, we need to be more American.'

'YES!' shouted Dee, getting in the mood.

I looked at my watch. I didn't quite know what I was prattling on about but the doors would open any second. 'We're in an American movie, this is one big high school. Ian, you're the jock – confident, and cool, and I want you to make everyone like you. Dee, you're head cheerleader – keep up the peppy attitude and rally anyone that comes near our booth. Abi, you're the brainiac – you can bedazzle everyone with facts and figures and bring home the trophies, I know you can.' She grinned at me. 'And Jasmine, why don't you play the gothy best friend – make sure you're speaking to all the shy girls and helping them realise how perfect they all are. Yes, the eye-rolling is perfectly in character.'

And suddenly the music was cranked up and a bell rang somewhere over a tannoy. The doors of the conference centre opened and in streamed the best sight in the world: crowds of people – both women and men – faces flushed with excitement and cold, all eager to be here and stand up for equality. Why had I ever been nervous? These people were me – they were on my side.

A girl appeared before me, a couple of years younger and with a face pink with anticipation. She looked up at the stand with a huge grin and spoke with a thick American accent. '"Girls of the World", I like it. What do you guys do?'

❄

Day one was rushing by and I realised mid-afternoon that I hadn't stopped for a bite to eat. My stomach growled just as I felt a hand on my back and I turned. Jon.

'Isn't this brilliant?' I said, before he could utter a word. 'These women are so inspiring; did you hear what Judge Williams said in her keynote about women building their own bridges across the pay gap? She was so cool! And look at all these people, I feel like this is the best conference ever, don't you think? I'm so hungry. Do you think I should run for prime minister?'

Jon was smiling at me. 'Do you want to run for prime minister?'

'Absolutely! Well, no, but I could.'

'You'd be a great prime minister.'

'I think I would too. You might need a penis to be powerful in this world now, but vaginas are having an uprising, now more than ever, like superpower stormtroopers. Not that vaginas want to crush the penises, just stand hand in hand with them on top of the world. Wait, what was I talking about . . . ?'

'I don't know. I'm left wondering if we're talking about sex or if I should put on a codpiece.'

'Are you having a good time?' I asked, shaking thoughts of penises – his in particular – from my mind.

'It's great, and it's nice to see you enjoying yourself so much, even without Kim. Nerves all gone then?'

'Completely. I have been having text-pep-talks from Kim in Antigua though. I feel just . . . full of energy. What's your favourite bit?'

'You.'

I scanned his face for a moment – what did that mean? Was he making fun of me?

'What?'

'You.'

'Why?' I hoped this wasn't about to become awkward. I felt myself start to blush.

'Because you're so ... *into it*. And you're standing here saying you're so inspired by everyone else and talking about your lady bits becoming prime minister or something, but I think *you're* inspiring. You've made me want my lady bits to be prime minister, too.'

'I'm not inspiring.' I brushed him off, embarrassed.

'Look,' he said, handing me a polystyrene container, 'I have to get back, but I picked you up a pulled pork burger from the Montana BBQ stand near HeForShe – I had one earlier and they are amazing. Knowing you, you've probably not eaten since breakfast.'

'When you're on a roll, you're on a— *mmmmohmygod*, these are amazing.' I chomped into the burger without even finishing my sentence.

'Dani's going to come over in a bit; she's really interested in getting to know you.'

'Me?' I said, mouth full.

'Yep.'

'Why?'

'Because I told her you're a lovable weirdo with a party trick of eating a whole burger in under thirty seconds.'

Jon was amazing. This burger was amazing. Dani's

hair was amazing. I was in love with everyone and everything right now; maybe I should calm down.

❄

The rest of the day went by in a blur of people, activities, speakers and fun. My shoes and my cheeks were killing me by the time we said goodbye to our final guest at the stand.

'What a day,' I said to nobody in particular, but all my team agreed with me nonetheless. 'Who's ready for the drinks and cultural show?'

Ian yawned and Abigail rubbed her eyes.

I popped a party popper at them. 'No time for sleeping, we are here in New York and we don't have long and we can sleep when we get back to the UK.' An image of my bed, my flat, my lovely, people-free flat flashed through my mind. Good things come to those who wait . . . 'Let's clean up the stand so we don't have to do it in the morning, and then let's have a well-deserved drink. Yes? Yes.'

❄

I was entranced. It was later that evening and I was watching some of the USA's finest young dancers and musicians perform an adaptation of *The Nutcracker* that took us through Christmas in different neighbourhoods of New York. When the performance finished I shot up to applaud so fast that Jon wobbled on his seat next to me.

'*Those* are the types of women I want to connect with if we bring Girls of the World to the US,' I babbled to Jon. 'Imagine how inspiring they would be to anyone with a dream to be a dancer? Look at their strong bodies, and their confidence!'

'Excuse me,' said a well-dressed woman with voice of silk who approached me. 'Are you Olivia Forest?'

'I am – hello!' I answered, admiring her immaculate hair. 'You have amazing hair. Are you from New York? I'm noticing more and more that New York women really are so well put-together, not just in looks but also in life. I'm sorry, I've been talking all day and I can't seem to stop, I think it's the adrenalin.'

The woman laughed. 'It has been a good day. I'm Lara Green, I run the Green PR firm here in New York – which is, yes, where I live. We have a meeting tomorrow, I believe?'

'We do! Lara, it's so good to meet you, Scheana's told me so much about you.' In particular, how important it was that this meeting went well. Lara had well-established and respected government connections, a great reputation, and Scheana really thought she might get on board with helping us branch out over here in the US.

'I literally love Scheana, she's the best. But listen, my calendar is *kerrazy* busy tomorrow; I swear it fills up more by the hour, even though it was already full. How would you feel about skipping the networking and movie screening tomorrow night and having our meeting over dinner and drinks?'

'That sounds great!' Whatever she wanted. I just hoped my team would be OK without me ...

I faced Jon once she'd left and he gave my shoulder an affectionate little squeeze. 'You just got yourself a date,' he said.

'She wants to spend the evening with me! That's a good sign, isn't it? If she thought there was no hope in our little company she'd have just left me as one of her short day-meetings.' This was better than I could have hoped. Now I just had to make her like me. A lot. 'What's my least likeable quality?'

'Wow, talk about putting a guy on the spot! I can't think of one.'

'Yes you—'

'Actually, yes I can,' he said. Hmph. 'I think you suck because you don't work at HeForShe, and I'm jealous that Girls of the World get you instead.'

I laughed. 'Maybe one day I'll come and do a key-note talk at one of your little seminars. You know, if you grow tired of Emma Watson or Kiefer Sutherland.'

'I have no doubt about it.' Jon grinned, shaking his head.

'Come on,' I said. 'I owe you for this morning – let me buy you a free drink.'

As we walked towards the bar, I gave myself a mental high-five, and threw in a mental hug too because why the hell not? I was doing OK – day one was nearly at a close and everything was going well. Really well. *Told you you could do it*, I told Olivia-from-the-past. I *would* be delivering keynote speeches one day . . . I'm coming for you, world.

16 December

1 week, 2 days to Christmas

❄

The second day of the conference began without any hiccups, and entirely in my own clothes. My suitcase had arrived with all pairs of knickers intact and accounted for. And that was pretty much the vibe for the day.

It was *Full On* though. Other than one small errand I had to nip out to do at lunchtime, the entire day was spent smiling, explaining, helping, motivating, encouraging and solving any little issue that came up, such as Abi's hair getting caught in one of the banners, and Ian asking a really irrelevant question during one of the seminars. I felt like we were spreading the word of Girls of the World like wildfire, and now I just had to hope it stayed alight.

Thank God we were going home in two sleeps. I was having a great time, but responsibility shaken-not-stirred with jet lag was taking its toll. Other than the first night foray, precisely one block across and three down to St Patrick's Cathedral, I'd barely seen New York City yet. I also hadn't seen Jon all day, which was rubbish.

But tonight was my dinner meeting with Lara. I'd asked the rest of my team to go along to the networking-slash-movie screening event in my absence, but actually I had other plans for two of them ...

As we tidied up the stand at the end of the day I took the pair of tickets I'd purchased at lunchtime out of my pocket, and pulled Ian aside. 'Ian,' I said, 'I don't know if you're aware of this, but it's actually Dee's birthday today?'

'Oh?' he squeaked, the voice of a man who had probably been up at the crack of dawn to wish his lady a happy birthday in his own special way.

'Yeah, and the thing is, I bought tickets to take her to The Rockettes tonight as a surprise – you know that Christmas "extravaganza" they call it over at Radio City Music Hall?' I sighed, forlorn. 'Only I bought them before I knew I had to go to this business meeting this evening.' Another sigh. 'I don't suppose there's any way you could take her, could you?'

Ian reached out and slowly took the tickets from me. He was very quiet. 'You want me to take out Dee for her birthday?'

'It would really help me out. Jasmine won't want to, and I think it would be good for Abigail to stay and network, but you're like me; you've met all these people before. It would be nice for Dee – for you both – to enjoy a New York Christmas treat on her birthday.'

He fingered the tickets for a moment and then looked up at me, searching my face with his eyes. I smiled, and he smiled back. He knew I knew.

'Thank you,' he murmured.

'You're welcome. Merry Christmas. And happy birthday to Dee.'

I looked around one final time to see if I'd have a chance to say goodbye to Jon, but he was busy chatting to Dani, a big smile on his face, telling some story in his enigmatic way. So I slipped out of the room and rushed back across Manhattan to the hotel for a quick change. I planned to arrive at the restaurant, which was uptown, twenty minutes early and make a great impression.

Sitting in a cool way doesn't come easy to me. I arrived at the restaurant early, as I'd intended, and in the minutes that passed while I waited for Lara I must have shuffled positions so many times that it probably looked like I had haemorrhoids. I needed to calm down. What kind of small talk would Lara enjoy? Should I open with '*So, do you come here often?*' No, that was a bit 'pick-up-line'. How about, '*I like the seating in this place. Did you know that the Chesterfield sofa might date back to 1574 and the fourth Earl of Chesterfield?*' Oh God, that was so boring. Maybe: '*When you travel uptown do you get the song "Uptown Funk" stuck in your head, like every time?*'

The door opened and Lara walked in, all cool and Noo Yoik, just like when I'd met her yesterday. I opened my big gob and hit her with a 'How you doin'?' For crying out loud, I just Joey Tribbiani'd my dinner meeting. 'So, do you live around here?' I asked, trying to rein it back in.

'Just a few streets away in an apartment block near the river. I'm sorry to drag you so far up town, it was entirely selfish; I just needed to go home first to unwind a little.'

'I completely understand, the conference is full on.'

'Right? It's amazing but, man, I crave my bed at the end of the night. When do you and your team fly home?'

'The day after tomorrow.'

'Looking forward to getting back for Christmas? I bet London is beautiful at this time of year.'

'It is . . . ' We took our seats and ordered a couple of martinis.

'All right,' Lara said, snapping her menu shut. 'Let's get into this. Scheana wants me to help bring you guys to America, but I can't invest unless I know what's in it for me. I don't have the time or the money for projects I don't feel connected to.'

'I completely understand,' I said, beginning to sweat from the responsibility. Come on, Liv. My eyes flicked towards the street outside where women and men strode through this concrete jungle as tall and as confident as the skyscrapers they passed. I could be like them; I *needed* to be like them. I straightened in my seat and looked Lara straight in the eye, businesswoman to businesswoman. 'What can I do to convince you?'

'What are your profit margins?'

Balls. I didn't know. *Why* didn't I know this? My heart sank and I felt like an amateur. But I would not quit. I never quit anything and I was not about to quit on myself now. 'That . . . is an excellent question. May I email you a comprehensive document that talks about our profit and loss per year when I get back to my hotel room?' . . . and write a comprehensive document that talks about our profit and loss per year.

'Sure,' said Lara. She signalled to the waiter and reeled off an order that seemed to basically boil down to chicken – plain – with hot sauce and salad on the side. I asked for a pulled pork burger, because they were turning into my every-meal staple, and prayed I wasn't already in her bad books.

'Let's change tack.' Lara cupped her hands around her martini glass. 'Tell me what your favourite thing is about Girls of the World.'

'OK, my favourite thing.' This I could do. 'Girls of the World does so many things for young women in Britain. We travel around the country, we speak in schools, we get these girls involved in so many activities that not only they might have not had access to but that they might never have even dreamed of having access to in the first place. And sometimes that's because they've never put themselves out there before, and sometimes it's because they've never realised that girls can do, well, anything. And that's all great, but my favourite thing about Girls of the World is how it makes *me* a better person.' I took a sip of my drink and glanced at Lara, who cocked her head in interest.

I continued. 'I know that sounds selfish, but it's true. These girls are inspiring to me. I watch them become engaged in things that truly fit their personalities and they just come alive. And they make me want to be better. I had a time in my life where I felt really low, and untrusting, and I didn't want anyone to be close to me, and in some ways I'm not sure I'm out of that yet, to be honest.' Where had *that* come from? I ploughed on regardless. 'But Girls of the World doesn't try and teach girls that you can snap out of hard times like they don't matter, that's not what we're about. We're about being who you really are, and expanding on that, and showing the world. So now I want to show the world who I am.'

Lara was nodding. 'All right, I see that, I like where you're coming from. Can you give me an example of what you help these girls achieve?'

'Sure. Well, we have a group of girls from around the country who make videos – vlogs – for us. The girls are all really different from one another but they all have an interest in computers, and the inner workings of things. So we developed a course for them to hone and tone their coding and editing and whatnot. They went from being geeky outsiders who were afraid they weren't being girly enough to these completely cool girls who vlog about tech stuff, but other things too, like standing up for yourself, teen life hacks, and sometimes beauty if that's the mood they're in. They're the next generation of Girls of the World staff, to be honest with you. A whole group of Scheanas.' I smiled. I loved those girls.

Lara was listening intently. 'I actually know the young women you mean – I checked out some of their videos on your site a couple weeks back. They're bright girls.'

'They're so bright. We don't ever want Girls of the World to just be about preaching to young people and telling them to "be better", we want them to be involved, and be part of it. Like a club. It's not about being better, it's about being what they want to be.'

'I like that,' said Lara. 'A club.'

I nodded. 'And it's a club that anyone can join.'

She lapsed into silence for a moment, a slow nod bobbing her head up and down. Suddenly she took a sip of her drink and asked me, 'I'm so sorry; how's Scheana doing?'

'Oh she's fine; the doctor just said she won't be able to walk around for a few weeks.'

'Oh my god! Is she in that much pain?'

'Yeah, I think so. I haven't seen her since it happened, she's been working from home, and I've never had it happen to me, but I gather it's pretty uncomfortable. Both when it happens and the aftermath.'

'When it happens ...' Lara seemed to be having processing problems.

'I mean, when the accident occurred it was just so slippy-slidey, I'm surprised it didn't happen to all of us.'

Lara blinked. 'Oh, it was an accident?'

'Definitely. She was pretty fed up about missing New York just because of it.'

'And you were all there?'

'Yeah, it was a sort of team-building, I suppose. Jasmine, who you may have met, she wasn't there, she's not really into anything dirty.'

'I can understand that . . .'

'Is it not your kind of thing either? I must admit, halfway through I was ready to have a shower and never see a big wet bit of wood to climb ever again, but I did want to finish.'

'Well, that is your right,' Lara stammered.

I nodded. That was a funny way of looking at it. 'Yeah . . . I had paid for it, after all.'

Lara downed her cocktail and signalled for another. 'You paid for it. Did you all pay for it? Did Scheana?'

'Absolutely, I think the money goes to charity.' I sat forward. 'We actually invited a group of our very own Girls of the World kids to watch us, and I think it really opened their eyes.'

'Of course it goddamn did— You did *what*?'

Uh-oh. Lara now didn't just look confused, she looked kind of angry. And a smidge disgusted. I know New York women are gorgeously polished but surely she wasn't that against a little outdoor activity? 'They came to watch us ... in the race. The obstacle course race where Scheana broke her leg ...'

'Scheana's broken her leg? Is the baby OK?' Lara gasped.

What?! 'Scheana's having a baby?'

Lara's hand flew up and covered her mouth. 'Oh, you didn't know. Wait, so you've been talking about a race all this time, one of those Tough Mudder things?'

'Yes, were you not?'

'No, I was talking about Scheana being pregnant. I thought ... I thought you were saying that the baby had been an accident, but then you said you'd all been there when it happened and it was team-building and that you paid for it, and ...'

I put my hands over my face. 'And I told you I never wanted to see wood again. I meant *wood*, actual *wood*, like tree trunks and things.' Oh this was horrible. If I thought I'd made a faux pas at the airport by forcing my colleague to picture me in a swimming costume, forcing a potential investor to visualise me 'finishing' was way way way way worse.

I collected my thoughts (my dignity was long gone) and took a huge gulp of cocktail, eventually looking back up at Lara. 'So. Scheana's pregnant?'

Lara thankfully was fanning her watering eyes, her blushes and laughter subsiding. She smiled at me, the misunderstanding very much forgiven, and took a deep breath. 'I feel just awful spilling Sche's secret, I shouldn't have said anything, I just assumed you knew.'

'No . . . I guess she's not at three months yet.'

'No, I guess not. It's the reason she didn't come to New York, so I guess I just assumed she would have confided in you.'

'Yeah. Except, she didn't come to New York because she broke her leg.'

Lara shrugged. I didn't know what was going on with Scheana, but we'd probably both done enough guessing for today. I took a breath and tried to rebuild what was now a strange, precarious relationship. 'So, Lara, we've talked a lot about me, and Girls of the World, and Scheana's body, one way or another. Tell me about you, how did you come to own your own business?'

17 December

1 week, 1 day to Christmas

I'd had a funny night's sleep, which was frustrating because my jet lag was making me reeeeeeeally want to snooze my head off, but my brain was all, *hell no, we have to think about Scheana and what this all means.* So I was lying awake early, and wondering if I should just give her a call and ask her what was going on.

I shouldn't ring her. If she'd wanted to tell me she would have; this was none of my business.

But ... why would she tell Lara and not me? Was there no baby? Was that just the excuse she gave Lara? I felt embarrassed about my meeting, and now I was worried her lasting impression of me was one of someone who wasn't kept in the loop by her senior management, and someone who accidently went on about slipping around on wood during a business meeting.

I blushed again at the memory. And after thirty more seconds of arguing with myself I thought, Bugger it, and called her before I could change my mind.

'Hey, Liv, how's it going?' Scheana's voice rang clear down the line.

'Good, really well. We miss you.'

'Awwww.'

'How's the leg?'

'Good, yeah, ouchy ... '

'So I had dinner with Lara last night,' I said.

'I *love* Lara! How was she? How did it go?'

'I think it went really well, though there was one thing she said which threw me a little bit, and I didn't know what she was talking about so I felt like a bit of a wally.'

'Don't be hard on yourself; I'm sure you did absolutely brilliantly.'

'Well, she wondered how you were doing ... and the baby.' I paused, holding my breath. I hadn't wanted to put Scheana on the spot, and I immediately wished I'd never opened my big gob.

After a gap of what seemed like for ever, Scheana

laughed, lightly. 'Busted. So Lara let the cat out of the bag?'

'She assumed I'd know. But, you know, I didn't.'

'I'm not at three months yet, so I didn't want to talk about it with anyone.'

'But you told Lara. We had this huge misunderstanding where she thought ... Never mind, I'll tell you all about it when I get back.'

'Sorry to have put you in that position. I've known Lara a really long time, so I told her the truth. You I've known a long time as well, but if anything had gone wrong, and I'd lost the baby ... I have to see you every day. I see Lara maybe twice a year. I was just protecting myself.'

That made sense. I wished she'd told me, but I got it. I can't imagine how hard it must be to say the words aloud if you lose your baby. I lightened my tone of voice. 'So is your leg even broken?'

'No. But my doctor advised me – medical stuff – that I shouldn't fly during my first trimester. So I feigned being a big old weakling at the Fearless Freeze to get out of it.'

I couldn't help but let a laugh escape. 'Did you even need to be on that stretcher at all?'

'No,' she replied. 'I basically hung out at the start until you'd all gone round the corner, rubbed myself in mud and then went and made friends with the guys in the medical tent. It's amazing what people'll do for you when you say you can introduce their daughter to an astronaut.'

'Who do you know who's an astronaut?'

'*My* daughter. She may only be five but it's all she talks about; I know full well she'll get there.'

Scheana was such a goddess; I wished *I* was her daughter. 'OK, last day. I've got to go – you take care and I'll see you after the Christmas hols.'

'And I'll tell everyone about my baby then, all right? Can you not mention it to anyone else?'

'Of course not. I might tell them your broken leg has gone gangrenous though.'

'Fair enough. Keep up the good work, lady – I'm going to make sure everyone sees what a shining star you are when you get back. See ya, Liv.'

'See ya, Sche.'

All right. I felt better now that Scheana had put my mind at rest. She *did* trust me. Everything was fine, and now I just needed to go down to the conference one last time, have a final day of plugging Girls of the World, and then work would be overrrrrrrrrrrr – for two weeks. I was excited as a child on Christmas morning – or at least that's how excited I assumed I was.

I decided to dress in all-out spangles for the gala evening. I looked like a holly-jolly Christmas tree, and I was proud of it. This had been such an unexpectedly great few days that all I wanted to do was to continue sparkling. Did I tell you that Laverne Cox made a surprise closing speech today? She was fantastic – utterly inspirational, and though I was mildly miffed that Amal hadn't showed, with George to carry her things, Laverne brought down the house. And tomorrow we got to go home! From tomorrow I would spend two whole happy weeks wearing pyjamas so this evening I was going to brave the cold and get my glitter on, once and for all.

I exited my hotel room and sashayed my sequinned self down the corridor, knocking at Dee, Abigail and Jasmine's rooms on the way. As I waited for them I tried to call Anne again. I'd been trying all week, and I'd had one missed call back from her – so I knew she was alive – but other than that we were simply disconnected.

Abigail emerged first, looking pretty and more grown up than usual in a white shift dress. 'Hi,' she said shyly.

I hung up after another no-answer. 'You look nice,' I said to Abigail. 'Excited?'

'About going home?' She nodded, enthusiastically.

'About tonight . . .'

'Oh, yes, definitely, sorry – it's just that my boyfriend is going to meet me at the airport and we're going to start Christmas festivities straight away. He says he's going to surprise me with something really fun.'

'What do you think it is?' That was nice that he was meeting her at the airport. I would be taking the tube home – separately from my colleagues – so in a way I, too, was starting my Christmas festivities from the minute we landed.

'I don't know . . .' But she instinctively looked at her hands. Abigail was such a fairy-tale princess. I wanted to describe her skin as porcelain and her lips as rosebuds, but that is not the way a boss – however temporary – should describe her team members.

Let me just clarify something: there's nothing wrong with a girl wanting to be a princess. There's nothing wrong with a boy wanting to be a princess. What you want is up to you, it's your life. It doesn't matter to me, and if anyone else gives a flying f*** that's their problem. It certainly doesn't make you less of a feminist, less of a man, a bit gay, a loser, a dork, a geek, vain, slutty or a whore. So, princesses all over the world, go forth, be and do whatever you want.

I climbed off my soap box and collected the rest of

my team. Jasmine actually smiled, briefly, so presumably she'd cracked into the minibar in her room. Dee had the hugest smile on her face, and Ian, who would only meet my eye very quickly, looked very dapper in his suit.

'I can't believe we leave New York tomorrow,' twittered Dee as we stepped from the hotel into the frosty breeze and waited for a yellow cab to come by. 'It's just such a fabulous place; I'd happily stay on an extra three weeks.'

'Me too, I heart New York,' I agreed. But I also love my PJs and my bed and my flat and my peace and quiet and my sleep.

Dee huddled in close to me, linking her arm in mine. 'Thank you,' she said so quietly the words nearly flittered away down the street like snowflakes. 'For yesterday. For what you did for my birthday. It was just lovely.'

I smiled and nodded at her. 'Merry Christmas-slash-birthday, Dee. OK, this is us!' I said, breaking away from her and holding open the door of the taxi that had pulled over to the kerb. 'Get ready for the best night of your whole life this week.'

We walked into that ballroom like we were the Real Goddam Housewives of New York themselves, all blinged-up and ready to celebrate another great conference. By now, so many faces had become familiar, and a small part of me would be sad to say goodbye to them tomorrow.

I was confident that the conference had been a success. I had reams of business cards and paperwork and follow-up actions and people to stay in touch with, and ideas for how to take Girls of the World forward. My plan for the plane ride home tomorrow was to get it all down in one place and make a plan. I love making plans.

We gave ourselves over to mingling, laughing, quaffing Prosecco and chowing down on appetisers. I waved at Lara across the room, who was looking resplendent in both outfit and attitude. She excused herself from the people she was talking to and made her way over to me.

'Olivia, I have been feeling just awful about letting slip yesterday and putting you in that position,' she said, kissing me on the cheek.

'Don't apologise, I cleared it all up with Scheana – turns out her leg is fine, and her secret is still very much a secret.'

'I also wanted to say thank you for the report you sent over last night – the numbers looked great. I was really impressed with the company, with you. I'll be in touch with Scheana, but I wanted to let you know that

I'm definitely going to see what Green PR can do for Girls of the World.'

I could have tongued Lara right there. I could have peed myself with excitement. I could have passed out with relief. But I managed to keep it together just long enough to say a gracious thank you. When Lara left I took myself off for a moment to let the magnitude of what had just happened sink in.

I'd done it. All my hard work had paid off, and I'd done it. Not only had I got us through the conference but Girls of the World was now one giant step closer to becoming an international company, and I'd helped make that happen. Well done, me, I thought. Well done, all of us.

Smiling to myself, I found myself thinking of Kim. I missed her! Last year at this very gala we'd sneaked a bottle of Jack Daniel's away and into the bathroom where we stayed, giggling, for over an hour, making huge, wild plans on what we would do when we moved out to New York together and got bit-parts in *Gossip Girl* (yes, I know that show ended in 2012). I missed my Kim. So I ordered a Jack Daniel's and got out my phone.

'Aloha!' she answered, in full spirits. 'Or whatever they say here. How are you, you big fat Noo Yoiker? I'm so sorry, you're not fat.'

'Haha, I'm very well thanks! Tired, happy, missing yoooou.'

'I miss you too! Why don't you fly out here instead of home tomorrow? Do you know England is snowy AF right now?'

'No way.' I cast my mind back to the weather report we'd all watched at Heathrow on the way out. 'That snowstorm really hit? I just thought the British media were flying into their usual panic.'

'It happened, sista; total white-out. So where are you right now?'

I looked around me. 'I am at the after-party, the grand gala. You know that meeting I had to go to, with Lara from Green PR?'

'The big important scary one?'

'That's the one. Long story short, it went OK yesterday, other than a misunderstanding about group orgies. Anyway, Lara just told me they're going to help represent Girls of the World!'

Kim started shrieking and there were a lot of *OMG*s and *fantastic*s before she calmed down.

'And you want to know something else?' I continued. 'I'm wearing sequins and everything – people totally think I'm into Christmas.'

'That's my girl!' Kim squealed. 'Where's Jon? Is he looking mighty fine in his tux?'

'He's ...' I peered through the crowd; I felt like I hadn't seen him all night. Then I spotted him, deep in conversation. He *did* look good. The jet black of the fabric made his hair and eyebrows look darker than usual, and the snow-white of his shirt made the skin on his neck and his hands look more tanned. And it fitted him really well. I cleared my throat, snapping myself out of it. 'He's talking to Dani.'

'Dani? Who the hell is Dani?'

'Oh, she's really cool; she works with him at HeForShe. Wow – she looks stunning.' The two of them looked good together.

'What's she wearing?'

'A sort-of silvery long dress, very Charlize Theron.'

'And what did you say you were wearing?'

'A sequin dress.'

'Wow – a whole dress of sequins?'

'I know, but I look OK.' I tugged on it self-consciously. I *felt* OK.

'I bet you look phenomenal. Better than Dani.'

I laughed. 'It's not a competition.'

'Get off your high horse, you bloody feminist,' Kim cackled down the line. 'It's always a competition, especially with people with names like Dani – that's a very cool name.'

'And she's really nice as well. Like, not fake nice or

sugary nice, like, I kind of wanna be your best friend nice.'

'Hey!'

'Only if you died or something.'

Kim *hmph*ed into the phone. 'Am I that replaceable?'

'That depends on what present you bring me back from Antigua. Anyway, why are we even talking about Dani and me being in competition?'

'You started it. I just asked where Jon was and you basically said, "He's talking to another girl waaaahhhh".'

'I did not.' I turned away from Jon and Dani and walked back to our table. 'So what did you do today in paradise, Vanessa Paradis?'

'Wouldn't you like to know, Jack Sparrow. We went snorkelling and Steve got a nosebleed, so then we went jet-skiing and he got another nosebleed. Poor lamb. But now he's right as rain and dancing with a woman in huge feathers at the Creole theme night around the pool.'

'And where are you?'

'Resting my feet on a sunlounger. I've been dancing with feather lady for the past two hours.'

'Are you having a good trip?'

'I am,' she answered, with what I could hear was a smile. 'I love you heaps, honeybunch, but this man does make me happy too.'

'I'm glad.'

'You have a few hours left in New York. Can I say one thing? It's just … I want you to be happy. If someone reaches out to you, maybe you should open up a little and let them in.'

My heart responded with a lonely thump. I was happy as I was, I didn't need a man.

'It's not about needing a man,' she continued, reading me like a book. 'It's about letting yourself enjoy someone who makes you happy. Not everyone's a Kevin … Liv?'

'Sorry,' I said, shaking myself from my thoughts. 'All right, Bo Derek, you go back to your scene from *10* and I'll go back to parading my be-sequinned body around New York in search of a man.'

'I didn't mean—'

'I know you didn't, and I'll think about what you said. Or kill Steve so you can go back to being the Thelma to my Louise instead.'

'Fair enough. Have a good night, cherub.'

'And you, shnookums.'

We rang off and I turned to survey the room, sipping on my Jack Daniel's. My eyes rested on Jon, who was now listening to Dani talk. I looked at his face, a face that made me smile, and … I just … he really did look incredibly dashing in his jet-black tux.

Suddenly, for no good reason, I imagined what it would be like kissing him and I closed my eyes. I imagined his face near mine, his hand on my cheek, his hair flopping onto my forehead. I imagined him growing serious, his chocolate eyes becoming more intense, but his features warmed by that slight, open-mouthed smile as he came in closer.

'Hi,' he said softly, and my eyes shot open.

'Kissing!' I yelped at him before I could stop myself.

'Well, all right.' Jon wrapped an arm around me and swept me into a low dip, hovering above me for a moment, our lips close while I tried to distinguish if this was actually happening or if I'd fallen into some strange jet-lagged dream in the middle of the gala. But within milliseconds he pulled me back up and chuckled, placing me gently back into a standing position and grinning down at me. 'What the hell were you thinking about, standing there with your eyes closed?'

'Um . . .' I non-answered.

'I was talking to Dani and I looked over and thought you were about to pass out, then as I . . . ' He started laughing. 'As I got closer . . . ' His laugh got louder. 'As I got closer I saw you were licking your lips and I was like, "YES, Olivia, you enjoy those appetisers, lady!"'

'I love food!' I shrieked, hiding my embarrassment.

'Um, so anyway, can you believe that's another New York conference done?'

'I know; it went too quickly.'

I nodded, and we stood in silence for a moment, with me looking anywhere but at him. 'Are you looking forward to going home? For Christmas?'

'Definitely. We should see each other again soon though – before the London conference. I've missed you and we've barely caught up on this trip.'

'I know. I'm sorry – I've been so busy lately, but yes, we should have a proper catch-up soon.'

'How about now?' he asked. 'The night is still young, the gala's almost over, I don't know about you but my jet lag has thrown my sleep patterns completely out of whack. Why don't we go and see a bit of real New York? Let's find a crap diner and sit by the window and drink a ridiculous amount of free-refill coffees.'

I looked around me. My work here was done. My team could make their way back to the hotel on their own, and other than getting everyone to the airport tomorrow I was nearly, very nearly, on me-time. 'Let's do it. We're not allowed to go back and get changed though; we have to go in our fancy-pants outfits.'

'I think we're dressed perfectly for a diner date,' he grinned, taking my arm. I flinched, just a little bit, at the word 'date'. I don't date. Dating is a precursor to relationships and they're more trouble than they're worth. This? This was just a late-night rendezvous, with a *friend*.

I walked into the diner and took a seat in a booth in the corner while Jon took some cash out of an ATM across the road. I gazed out of the window, finally feeling on wind-down, and finally beginning to appreciate where I was and what season it was; outside, the streets were ink-black, sprinkled with the bright lights of office and shop windows. Snow fell gently, lazily, as if out of habit rather than it really needing to.

The door opened with a tinkle of bells and in walked Jon, all thick-wool coat and snow-dusted hair. He strode to the table and removed his coat, peppering me with snowflakes.

'I'm so happy we're doing this,' he said. 'Catching up, properly. Did you hear the news reports, by the way? I was just checking the BBC app when I was in the queue.' His cheeks were flushed from walking fast through the cold New York streets and under the table his knees knocked against mine and immediately my legs, clad in nothing but thin shiny tights, began to warm with his body heat.

'What news reports?'

'The snow in the UK has got worse, and they think it's going to go on all night. The biggest snowfall in six years, they're saying.'

'Kim mentioned the snow on the phone, but surely it can't be that bad across the whole country? Are you sure this isn't just in the north?'

Jon ran a hand through his hair, shaking out the last of the snow and leaving wet tousled strands in his wake. 'Nope; all over. I spoke to Mum and Dad earlier in Cornwall – they say it's even beginning to settle on the beach, which is rare.'

'I've never seen a beach in the snow – how cool is that?'

'One day you can spend Christmas with me and I'll show you.' He smiled.

I laughed. 'You don't want to spend Christmas with me; Kim says I'm so un-festive that I wouldn't even notice if Santa plopped down my chimney.'

'That can't be true. I know you're not the first in line to sing carols or hang candy canes, but do you actually not like Christmas?'

'No, I like it – I like having time off work, I like the good TV, I like seeing family at some point over the break, I'm just not your typical Christmas traditionalist.' At that point a waitress arrived, and looked at us until we put in an order. 'Can we have two coffees, please?'

I said. 'And some of these buttermilk waffles? With bacon? And maybe ... have you had any New York cheesecake since you've been here?'

Jon shook his head.

'And a slice of cheesecake please. What else shall we get?'

'Do you have any pretzel dogs?' asked Jon, and the waitress shrug-nodded so we took that as an affirmative.

'What's a pretzel dog?' I asked him.

'I don't really know, I've just always wanted to try one.'

'Cool. Two of those, please.'

We people-watched, made comfortable small talk and sipped our coffees, eagerly awaiting our weird and wonderful feast, which when it arrived took up the whole table.

'Wow. Do you think I can put this on expenses?' I smiled, stretching out my sequinned dress in anticipation.

'This one is on me.'

'No it's not. It's on me.'

'No it's not. It's on me.'

Hmm. We'd sort this out at the end.

'So,' said Jon. 'What's going on with you? Last time I saw you, you were saving for a house, drawing up some kind of plan ... ?'

'Yes, the plan is very much in place. It's hard – there were setbacks to my plan a few years ago but I'm getting it back on track, slowly but surely.'

'Setbacks?'

'A douche-flop of an ex-boyfriend, but let's not get into that. The plan is going ahead!'

'All right, so what's the plan?' Jon cut the immense waffle into two and poured most of a jug of maple syrup on his side.

'It starts with a two-week staycation in my pyjamas, beginning in just over twenty-four hours.'

'That's a good start.'

'Then I'm going to go back to work in the New Year, all refreshed, and take all my ideas to the directors on how to expand Girls of the World globally. Then I'm going to get a raise, then within the next couple of years I'll be a director myself, another raise, I'll become best friends with Tina Fey or Amy Poehler or Lena Dunham or someone, and hopefully, I'll be able to buy a house in the countryside, with five dogs and a library, by the time I'm mid to late thirties, which I know is late to be getting on the property ladder but I think it's doable.' I took a breath and a gulp of my coffee, watching him over my mug for his reaction.

Jon grinned at me. 'That's a big plan, good for you. A house in the country, hey? Would you commute?'

'I guess so ... if I'm a director I suppose I could do what I want.'

'What makes you want to move out of London?'

I hesitated. 'Because that's what I've always planned to do. It's in the plan. Because I'll need at least three bedrooms if I have kids, and I can't afford that in London.'

'So the plan includes buying a house away from somewhere you know and love, for a fictional family?'

That stung. 'They're not fictional, they're just ... missing.'

'Hey, I'm sorry,' Jon said, realising his mistake. He reached across the table and covered the length of my forearm with his own, cupping my elbow and leaning closer. 'I didn't mean to be mean. I think I was just misunderstanding, because you hadn't mentioned finding that family in your plan.'

I was quiet, watching my coffee swirl in its mug.

'Are you ... ready ... for a family?'

'Oh no, I'm not looking for someone yet,' I said quickly.

'OK.'

'It's just, you know.'

'Totally.'

'Relationships – blurgh.'

'Yuck.'

'They're just so . . . ' I looked out of the window at the window display opposite, the lights appearing bulbous against the wet windows. What was the word? 'Tricksy.'

'Are they?' Jon sipped his coffee and watched me. When had he moved his arm away?

At that point the door tinkled open again and a couple came in, similar age to us, shopping bags first, laughing their heads off and banging their purchases against themselves, the counter, everything they came into contact with. I watched them, all happiness and excitement, as they danced their way towards a table.

Jon followed my eye line and smiled at the couple. 'So you don't want to go Christmas shopping and wear matching mittens with someone?'

'I don't know . . . ' I crinkled my nose. 'Maybe one day but at the moment I don't have anyone to wear matching mittens with, which is fine, by the way.'

'What about me?'

'Would you like to get some matching mittens, Jon?'

'Maybe I would. Would you?'

My heart slowed and I was suddenly afraid of making a wrong step. Was he flirting? And if he was, did he mean it? 'I think you should share mittens with some-one a bit less Scrooge-like,' I said carefully. 'So what will you and your family be doing over Christmas?'

I smiled, trying to lighten the mood and push bitter thoughts of Kevin to the back of my mind.

'Home!' He smiled that big smile. 'My parent's house is going to be mad this year – my two sisters, and my brother, and my other brother and his husband will be there. All of their kids, who range from one and a half to eight, have apparently already devised a play for us, which goes on longer than *Lord of the Rings* and is largely plagiarised from *Frozen*. My aunt is joining us because my uncle passed away earlier in the year—'

'I'm so sorry!' I interrupted.

'Thanks. Then there'll be me, slurping on the port and watching the madness unfold.'

'Do you like spending Christmas with all those people?'

'Of course!'

'Don't you just want some alone-time?'

Jon laughed, looking puzzled at my silly question. 'Not at Christmas. It's not allowed at Christmas. Why, what are you doing? Are you having people over to yours or is your staycation based at your parents' house?'

'No, my parents are away – Tenerife this year. They always take a winter sun holiday over Christmas.'

'Wait, but isn't one of your sisters in Miami? And Kim's in the Caribbean. Who are you spending Christmas with? Your little sister?'

'She's going to Thailand. I'll be spending Christmas with myself.'

Jon picked up a spoon and then dropped it for dramatic effect. 'You're spending Christmas alone? Who do you think you are, the man on the moon?'

Who's this man on the moon people keep talking about? Neil Armstrong? 'I won't be alone, I'll have the future prime minister with me – me.'

'Why aren't you going to Tenerife with your folks?'

I shrugged. 'I didn't feel like it. It's fine – Anne, my Florida sister, is coming over in January so we're having a family Christmas then. Well . . . '

'Well?'

'I mean, we won't make it very Christmassy in January, but it'll be a nice get-together.'

'Do you want to come to mine for Christmas?'

I looked at Jon for a minute, unsure if he was joking.

'No, I'm serious,' he continued, reading my mind. 'Oh it'll be great!' He jumped up and swung around to my side of the table, sliding in next to me and angling his body towards me. His scarf flopped on my knee, leaving a small warm patch. 'You should definitely, one hundred per cent, spend Christmas with me.'

'Why should I do that?'

'So many reasons. Firstly, you can pretend you're my girlfriend, which would make my mum so happy, would give my aunt something to gossip about – and remember she's a poor grieving widow so she needs this – and it might also shut up my brother's husband who has never even seen me talk to a girl and is convinced I'm "one of them".'

I laughed. 'Those are good reasons, but—'

'Wait, I have more.' He edged closer still. 'You … you … can still have downtime, I'll keep out of your way other than when we're pretending we're madly in love, or eating Christmas dinner, or sharing a bed, of course.'

'What?'

'Fine, the bed's yours. Um, you don't have to like any of them, I only like about half of them, and only about a third of the kids, but I promise all of them will like you, and they'll love having you there.'

'Jon, this is very sweet of you, but I'm not spending Christmas alone because nobody else likes me, or because I don't have any other imaginary boyfriends, I just don't …'

He waited while I found my words.

'I don't have any experience in a traditional Christmas, so to me, I'm not missing out on anything. It's been a tough year, dealing with an awful lot of people and their quirks and dramas and successes and you have no idea how many secrets you end up knowing about people and their genitals when you're a manager, I found that out within the last month, and I'm really, truly, just looking forward to some time off. By myself.'

Jon thought about this for a while before peering back up at me. 'The offer doesn't go away, if you change your mind.'

'Thank you.' I flipped his scarf in his face, embarrassed by the lapse in conversation.

'So you've *never* had a traditional Christmas?'

'No.' I shrugged. 'What's the big deal?'

'The big deal is that we're about to leave New York and there's a whole city of festivities going on out there that you're missing, while you sit in here like Scrooge gagging to get back to his chambers.' He dodged my hand that went to slap his leg.

And then I stopped short. 'Pissflaps.'

'Pardon?'

'Son of a nutcracker, we need to go to Rockefeller!'

'Now? OK then.' Jon stood and pulled his coat back on.

'I promised Kim I'd go and see the tree,' I babbled as we threw down some dollars and shuffled our way out of the diner and into the cold night air. 'You don't have to come, but I have to go.'

'Of course I'm coming! I'll be Kim for the evening.'

166

I swathed my parka around me, the sequins on my dress crunching underneath the waterproof, padded fabric. 'New York is cold when you're wearing a dress.'

'Tell me about it,' Jon said, wrapping an arm around me.

As we walked briskly up Fifth Avenue towards the Rockefeller Center, I found my thoughts sneaking over to Jon again. I wish he wasn't so nice, and I wish everyone stopped trying to put us together . . . it made things feel very complicated.

We saw the angels first. Two long rows of pale gold, fairy-light-covered statues holding trumpets to the heavens that no matter your religion or attitude towards Christmas couldn't help but evoke a feeling of calm and magic. And framed at the end of the walkway, nestled at the bottom of the Rockefeller building and overlooking the famous ice rink . . . 'There it is!' I smiled.

The Rockefeller Christmas tree – vast, tall, fat, covered in a million twinkles and topped with a Swarovski star – was everything I remembered it to be. I can't believe I nearly didn't come here . . .

My eyes trailed over the humans of New York, all these people, embracing selfie heaven and thoroughly enjoying the city at Christmas. A huge family of what looked like four generations were bunching against a railing with the ice rink in the background, arguing good-naturedly about who should be more prominent in the family photo. A couple were sharing a static kiss in front of the tree while one of them held out their phone to try and selfie the moment. A woman in her early twenties was absent-mindedly bopping away to the Christmas music blasting up from the ice rink while she played on her phone, a hundred shopping bags hanging from her arms.

I sighed and looked up at the top of the tree, far above me, with 30 Rock towering far above *it*.

'You OK? Are you making a wish?' Jon said.

'What?' I laughed.

'You're staring up at that star pretty hard. Are you wishing Kim was here?'

'I wish Kim was everywhere I was, but that's not what I was wishing. And besides, you make an excellent Kim substitute.'

'So can you tell me what you were wishing? Or will that break the spell?'

I tried to form my words. 'If you laugh at me I'll tell Carl you really want to hear about his favourite buses on the way home.'

'I won't laugh.'

'Fine. I was wishing that I was like these people.' I gestured towards the large family.

'What, American?'

'That's not what I mean, not like them specifically. Like anyone here. Look how happy they are and how excited they are about being in New York at Christmas. I just . . . I wish I was like them. I feel like I didn't make the most of it and now we're going home.'

'But you're not into Christmas. And that's OK. You don't have to be like everyone else if that's not you.'

'I know, and that's what I'm telling people all the time, but they do all look happy and maybe there's something in that. I don't know. In hindsight I just kind of wish I'd been a bit more open-minded, seen what all the fuss was about, and given being merry and bright a go. Then if I was still not bothered, at least I'd know. And it would have made spending Christmas holed up on my own in my PJs even sweeter than I already know it will be.'

Jon pulled me into a one-armed hug and we gazed up at the tree together. 'So what you're saying is you want the George Bailey experience.'

'Who's George Bailey? The photographer?'

'No, my festively challenged friend. George Bailey is the star of *It's A Wonderful Life*, have you seen it?'

I shook my head.

'In it, George wants to commit suicide because . . . Well, I won't go into it because I don't think that bit is relevant to you. Anyway, this angel called Clarence visits him. You can call him Jon. And he shows George what life in his town would be like if he'd never been born. Which again, is not quite what you're going through, but he has a couple of days of seeing things from the other side so he can carry on with his life and be happy.'

I nodded slowly. 'Well that sounds nothing like my problem really, but thanks anyway.'

Jon chuckled and waved towards the angels. 'What you need is for me to be your Clarence, your Christmas guardian angel. Come to my family home and let me show you how we do things over on the festive side, and then you'll know what all the fuss is about. And how you celebrate from then on is up to you.'

'I don't know. What I need is to have two weeks of sleeping in, letting my hair air-dry, watching the type of TV normal people are ashamed to watch, reading a hundred books and stuffing my face full of breakfast food at all times of the day. I'm just thinking out loud really.'

Jon clapped his hands together. 'OK, how about this? I'll show you my version of Christmas, then you show me yours.'

'My Christmas involves being on my own, no offence.'

'Tough luck, because my Christmas involves never having a moment of peace.'

'What if you need to go to the loo?'

'Going to the loo is the busiest time! The nieces and nephews will just bang and scream at the door, the lock won't work properly, a mum – any mum – will be yelling from the kitchen about whether you want a glass of wine or if she can put it in the gravy instead. It's really fun,' Jon said happily.

'It does sound fun,' I half joked. Actually there was something about it that sounded kind of nice. In an awful way. My family were going to be so spread out – again – what with Lucy in Thailand, Anne in Miami, me at home in London and my parents in Tenerife. But that's what I wanted: solitude.

I looked back up at the tree, pleased I'd made it down here. 'Maybe one day,' I said. 'One day you can show me your Christmas, but this year I think I'd better stick to my plan. Goodbye, New York,' I whispered into the falling snow and the night air. Sorry I didn't let you in this year. 'See you next Christmas.'

18 December

1 week to Christmas

I woke with a whopping great snort to a pitch-black hotel room and a rapping at my door. Did I oversleep? Had I missed my flight? Was I about to be murdered? At least the murderer was polite enough to knock, especially since apparently I'd been too hot at some point in the night and thrown off my PJ bottoms. Where the hell were they?

Knock-knock-knock-knock-knock. 'Olivia?' someone hissed.

Not wanting to show off my own full moon, I hauled myself from the bed and wrapped the sheet around my lower half like a meringue wedding dress skirt, and shuffled towards the door. Maybe it was surprise room service. Mmm, I could definitely eat a Philly cheese-steak right now ...

'Who is it?' I yawned as I opened the door, negating the point in asking.

Abigail stood there, twitching about like a baby deer, wrapped in a dressing gown and an air of distress.

'Abi, hello ...' I peered past her and down the deserted corridor. 'You didn't bring any room service with you, did you?'

'No,' she said in an almost whisper. 'Did you order some? Do you want me to go and check for you?'

'No, don't worry about it. What's up? Isn't it the middle of the night?'

'It's seven a.m. My boyfriend's still up at home watching weather reports because the snow is really bad in England, and he just called me because *look*.' Abigail held her phone up to my face, and I squinted in the bright light. When I could focus a big red word jumped out at me. CANCELLED.

Abigail scuttled past me and into my room, tapping away at her phone.

I closed my door and followed her back inside, pushing yesterday's knickers towards the edge of the room with my foot. 'Cancelled? Our flight? That's a pain. We'll squeeze onto the next one, I'm sure. At least you'll get to see New York in some proper, thick snow.' I wondered if it would be unprofessional to climb back into bed with Abigail still in the room. Given my business-up-top, party-down-below state of undress, I concluded that yes: it would be unprofessional, and a touch sex-pesty.

'No, here's not the problem.' Abigail hurled open the curtains to show nothing more than some flittery-fluttery snowflakes that wouldn't look out of place at a Disneyland Christmas. 'It's the UK, it's snowbound.'

'Well that's impossible. This is England we're talking about, not Alaska. Maybe Scotland and the north, *maybe* London, are actually snowbound, but if all else fails I'm sure the south-west will be clear enough and I think some flights go from New York into Bristol. But it'll be fine, I bet we'll just get on the next flight. Now why don't we meet at breakfast in half an hour or so and we'll come up with a game plan ...' I led Abigail towards the door, but she whipped back around at the last minute and my toga-skirt wobbled precariously.

'I don't know, my boyfriend said it's all over the country – he said over fifty per cent of flights are cancelled.'

Over fifty per cent?

I felt like Kate letting go of Leo after the *Titanic* sank. Only Leo was my holiday leave and I was stuck with my workmates rather than on my own, like lucky Kate. An image of myself floated into my mind: coming in through my door, kicking off my shoes, dumping my suitcase in the hall to be unpacked a few days later and not having to hear or see any workmates for two peaceful weeks. And then it floated away, into the dark, drifting like a snowflake.

I held back a sigh. As the acting-manager, people expected me to have all the answers and come up with all the solutions and figure it all out, and as tired as I was it looked like that still had to be on me for a bit longer than expected. 'OK, well … let me get dressed and then we'll round up the troops and find out exactly what's going on. From someone at BA, not from your boyfriend.'

I gently shoved Abigail out of my room and then flopped down on the bed, a sense of foreboding creeping over me. If I couldn't get everybody home for Christmas, would that mean we'd have to spend it together? I couldn't organise Christmas. I didn't know how – walking in a winter wonderland was foreign to me. And I didn't have the strength, or energy, to do it for the people I'd been counting down the days to have distance from. All I wanted for Christmas was to be home, alone.

Part 2

Dashing through the snow, in a one horse open sleigh
Over the fields we go, laughing all the way.

18 December continued ...

1 week to Christmas

❄

'Hi!' Jon's voice chirped happily down the phone at me.

'Good morning!' I replied, scrutinising the contents of my suitcase, most of which were strewn across the floor. I kicked a pair of knickers out of my way and uncovered a clean pair – *yes!* 'Is your flight on schedule?'

'That's what I was calling you about – no, Virgin have cancelled it. And the one after it, but it looks like the flights later in the day are going, so they must be busy shovelling snow, Old Man Marley-style over at Heathrow. And you?'

'Cancelled, but lots are still showing as on schedule. I think we'll head to the airport anyway, see what's going on and wait it out. How about you and Carl?'

'Yeah, we'll come to the airport with you . . . ' There was a shuffling noise and what sounded like Carl protesting with the words *'seven hours?'* and then Jon came back on the line. 'Carl's up for it, he loves airports.'

❄

With seven of us squeezed into a mini-van, trying to make light small talk but with minds elsewhere, the trip to the airport was a little sombre. Abigail was staring out of the window searching for planes to take her back to her boyfriend, and Dee and Ian were sitting in the back of the people carrier in silence, pretending they weren't holding hands under their coats. Jasmine was intermixing texting, tutting and shooting dagger stares at me in a way that said, *I can't believe you fudged up like this.*

'Never had this happen before,' she muttered.

I ignored her and turned to Jon. 'So you're not flying back with BA?'

'We're flying back with Virgin,' Jon explained, stretching over me to look out the car window at the sky, laying a hand briefly on my leg. 'Or so we thought.'

Carl nodded his agreement while nibbling on half a pretzel he'd found in his pocket.

Jon went on quietly, 'Maybe we'll get to have the George Bailey experience in New York after all.'

I thought about the night before, about how relaxed and fun it had been. I'd needed that, and I felt closer to New York and Christmas because of it, because of Jon. But I had to get these people home.

'Just a little longer to wait then we'll be home.' I was trying to cheer myself up as much as anyone else. 'I'm sure the airlines have it all under control.'

❄

As we walked through the doors of JFK airport we were faced with a scene straight out of a disaster movie, minus the actual disaster. The vast crowd had formed itself into spaghetti-junction queues, and everyone was talking loudly into their phones, slurping from water supplies and fanning themselves with rapidly outdating boarding passes. There was also an unsettling lack of staff behind the long rows of check-in desks, just forlorn Christmas wreaths hanging where the workers should be.

'Right.' I surveyed the scene, trying to keep my voice light. 'Come along then.'

We wheeled our suitcases in and out and over

people's feet until we were in the British Airways zone. I picked a queue and we settled into it, because being British we knew this was how best to handle a crisis. Jon and Carl ambled off to find the Virgin desks, and as Jon left he hurled a grin at me and I realised he didn't seem quite as bothered about the delay in returning home as the rest of us.

'Hey,' I called after him, and he turned.

'Yep?'

'You aren't gagging to get home to that big family Christmas?'

'Christmas is nearly a week away, we have loads of time to get home. I'm quite happy if we get to stay here a bit longer.'

So here we were, in a queue that looked like it belonged in Disneyland in the height of summer, weaving, stretching, snaking its way back and forth in front of the check-in desks. Above us, long banks of TV screens with departure information on them were showing an awful lot of red. I stood on tiptoes and searched the crowds for someone in BA's trademark navy blue, but I couldn't see anyone. For now, at least, we were on our own.

'All right,' I chirped. 'Let's just wait it out here for a while and I'm sure someone will come and tell us what's going on soon.'

'Do you want me to just go and find someone?' sighed *guess who*. 'Then we'll actually have some answers?'

'No, I don't want you to go anywhere. If BA had answers they'd come and tell us. I'm sure they're working their arses off – wherever they are – to try and figure out what to do with all these people, so we need a little patience.'

Jasmine sat down on her suitcase and looked away.

'Oh no,' Abigail wailed and stepped forward, breaking apart Dee and Ian, who were standing as close as two people could without touching. 'My boyfriend just texted me and he says they're cancelling flights all over Europe – the snow is just getting worse!'

This rippled up and down the queue and before long everyone was swapping stories on how *they'd* heard the snow was three foot thick at Heathrow, that there wouldn't be any flights until January, that it was all a BA conspiracy, that Christmas was *ruined* and that none of this would have happened if we hadn't legalised gay marriage.

'OK, OK, calm down everyone,' I said to my colleagues. 'I think it's pretty likely that we won't be going home today . . . ' I tailed off. We weren't going to be going home today. I'd guessed that, really, but now I knew for sure. My little flat, with its slippers and its silly little Christmas tree and its pizzas in the freezer suddenly seemed even further away than they'd felt all week.

I shook myself out of it. So we would be here for another day. Heathrow will have the snowploughs in by tomorrow, and New York City really wasn't the worst place to be stuck. 'As soon as a BA rep comes along we'll find out if they have any idea when planes will be flying again, and if they have a plan for us to go to some airport hotel or something.'

Dee and Ian exchanged a sideways look, Jasmine remained silent and picked at her nails, and Abigail pulled her phone out to search her Twitter feed for *#SnowmageddonUK*. I watched her chew her bottom lip. 'Abi, we'll be heading back tomorrow, I'm sure. It can't be that *all* the airports in Europe are closed. Maybe we'll have to fly into Amsterdam or something and then get on a Eurostar back to London. You'll see your boyfriend really soon.'

Abigail nodded without meaning it. 'I know, it's just that we had all these plans. Tomorrow he was going to pick me up from the airport and he had that surprise planned. Then we were going to visit his family, then we've got tickets to Somerset House – for the ice rink – the day after. If our flight doesn't go then Christmas is—'

'Don't you dare say "ruined".' I stopped her.

'Christmas is whatever you make it – contrary to popular belief, it's not only Christmas if you follow a certain procedure.'

'Damn right,' said a man in front of us in the queue without turning around. He wore a scruffy leather jacket and was leaning against a piller, nose-deep in a magazine article.

I blinked. Was he talking to us? I studied the back of his neck for a moment before turning back to Abigail.

'So, um, let's not jump to conclusions. Christmas is still on. We're still going home. Everything will be fine and ... ' My stomach growled. 'And everyone needs to calm down so I can think about food for a minute.' Yes, food. That's what we needed. I had always found thoughts of food soothing.

The man in front of us straightened up and stretched, cracking his neck joints, before turning around with a grin.

HELLO. My eyes met his and I found myself smiling back. He had a lovely face – a face that combined the best bits from that guy from *Game of Thrones* and *Nashville* with that other guy from *Star Wars*. You know the ones. A face with stubble and dark eyes and perfect snog-lips that looked like they'd bite you mid-make-out, in a good way.

Dee and Ian went back to chattering intimately, while Abigail returned to her phone.

'There's a lot of motivational speaking going on in your group,' he commented in a soft American accent. 'Can I make a wild guess that you're the boss?'

'I am,' I laughed, and checking the others weren't listening, added, 'And I'm looking forward to getting everyone home.'

He nodded, catching my drift. 'You need a break?' He handed his magazine to me. 'I've got the latest *People* right here and there's a pretty juicy story on Katy Perry and Taylor Swift that's worth a read.'

I took the magazine, my brows furrowed. 'Thanks . . . are you sure you're done? Did you have a chance to read this one?' I pointed to a story on the cover called 'Could All the Real Housewives be Off to Prison?'.

'I read it,' he nodded. 'But it was a little sensationalist. Nothing more than them breaking contract by refusing to film a whole episode in Cabo at a funeral. So it's yours, take it.'

'Thank you.'

'It's made its way down the line and I think I've had it for more than my fair share. And besides, you mentioned food, and that's a sure-fire way to get a guy to stop reading and give up his magazine.'

'Oh, I wasn't trying to get your attention!' I said, mortified.

'I know.' He grinned again. 'But my stomach listened anyway. I doubt we're leaving here anytime soon so could I ask a huge favour?'

'Maybe,' I replied.

'Could you watch my bag for like, five minutes while I grab something to eat?'

'Sure.'

'You're the best.' He held out his hand. 'I'm Elijah.'

'Olivia, lovely to meet you,' I said, becoming all Queen of England-like around this foreign scoundrel. I shook his hand, and the physical contact made me want to phone my mum, and Kim, and say *Look here, you lot*, this *was the spark I kept banging on about*. I knew you needed it – I knew that being a perfect match to someone on paper wasn't enough.

Off he wandered and I watched him leave like he was Kenickie and I was Rizzo and I'm not ashamed.

I let out a long, low whistle and when I caught Dee's eye she gave me a subtle thumbs-up. Flicking through the magazine and not focusing on any of the pages, my mind and gaze wandered to Elijah's tatty suitcase and I fell into a daydream about what type of underwear it might be holding. Would we carry on talking when he was back? Perhaps we'd be sat next to each other on the plane, and he'd fall asleep on my shoulder, and I'd let him and then make some joke about how he had to now buy me breakfast. Ha, who doesn't love a pervy joke with a near-stranger?

Five, ten, fifteen minutes. He was taking a while to pick up some food ... Perhaps he was sitting in somewhere. But what if he wasn't? What if he was a devastatingly good-looking terrorist who'd just left an unattended bag full of bombs with me? Ooo, here come the sweats. I was going to be on the news. Oh lord.

As my watch ticked around to the twenty-minute mark I fanned my armpits and looked up and down the terminal. Where was he?

'What's wrong with you?' Jasmine piped up, glaring up at me from her suitcase throne.

'Nothing, everything's great. Go back to sleep.'

'What?'

I ignored her and crept an inch closer to his bag, leaning down, just a little. Was it *ticking*?

'Ian, do bombs still tick?' I hissed.

He looked up, eyes wide. 'What are you talking about?'

'Bombs. Do bombs still tick, like a clock, or is that an eighties movie thing?'

'Why the hell are you asking me?'

I ignored him and knelt next to the tatty holdall, pressing my ear against it. And of course, that's when Elijah reappeared. He stood over me, smiling curiously, looking like Chris Hemsworth after a trip to Zara Men, following a day of hard manual labour. I bet his arms were a bit filthy and sweaty under that smart jacket. God he was a fox.

'Thanks for looking after my bag,' he said, still smiling. 'You didn't have to keep *quite* this close an eye on it, you know.'

I stood up, feeling like a prize twonklodite. 'At your service, guvna!' I saluted. I hate myself sometimes. 'So what did you get to eat?'

He opened a Subway bag. 'I didn't know what you guys liked, so I just got a whole selection of sandwiches.' He looked up at me, and then at Abigail, Dee, Ian and Jasmine, whose ears had pricked with interest at the prospect of free stuff. Even Jasmine was edging forward.

'You bought Subways for us?'

'Yeah.' He shrugged, his eyes remaining on me. 'Gotta be hospitable and feed the Brits, right? Merry Christmas.'

I didn't know what to say. What a nice gesture. I thought he was leaving me with a suspicious package and all along he was buying us food. FOOD. Mmmm. I fumbled in my handbag. 'Let me give you some money for these—'

'No, don't be crazy.' He put a warm, rough hand on mine. 'Now, you look like a girl who'd like a pizza sub, am I right?'

'They do a pizza Subway? How do you know me so well already?'

'I know a kindred spirit when I see one.' He turned to the others and pulled out sandwich after sandwich. 'Girl on the phone, you look like you could do with a pick-me-up. How does a bacon melt sound?'

Abigail took the gift and practically teared up. 'It sounds like comfort food.'

'And for the happy couple, how about matching turkey and black forest ham?'

Dee and Ian leapt further apart. 'We're not a couple!' they cried in unison. Dee started laughing like a hyena sprayed with laughing gas. Ian reached forward. 'We will take the Subways though, thank you, sir.'

'My pleasure. And you.' He fixed Jasmine with a smouldering look and she flipped her hair. It was all very Coca-Cola advert.

'This is really cool of you, I didn't think we were going to get to eat today,' she remarked, glancing at me.

'You look like you need something to put a smile on your face. So how about a big ol' greasy meatball marinara?' He handed her the sub and she unwrapped it, uncertainty on her face. Was that an insult? Elijah turned back to me.

'Thank you for these,' I said, chomping into my pizza sub. *A pizza sub!*

'You're welcome. All I need from you is to keep me company in this queue.'

'Lucky for you, queueing is one of my fortes.'

'That is lucky for me. You look like you're enjoying that sandwich.'

'Hell yes, I am.' My inner goddess began to salsa – haha just kidding, I don't have an inner goddess. But I hadn't felt chemistry in a long time and it was like all my nerve-endings were waking up.

'So, Olivia,' he said, as we both chowed into our respective Subways. 'What brings you and your friends to New York?'

I sat down on my suitcase and he did the same on his bag. I remembered an article from *Sugar* magazine from when I was about fourteen that said a boy fancies you if he mirrors your actions. Elijah and I were clearly meant to be together. 'Work. I'm a temporary manager at a company called Girls of the World, this is my team, and we were here for a conference.'

'A conference about girls?'

'A conference about equality. My company helps

young girls stand up for themselves and have opinions and be confident in themselves and their brains. We go to schools and clubs around the country but also set up groups and days out and courses where people can meet new people and get involved in whatever makes them shine.'

'That's good spiel. A New York conference at Christmas, that's a sweet free ride.'

'Well, we're a pretty big community in the UK, and online we have hits from all over the world, but we're still trying to break through a bit more internationally. I didn't really have a lot of time to make the most of Christmas in this city. Do you live here?'

'I do, I live just below midtown, in the Meatpacking District. Did you get down there at all?'

'No, I don't think so. What do you do there, I've always wondered about that area? Is there a lot of ... meat to be packed?'

He laughed. 'No. I'm a musician. I play drums for a rock band; we do gigs around the city most weeks.' Of course he'd have a yummy profession. Of course he'd turn me into an eighties music video-style groupie.

'Is that why you're flying somewhere? Are you off to play a Christmas concert?' I asked him, chomping into my sandwich, which was rapidly disappearing.

'No, I'm just getting out of the city until the new year.

New York is crazy with tourists during the holidays – no offence.' He looked bashful. 'But I have a buddy in Manchester in the UK so I'm flying over to visit him for a couple of weeks.'

We talked for a while, eating our sandwiches and trading anecdotes, before a wary-looking British Airways employee appeared from nowhere and clapped her hands together to get the queue's attention. 'Ladies and gentleman, if I could have your attention please?' We all fell silent and shuffled into a semicircle around her. My right arm became pressed against Elijah's as we stepped forward, which I pretended to ignore.

'I'm afraid there won't be any more flights to the UK today . . .' the BA lady started, and a low grumble began to rise from the queue. Her face fixed into a smile that was ready for battle. 'The weather is just not letting up across the pond, and the most important thing is that you're all safe. So we don't fly until it's safe, simple as that. Other airlines are facing the same cancellations, and we estimate that nobody will be flying into British airspace for at least another twenty-four hours.'

Behind me, I heard Abigail whimper.

Beside me, Elijah turned his head slightly and caught my eye, a small smile playing on his lips, which I couldn't help but echo. Another twenty-four hours in

New York? All right, so maybe that wasn't the worst thing after all . . .

'You're welcome to stay in the airport if you want to, but I'd highly recommend you take the complimentary hotel service we'll be providing. I'll be coming down the queue to check how many are in your party and how many rooms you'll need, and then we'll be moving you to the Brooklyn Marriott, where your dinner and breakfast will be provided.'

'Excuse me?' I piped up, upon seeing Abigail's sad face. 'I just wanted to check – there's no chance of us getting a flight to France or anything today instead?'

The BA woman shook her head. 'Not today, not with the weather how it is over Europe. I'm sorry. Hopefully we'll be in the clear tomorrow.'

I faced my team and slapped on a smile. 'The Brooklyn Marriott, that's not bad. At least we're not stuck in an airport hotel. Think of it like a free holiday night in New York, no work or anything. You can do whatever you want.'

I saw Dee look over at Ian and smile a small, tender, smile. Good for them. As the woman started moving down the queue with her clipboard, my team began gathering their things, folding their magazines back in their bags, stowing away their snacks and slipping back on their discarded shoes.

Elijah slung his leather holdall onto his shoulder and looked directly at me. 'Well, Olivia, I hope we get to do this the same time tomorrow.'

'You're not coming to the hotel?' I accidently whined.

'Nah, I live so close, I might as well go home for the night.' He kept his eyes on me as he leaned in to kiss me on the cheek. 'But thank you for the company; it was great to spend time with you.'

'Ermanyu-nyuto,' I said. What I meant was 'oh, you too' but I was still sparkling like a teenager from that stolen kiss. 'Thanks for the chatter.'

'Thank *you* for the chatter.' He hovered. Was this like the end of a first date? Should I signal for him to kiss me on the *mouth*? This was not something I was completely averse to, though it was perhaps a little forward ...

'Thanks for the advice on looking after your hands, I'll remember that,' I said.

'You're welcome. Thanks for talking me through biscuits versus scones.'

'Thanks for ... ' Oh lord, this wasn't an Oscar speech. What I wanted was for him not to go – it felt too fleeting and too soon. He was hardly the love of my life after just two hours of talking, but I liked his company and it had been a while since that spark had actually sparkled. Why wasn't he asking me out?

Urgh, I could have slapped myself. What was I

always telling the girls in school? Be confident, have an opinion, don't be afraid to speak your mind about the things you like or the things you want. And now I was all 'why won't he ask me out?' like a big fat wet-wipe.

Elijah leant in for one last one-armed hug and I grabbed his arm as he pulled away. He looked at me expectantly, amusement in his eyes.

'Do you want to meet for a drink tonight?'

He grinned. 'Hell yeah, I thought you'd never ask!'

'Why didn't you ask?'

'Because you're here with all your friends and I'm the weird loner. Ball's in your court.'

'Fair enough. Where would you suggest we meet?'

'What are you into?'

In my mind Jon's face appeared, telling me about all the things New York at Christmas had to offer, all the things I'd never done. 'I have one more night in New York, so I want to do something traditional and Christmassy.'

Elijah laughed. 'Something touristy?'

'Well, I am a tourist.'

'All right … meet me on the corner of Fifth and Thirty-Third Street, outside the Empire State Building, at eight p.m.'

The Empire State Building? A ripple of excitement

went through me. I'd never been up it, and I'd seen from my hotel that it was lit up red and green for Christmas. Hang on, was this what it felt like to be excited about Christmas? Or maybe I was just excited about Elijah.

The staff from British Airways were beginning to usher us towards the buses. I suddenly had a thought and stopped short. 'Wait,' I said to nobody in particular. 'What about Jon and Carl?'

'What about them?' said Jasmine. 'You do know they don't work for us, don't you?'

'Of course, but we should see what they're doing, let them know we're going back to the city.'

'Who are Jon and Carl?' Elijah asked, picking up my case for me and shuffling closer to the door with us while I craned my neck behind me.

'They're our good friends and their flights were cancelled too . . . '

'Everyone on buses one to three please exit the terminal using the doors to the right and head straight to bus stop five, where you'll be directed onto your coach.' The BA woman rubbed her eyes, tiredly. 'I'm sorry, sir,' she called to a man who'd broken free of the group. 'The buses can't wait; they have to do many trips between the airport and the hotels this afternoon.'

'Can I just—'

'*No*,' she snapped, and he shuffled back into the group.

'Come on,' Elijah said, edging me forward. But I hadn't said goodbye to Jon. I hadn't told him Merry Christmas.

'Chop-chop,' shrilled the BA attendant, her patience wearing thin, and who could blame her? Perhaps she too thought she was about to finish for Christmas, and now she had to stay in New York, with everyone looking to her for answers and expecting her to sort everything out. With a final look back at the terminal I followed orders. *I hear ya, sista.*

Outside the coach I said goodbye to Elijah. 'See you tonight then!'

'Sure will. I'm looking forward to it.'

'Me too. And thanks again for the lunch – dinner is on me.'

'You're more than welcome, and I wouldn't dream of it. It's not every day a struggling musician from New York gets to take out an English rose.' He leaned over and for a moment I thought we were going to snog (I was feeling bizarrely up for it, even in front of my colleagues). My mouth curved into a smile as he came closer and I drew in my breath, but instead he met my eyes and then moved a fraction to the right to give me another cheek kiss. I exhaled and shook my head, just a tiny amount, as he walked away. Santa *baby* ...

❄

The drive back into the city was surreal; hadn't I just left here? The yellow taxis, the road signs, the skyline, it was all coming back to me like it was yesterday. Only it wasn't, it had been this morning. I sat in comfortable silence, excited at the prospect of one more day in the city, Jon and Kim would be proud. Behind me Abigail was murmuring into her phone. I knew she needed her privacy, so I only half strained to listen in to her conversation. Well done, me.

'I just want to come home and see you,' she was saying. 'Do you think your mum will be OK with us coming a day later?'

I thought about what Jon had been telling me about his big family Christmas. Would his family, and all his brothers and sisters and nieces and nephews, be OK with him being delayed? I knew if it were my family they'd barely notice. Well, that's not fair. They'd *notice*, but there wouldn't be any chewed fingernails, or worries about missing out on Christmas activities. I, however, was a bit worried on missing out on my downtime.

Thinking about Jon I pulled out my phone and tried to call, but just got his answerphone. So after a text to Anne to update her, if she was interested, I called home instead.

'Hello?' barked Dad down the phone.

'Hi, Dad, it's Liv.'

'Hello, love. How's New York?'

'Good thanks, looks like I'm stuck here a bit longer – the flights are all cancelled.'

'Oh dear . . . you'd better speak to your mother.'

'*Oh, for God's sake, Lucy, just eat the bloody apple.* Livia! How are you doing, sweetie?' Mum said, coming on the line.

'I'm fine thanks – we won't be coming home today though, because of the weather. BA are putting us all up in a hotel back in Brooklyn and hopefully we'll be on a flight tomorrow. Lucy's still there?'

'Yes, her flight to Thailand is delayed until who knows when, and she's being the world's stroppiest teenager. Do you know she only wants exotic fruit because she wants to "at least pretend she's on a South-East Asian beach and not stuck here"? And I'm paraphrasing – she was *much* ruder than that.'

I couldn't help but smile at the thought of my mum and my sister spending this 'quality' time together. I bet it would be quite fun to be at home right now. 'So is it really that bad in England, the snow?'

'It's pretty thick – more than I've seen before around these parts. Very Christmas card-like. It's quite pretty actually. The neighbours have been sledding like mad.'

'Is it snowing now?'

'Oh yes, it hasn't stopped all day.'

Hmm, that wasn't a good sign for tomorrow. 'OK, I'd better go, Mum, but I'll keep you updated. Let me know if Lucy gets her flight out.'

I sat back in my chair and watched a yellow taxi whiz past the window, fairy lights entwined around its sign, and smiled at the thought of Elijah.

I might still technically be the boss, but work was over. We were off the clock and into the Christmas holidays. I leant over the back of my chair.

'You guys?'

Abigail put her hand over the mouthpiece, Dee and Ian looked over and Jasmine raised her eyebrows at me without looking up.

'It's half past two, and I think I'm going to leave you on your own for the rest of the day. I have some things I'm going to do while I'm here, so feel free to sightsee, hang out in your room, whatever you want. After we've checked in, I'll see you at breakfast tomorrow. Sound good?'

'Yep,' said Jasmine, very quickly. After the others

agreed I sank back down. I might not be home, but at least, just for a few hours, I was going to be alone.

❄

There was a definite festive spring in my step as I pottered about my spacious beige and red hotel room. It may only be for a day, but I was on holiday. The only thing, really, I needed to do work-wise was make sure nobody got lost on the way back to the airport tomorrow. I tuned my bedside clock radio into a Christmas music station and hummed along to 'Let It Snow'. Come on, Christmas; show me what you've got.

I was just sniffing the selection of Marriott complimentary toiletries when there was a knock on the door.

'Go away,' I muttered, assuming it would be Jasmine ready to complain that her towels weren't soft enough or the pole up her arse was getting uncomfortable.

But I opened the door to Jon! He was here! I made a loud 'yaaaay' noise like people do when they're pissed and a friend walks in the room, and threw my arms around him. 'What are you doing here?' I asked.

'Didn't you know that all the flights were cancelled?'

'Yeah, but I didn't think we'd end up in the same

hotel – how cool is that? How do they have space for us all?'

'I don't know, maybe because though the BA passengers have all been given separate rooms, I have to bunk in with Carl?' he said, coming into my room and plonking himself down on the bed. He pulled two bags of mini-pretzels from his pocket and handed one to me. 'I nabbed these from reception.'

I climbed onto the bed and we sat side by side, cracking into the mini-pretzels. 'Hey,' I said between mouthfuls, 'talking of free food, you would have loved this. We met a guy in the queue at the airport – a New Yorker – and he asked me to save his space while he went to get something to eat, and he came back with Subways for all of us!'

'For all of you?' Jon said, impressed. 'That was nice of him. So you're full then, I'll take these back.' He reached for the pretzels but I wriggled away, stuffing them frantically into my gob.

'He was nice,' I said slowly. I was watching Jon's reaction carefully. It didn't matter what he thought, not really, it's just . . . it kind of *did* matter.

'Cool. So, Miss I-Hate-Christmas-and-New-York-At-Christmas, we've just been given twenty-four work-free hours here, and I spent the whole journey to the hotel ignoring Carl and coming up with a total bucket list for us to do together, guardian angel Clarence-style. We need to head off while it's still light to fit it all in, but I guarantee that by the end you'll be feeling so Christmassy you might as well call yourself Jesus.'

'Oh . . . ' He made a whole itinerary? That was sweet, which made this all the more awkward. 'I can do a couple of hours now but I have plans this evening.'

'With your team? Can't they go it alone for one night?'

'Actually, no, with the guy from the queue.'

'The Subway guy?'

'Yeah. Elijah.'

'But isn't he like, fifty?'

I couldn't help but laugh at Jon's aghast face. 'No, why would you think that?'

'Because he talked to people in the queue, which is weird anyway, and he bought you all lunch for no reason, which is like a rich old dad thing to do. And who's called Elijah, other than Elijah Wood anyway?'

I stood up off the bed and brushed the crumbs off me. 'You're so odd. But stop sulking just because we can't do everything on your list, I really want to at least do some of it this afternoon, and I'm all yours tomorrow morning.'

'What if he'd put date rape drugs into your Subway?

You shouldn't just accept food from strange men.' Jon stood also and I began pushing him towards the door, my hands on his lower back.

'He wasn't strange, he was very nice.'

'Serial killers are nice when they're not killing, you know. It's how they lure you in.'

'Elijah is not a fifty-year-old rapist serial killer; he's just a nice guy who's taking me out this evening.'

'Somewhere public?'

'At least to begin with!' I raised my eyebrows.

'Just be careful, OK?' he said quietly. I grabbed my handbag and shut the door behind us. He stood close and rested his hand on my upper arm and I looked up at him. Was that sadness on his face?

I'm fully aware that there's always been a smidgen of chemistry between Jon and me. But it's never been any more than a flirty fondness, more 'lovely' than *love*. You know how there's always someone – whether it's the boy you used to fancy at school, that person in your office that you always like being near on nights out, the nice barista at your coffee shop who makes you smile when he or she remembers your name. But have I ever thought about it becoming anything more? No, not really. Apart from occasionally when I have rudey dreams about him, but I seriously have rudey dreams about everyone.

'I will be careful,' I said, kindly, and he thought about this for a moment, with his funny, lips-rolled-in thinking smile.

'All right.' He snapped out of it. 'Well, if I only have you for a couple of hours, let's make the most of it. Let me see ... we won't have time to queue for the ice rink now, but if we stay any longer than tomorrow we will. How about Central Park?'

Wait – I just remembered that I'd wanted to be alone. But being with Jon was the same, really. In a nice way.

'Central Park sounds great. Is it Christmassy?'

'Are you kidding me? Yes, it's beautiful at Christmas. Let's go.'

I didn't need to be alone right now, wishing it was the Christmas-future. I needed to be in the Christmas-present.

❄

A ride on the subway later and we emerged into the frosty afternoon air with Central Park stretching in front of us and the Plaza hotel behind. As we moved from the street and into the park, the ground beneath our feet changed from salty grit to an icing-sugar dusting of snow. The trees were a carbon-grey, pops of colour

206

in the form of neon running-wear on pink-cheeked joggers bobbed up and down along the paths, and dogs of all shapes and sizes bounced about, tangling their leads around their owners.

I loved it. We started walking and I soaked in the view with every step. 'I've been to Central Park once, I think, but Kim and I literally only had time to grab— Ooo, nuts!'

'Pardon?'

'This is what we grabbed!' I pulled Jon towards a man standing next to a small cart. The most glorious smell was wafting from it: caramelised almonds. Or cashews. Or peanuts! The choice was yours. I bought two bags of the almonds and forced one into Jon's hand. 'These are amazing, taste them. Just smell them!'

He crunched into the sugar-coated almond, which was warm and sticky in all the best ways. 'Well look at that,' he said, as we walked on through the park, snaffling them down. 'You just imparted a little New York winter wisdom on me; these are delicious.'

On we walked, our movie-like soundtrack being a saxophonist who stood under a bridge playing beautiful lazy melodies of Christmas classics.

'I can't believe *this*' – I opened my arms wide, speaking through a mouthful of almonds – 'is right in the middle of a city like New York. It feels like Hyde

Park. Actually, it feels nothing like Hyde Park. New York is so big and busy and epic, and I love that about it, and then Central Park is a slice of countryside. Do you know what I mean? I don't know if it's all the paths or the sports fields or the lakes or the little hills but it feels like lots of small parks sewn together.' I stopped and looked left and right at the scene, all silver, leafless trees and white powder, straight out of a Christmas card.

'I wish I'd thought to get us takeout coffee,' said Jon. 'Then we'd be proper New Yorkers right now— *Whooooooa!*'

I was just about to chow into the rest of my almonds when we hit a patch of ice and Jon skidded sideways away from me, his arms flailing in the air.

My nuts dropped (so to speak) and I reached out for him. Before we knew it we were both Charleston-ing in the middle of the path, all kicky-legs and swingy-arms. Eventually we slowed, gripping each other and laughing, and he wrapped his arms tightly around my shoulders. We were squeezed together, steadying each other, and it occurred to me we'd never been this close before. It was stronger than a quick hug, or a goodbye kiss on the cheek. We breathed against each other, afraid to move a foot wrongly, but Jon held us both steady, balanced against his warm frame. 'I'm not letting go.' He smiled, his face close to mine.

I chuckled lightly and an unexpected blush crept across my cheeks. I pulled away from him, gathering my nuts and stuffing them and my hands in my pockets, and we continued a long, careful, walk through Central Park together. Like proper New Yorkers.

❄

My Jon-time sped away from me and before I knew it our Christmas-in-New-York adventure was over. After we left Central Park we zoomed back to Brooklyn on the subway, and said our goodbyes.

'What are you going to do this evening?' I asked before we departed to our separate rooms.

'I don't know yet.' He dawdled. 'I'll find something. Do you know what you're doing with Elijah?'

I nodded excitedly. 'I think we're going up the Empire State Building.'

'Impressive. Very cool. I'm glad you're making the most of New York.'

'And Christmas. Have you seen it's lit up all red and green at this time of year?' I wanted him to know I'd listened to him, that I was trying.

We went our separate ways, and it was early evening

by the time I was waiting below the Empire State Building, staring up at it in awe just like I was Kimmy Schmidt straight out of the bunker. I didn't spot Elijah jogging over until he was right in front of me, all scruffy-chic and sexy-mexy. He greeted me with a 'Damn, girl', which honestly NEVER HAPPENS.

He stepped back, making a show of appearing to find my poncho, boots and jeans combo the hottest thing since hot sliced bread (aka toast). So I once-overed him and 'damn, girled' him back.

Elijah laughed. 'I forgot for a second that my best lines wouldn't work on a girl like you.'

'A girl like me?'

'Sorry, a *woman* like you.'

'Ha – that's not what I meant. I want to know what you think I'm *like*.'

'Smart, honest, a feminist.'

'Well thank you. Feminists still like compliments; we just don't survive off them. I am interested in your other "lines" though, because "damn girl" can't be your best.'

Elijah took my hand and kissed it, in an unexpect-edly gentlemanly and romantic gesture, and began to lead me down the street. 'All in good time, good woman.'

I looked back at the Empire State Building as we walked away. 'Are we not going up?'

'Oh, you wanted to go up the Empire State?' he asked.

'Yeah,' I replied.

'Believe me; you do not want to go up there. One week to Christmas and there'll be tourists queueing up all eighty flights of stairs. No, I'm taking you to dinner nearby. I know this great place, it's pretty quiet and it serves amazing steaks.'

'Could we go up after dinner?' I pressed, disappointment on my face.

Elijah looked down at me as we walked along. 'How about we do it tomorrow, if we're still here?'

I nodded. 'Yes please. I want to make the most of Christmas in New York. I do like steak though,' I added, not wanting to appear ungrateful.

'Then this place will make you fall in love.'

OK, no bother. I may not make it up the Empire State Building tonight, but I was still in New York, and less than twenty-four hours ago I was wishing to the star atop the Rockefeller Christmas tree that I could have extra time here. And here I was, ready to be open-minded and *believe* in Christmas, and the Big Apple, and everything it encompassed.

'Tell me about your family,' I instructed as we weaved down 34th Street.

'All right,' Elijah said. 'My mom's an alcoholic and

she left when I was two, and my dad is in prison for second-degree homicide. I raised myself, helped my cocaine-addicted sister through college and became a male stripper at sixteen just to pay for food.'

Oh. He's different from the usual boys I meet, and his underdog tale kinda made me want to be his sugar-mama. 'What kind of food could you buy on a stripper's salary?' I asked, as if this was remotely important.

'Pretty much just mac and cheese. Every night, mac and cheese. I think that's why my sister turned to drugs, just to try and escape that taste of microwave cheese.'

'That's a . . . ' I struggled for what to say. I was ninety per cent sure he was joking. Maybe ninety-three per cent sure. But imagine if I burst out laughing and it killed him, and he never told anyone about his horri-fying home life again? 'That's one gritty family story.'

'Suits me though, right? As a musician?'

OK, ninety-six per cent now. 'Yeah . . . so, is it all true?' One thing I was learning about Elijah was that he was hard to figure out.

'Nah,' he laughed. 'My folks are divorced, my mom lives over in Connecticut and my dad down south, but I'm an only kid so no cocained sister. I did live off mac and cheese for a long time though.'

'Because of stripping?'

'I don't think anyone would pay me to take off my clothes.'

I raised my eyebrows at him, and at that point we arrived at the restaurant, a small Italian place between a hotel and a souvenir store. The frontage was nondescript; nice enough but pretty standard. Huh. I mean it looked cosy, friendly, I certainly wasn't expecting somewhere all glitz and glamour, but ... I glanced down the street where I could see some traditional brownstones the next block over, steps leading both up and down to fairy-light-strewn basement and first floor eateries. They looked so *New York*.

Anyway. I shook off those thoughts, cursing Jon for getting in my brain with this 'you must experience Christmas in New York' blabber.

We took a seat by the window, so that was nice. With the yellow cabs whooshing through the darkness like bumblebees, I could remember where we were. Elijah smiled at me, my American Boy, for tonight at least. And when the steak arrived it too was delicious. I ordered the New York strip as a compromise with myself, and a glass of wine later I'd relaxed into the evening.

'I'm really glad I met you,' he said, all of a sudden as I was mid-chew.

'You are?'

'I could have been stuck between families full of screaming kids in that queue, but I was next to you. And you're interesting, and funny, and I don't know a lot of English girls.'

That was unexpected. 'You're interesting and funny too,' I said, my Englishness struggling to accept the complimentary nature of Americans.

'Full disclosure: I did date an English girl once, just briefly, but you're not a rebound or a replacement.'

'What happened?' I asked, being nosy.

'She was just here on vacation, but we hit it off. I was all booked to go visit a couple months later and she stopped answering my messages, or phone calls. I think she might have had another life at home.'

I studied him for a second . . . but I was certain this time it wasn't a joke. He looked quite forlorn. 'That's horrible! On behalf of Britain, I apologise.'

He laughed. 'Thank you. I'm over it now but she did inspire an album full of break-up songs.'

'Harsh, angry ones?'

'Soppy, "she's out of my life" ones,' he corrected me, then laughed again. 'But don't worry, I don't get attached generally unless it's a mutual feeling, I'm not hinting that I'm going to go bunny boiler-obsessed on you.'

The more Elijah and I talked, the more I liked him.

He felt like a mystery novel – confident, secretive, I was never sure when he was joking or when he was serious, but his charm made me want to turn the pages and dig deeper into his story.

As dinner drew to a close, he ordered us some whiskeys. I had the feeling he was testing me, assuming I would be a girl who didn't like whiskey, but would drink it anyway if he told me to.

'Jameson, huh?' I held my glass up to my face, the ice cube sparkling against the amber liquid.

'It's the best,' shrugged Elijah, watching my every move.

'Irish, though?'

'You don't like it?'

'I like it.' I drank it, slowly, but in one. 'But you surprise me, because to me, nothing beats one of your American bourbons. It's Woodford Reserve Double Oaked for me, any day.' I signalled the waiter to bring us a couple of those, and luxuriated in Elijah's dropped jaw. That's right, honeybunch, the English rose has many layers indeed.

I turned back to him and he leaned over the table, no messing around, and kissed me right on the lips. The Jameson stung, and his stubble scratched, but I kissed him back, my mouth curled into a smile.

He broke away and sat back down as the bar staff

appeared. My heart was racing, the blood was bounding in my ears and I could feel the whiskey burning in my belly. Lost for words but keeping my poker face in place, I picked up my glass and clinked Elijah's, before raising it to those recently used lips.

❄

I was exhausted by the time I unlocked my bedroom door, and so ready to take my bra off. What an evening! It had been a while, *believe me*, since I'd felt so drawn to someone so quickly. Elijah was fun, and sexy, and new. He was a distraction, who'd be gone before anything could even think about getting serious, but he was here now, and I could still taste his whiskey lips on mine.

I stepped over the threshold, already reaching up the back of my coat with one hand to unlock the gates of my own personal boob prison, when I stepped onto a piece of paper lying on the carpet.

It was a note from Jon. I thought of him for a moment. We were OK, weren't we? I really didn't want it to be weird between us, because it shouldn't be – if he met a girl I'd definitely be chuffed to bits for him.

Hello! I'm not sure when you'll be getting back in, but do you still fancy meeting up for some bloody *good last-minute sightseeing tomorrow? Crap diner coffee is on me? If so, meet me in the lobby at 7.30 am (I know it's early, but trust me . . .) J x*

I yawned at the note. Seven thirty a.m.? OK, I could do that. I kicked my legs jive-style until my boots hurled themselves across the room and then climbed into my bed, fully clothed, and with my bra just dangling about under my jumper. I needed to tell a certain someone about Elijah, and so I reached for my phone.

FaceTime connected after just a couple of rings and there was my Kim, all lit up under fluorescent lights.

'Olivia!' she cried, her face pink-tinged and make-up free. She was smiling a big smile.

'Hello, hello! How's Antigua?'

'*So good.* The weather has been perfect and all-inclusive is the best thing in the world. Do you know you can have pizza and a mojito for breakfast, if you want? I mean I haven't but you could. OK, I had it one morning. Hang on; shouldn't you be on a flight? Are you back home already?'

'Nope, still in New York, our flight – all flights – were cancelled so now we're staying until tomorrow.'

'Oh bugger! Oh well, if you've got to be stuck somewhere, New York's not a bad option. Now you can go to Rockefeller! You have no excuse!'

I laughed. 'Been there, done that.'

'You fitted it in?'

'Before I even knew we were staying on longer, I took a photo for you – I'll send it in a bit. Jon came with me, last night.'

'Ahh, and how is the lovely Jon?'

'He's OK. Actually you'd be very pleased with him – he says he and New York City are going to force me into loving a proper Christmas by the time we leave. He's been put up in the same hotel as me, and I'm meeting him in the morning.'

'Now I love him even more! That's my boy. Be open-minded, OK, Liv? And don't be tight with the money – live a little. And if you see some mistletoe and wanna just grab Jon – I mean life – by the balls then go for it.' Her face contorted into a wide-mouthed laugh.

'Where's Steve?' I asked, trying to change the subject.

Kim composed herself, mopping her eyes. 'He's snoring off the too-much-free-whisky he drank. He's dead to the world.'

'Tell him I say hi when he wakes up.' Then I said, a little shyly, 'So ... you know, I met a rather nice man here in New York.'

'You did WHAT?' Kim dropped her tablet and for

a moment I had a nice view of what appeared to be a hotel bathroom ceiling. Then her face reappeared. 'Who?'

'His name's Elijah, and he's a New Yorker, and he bought everyone Subways at the airport and then he took me out to dinner tonight. We had steak.'

'You had sex?!'

'*Steak*. But Elijah is really really really sexy, and he's all-American and all I can think about is sex with him because he is Sex.'

'Ohmygod, you said sex so many times to me just then. I need to know what the fuss is about – can you send me a picture?'

'No, I don't have one of him yet.'

'Text it over as soon as you do. I need to know if this man who's getting you all hot under the collar is really worth it, or if this is no different from your weird Paul Hollywood crush. But in the meantime, you should go for it.'

'Do you think?' I asked. My insides fizzed at the thought.

'Of course. I haven't heard you this excited about a man since that Draco Malfoy lookalike in that club last year.'

'It was a shame that was a gay club . . . '

'This Elijah is basically perfect for you. You can have

a great time with him with zero commitment, what with him living an ocean away and all.'

'Is it sad that that's true?'

'Not at all. Have some fun and maybe you'll come out of it feeling like you're ready to start dating properly again. Anyway, there's no rush. And don't overthink it. If you're both happy with no-strings Christmas canoodling, then treat yourself. Pull up those Christmas stockings and put an unexpected item in his bagging area.' Kim pulled a face. 'Urgh, what am I talking about?'

'You are quite disgusting,' I laughed.

'But . . .'

'What?'

'If you do decide you want something, er, *sexy*, you know you really don't need to look any further than the man who's sleeping down the corridor from you.'

'OK, I'm going to hang up now, I'm sure you have some couples massage to go and look smug about.'

'Nooooo, don't leave me, I'm bored,' wailed Kim.

'I'm so sleepy and I have to be up early.' I yawned at her face.

'I'll sing you to sleep, it'll be like the old days when you'd drunk a little too much and your head was spinning and the only thing that helped was me singing Disney songs and stroking your head.'

Mmmm, that did sound nice. I snuggled down in the bed and propped my phone so that Kim and I were facing each other. I closed my eyes and she smiled at her choice of song, as she launched into a soothing version of *The Little Mermaid*'s 'Kiss the Girl'.

19 December

6 days to Christmas

❄

I woke up to the sound of my alarm, and my first thought was of Elijah. It was nice to have met a man, even if it was only fleeting. But that was OK, that was how I liked it. Relationships are hard and involve too much leg shaving and sharing and trust.

I yawned and made myself get out of bed. Jon's note had said 7.30 a.m., so I piled on some winter woollies and my lovely mac, and paused just before heading out the door. Should I try Anne again? I hovered with my phone in my hand. No, it was too early.

I reached the near-deserted lobby and was mid-yawn

when Jon swung through the revolving door, bringing in a gust of cold air, dark and snow. He was carrying two takeaway coffee cups, a paper bag dangling from his wrist, and a big smile.

'You made it! Good morning, sleepyhead!' He leaned over and kissed my cheek like it was the most natural thing in the world and I flash-remembered Elijah's face and lips from last night. Kissing was nice ... I snapped out of it, realising I was staring at Jon's lips. Could Jon tell from *my* lips what I'd been doing last night?

'Of course,' I said quickly. 'Mmm, coffee ...'

'And breakfast. Almond croissant OK?'

'Perfect,' I yelped, my stomach growling on cue.

'We have to go, you ready?'

'Yep, where are we going?'

He motioned for me to exit the hotel first and though I was steady on the sidewalk outside, his long legs slipped immediately on the ice and he had to steady himself on me. 'Careful out here,' he smiled, and took my hand.

'Haha, get off, you baby.' A little nervous laughter escaped and I looked behind me back at the hotel. The last thing I needed was Jasmine or Abigail or someone catching me holding hands with Jon and giving me 'we knew it' faces.

I adjusted my earmuffs, pushing my rapidly frizzing

hair up and out of my eyes, and slotted an arm through Jon's for balance, freeing my hands to hold my coffee cup in one and stuff croissant into my mouth with the other.

'Nice, huh?' Jon smiled at the sight of my scarf covered in flaked almonds and icing sugar. 'I got them out of a bin just around the corner.'

I laughed. 'Yum. Hey, did you look at the UK weather this morning?'

'I did – it still looks pretty grim. I'd be surprised if we fly out today.'

I sighed. 'The BA woman said they'd send a rep to the hotel at eleven thirty this morning to give us an update one way or another. How about Virgin?'

'Twelve.'

'So we have this morning at least. Can I know where we're going or not?'

'You can! Now I know you went to the Empire State Building last night, that Elijah totally stole my plan, but if you can handle one more spectacular view I've got something I think you'll love.'

I looked up at the dark sky and watched the white speckles of snow appear as if from nowhere and float down around us. I chose my words carefully, not wanting to sound insulting about Elijah or the date. 'Actually, we didn't go up the Empire State in the end – I made a mistake. We just met there and then went to dinner.'

'He met you at the Empire State but didn't take you up there? Wow, that's ice-ice-baby-cold.' He peeped a look at me, smirking. 'What a tease.'

I shoved him with my elbow. 'We had a really nice dinner, the restaurant was apparently some New York staple, so it was, in fact, a great experience, and I feel richer for having done it. So there.'

'Then he's done me a favour – now I don't feel like you'll be too bored doing what we have planned.'

We reached the Brooklyn Bridge. In front of us New York was waking up, its lights coming on and the sky slowly turning lighter. I stopped and took in the view of Manhattan.

'I love looking at this city.' I breathed in a lungful of frosty air.

'I'm very glad to hear that.'

'What *do* we have planned?'

'What's your favourite place in New York?' he asked, and we continued walking over the bridge.

I thought. 'Central Park?'

He smiled at me. 'Really? We only went there yesterday.'

'I know, but it was so relaxing – no, screw Central Park: Rockefeller! Rockefeller will always be my favourite – *sorry, Kim!*' I called into the early morning air.

'Correct! So you and I are jumping on a subway to 30 Rock, and heading up to the top.'

'To the top of the 30 Rock? Is that allowed?'

'Yes, it's called Top of the Rock and you get these amazing views across the city, and you can look down at the tree which will make Kim jealous, and the best thing is that when you go up 30 Rock your view *includes* the Empire State Building, which is pretty cool. So to hell with Elijah and his not-taking-you-up-the-most-famous-building-in-the-world. This is going to be even better.'

'Wait. You can really go to the top of the Rockefeller Center?'

'Yes you can, if you want to?'

'Hell, yes, I want to! Jon, you're the best!' I took off in a speed walk across the rest of the Brooklyn Bridge, snow blowing into my face, and Jon jogging to catch up with me. 'Come on, Jon,' I called back into the wind. 'We don't have all day.'

❄

Being inside the Rockefeller Center made me feel like Liz Lemon. I took about a dozen photos before we even got up to the observation deck so I could send them to Kim.

But then I saw the view from the top and ... it was everything. Pale yellows and blues danced off glass skyscrapers as the morning sun washed over the city with an icy calmness. Building tops were white with overnight snow, and in the distance Lady Liberty's flame glinted over the New York harbour. And front and centre was the Empire State Building, standing tall and iconic. I found myself thinking, not for the first time on this trip, I love this city.

Jon turned to face the view and take a photo on his phone. 'So if we don't go home today, if we get another night in New York City, will you be free for the rest of the day or will you be seeing Elijah again?'

I examined Jon's profile. 'I might see him again. Assuming he wants to as well. I farted on our date, you know.'

Jon did a double take that nearly had him lobbing his phone over the side of Rockefeller Center.

'You farted? Did he ... notice?'

'I don't know. It was only a small one and I was laughing quite loudly so maybe not.' I shrugged. 'Everybody does it, we're all human and I'm not ashamed. But maybe he's not into a modern woman.'

Jon chuckled and went back to taking photos. I stuffed my gloved hands into my pockets and exhaled a cloud of chilly vapour into the cold morning air. 'But yes, if he wants to hang out again I think I will. It's good to make the most of people if you're only with them a short period of time.'

'Says the girl who's been longing to get home and have some time to herself ever since we arrived. What's so special about *Elijah*?'

I rolled my eyes at his tone of voice; I didn't know what he had against the name 'Elijah'. 'I can't say if there's anything special about him yet, but I'm just dying to find out,' I laughed. 'Or maybe I'll just hang out by myself. You're right; me, myself and I are frankly gagging for each other's company. We might go Christmas shopping, like a normal person in December. But thank you for this,' I added, afraid he'd think I was ungrateful for what he was trying to do for me.

I waited for him to turn his gaze to me.

'I mean it,' I said. 'Thank you for bringing me here. Thanks for being my guardian Clarence angel and showing me a bit of what New York is really all about.'

'What New York *at Christmas* is all about,' Jon clarified, 'and we're just getting started. I have plenty more up my sleeve if we don't go home today.'

'Are you worried at all?'

'About what?'

'About the snow. About not getting home for Christmas.'

Jon shook his head, beaming a smile out over Manhattan and jiggling on the spot to keep warm. 'Nope, I'm quite happy. Besides, the UK has the silliest weather in the world. It may be a white Christmas now, but give it a couple of days and it'll be washed away by rain and by New Year's we'll have a heatwave. Then it'll hail and go back to cold again. So no, I'm not worried, we'll get home.'

'It's Boxing Day one week from today, you know.' We walked around the observation deck to face Central Park; a patchy white blanket draped over seven miles of the city.

'So it is.'

'What do you think you'll be doing this time in a week? It's about one thirty in the afternoon at home.'

'I'll be long gone. My whole family will be. We'd have recently finished a huge lunch of leftovers, and something will be showing on the TV, like an Agatha Christie adaptation or *The NeverEnding Story*, and whoever had got stuck with the washing up will have full use of the two sofas to lie back on. Everyone else will be in some overstuffed state of coma draped over the armchairs or in a pool on the floor. The wrapping paper from Christmas Day will still be in disarray around us, someone will have trodden chocolate orange into the carpet, which one of the dogs will be licking at, and the kids will keep falling asleep and then waking up to either play with presents or ask why they don't have any presents left. Ahh, it's the best time of the day.' He smiled. 'What do you think you'll be doing this time next week?'

'Well, I have a Christmas tree, which is a first for me,' I said, proudly. 'But there won't be presents or wrapping under it. Which is *fine*, by the way. So I think I'll be munching bacon, curled on my sofa, reading some grisly book about murder which I'll love, and probably taking frequent naps in various places around the house.'

'Like a cat.'

'Indeed.' I looked at my watch and sighed. 'But I don't know, maybe I'll stick on a Christmas film after all – something New Yorky, something like *Elf*. Now, I really don't want to leave, but we need to get back to the hotel soon.'

Jon sighed. 'It's that time already? All right.' We began making our way towards the elevators down. 'I don't want to leave either,' he said. 'Not at all.'

We squished into the lift with a whole lot of other people, and I was pressed against Jon, eyeball to pec. 'Rockefeller, or New York?' I asked.

'A bit of both. It feels like there's a little magic in the air at the moment.'

'Because of Christmas? I can't believe I'm saying

this but I think I'm beginning to understand what you mean.'

'Yeah,' Jon agreed. 'Because of Christmas.'

❄

Back at the hotel, Jon and I hung around the lobby looking at the photos from this morning on our phones and drinking the free coffee, waiting for the BA rep and the other members of Girls of the World to arrive. Abigail arrived first, bags under eyes and make-up free. She looked worried, and sad. Before I could go to her, Dee appeared, with Ian strolling over casually moments behind her. They did not look sad. They looked like they could be on their honeymoon, with their easy smiles and relaxed demeanours. Jasmine was last, wearing her flight outfit again, fully intending to go home as soon as she possibly could, through hell, high water, or deep snow.

Since the Virgin rep wasn't due for another half an hour, Jon hung about close by to earwig, and Carl joined him.

The BA rep arrived and began with a sigh, which is never a positive start. 'I'm sorry to say that, as yet, there's no improvement with the weather in the UK.'

There was a collective groan from the group of

passengers, but I did spot Ian lightly stroke the back of Dee's hand with his.

'Is it getting worse?' asked Abigail.

'Well ... yes. There is definitely a disimprovement, to be honest. No flights will operate today. If there's any change whatsoever we'll attempt to reach you all by phone, and will also contact the hotel here who will post any updates on that flipchart over there by the coffee machine.'

'So we, um, could we fly somewhere else and then get a train into the UK?' Abigail pressed. 'If it's not improving how are we going to get home for Christmas?'

The BA rep shook her head. 'I don't know. We have considered diverting our flights to elsewhere in Europe, but many of their airports are closed too. Their train stations are closed. Their roads are closed.' She looked at our faces as this sank in. 'Europe is under a blanket of snow.'

As a group we stood silently, digesting this information for a moment until one woman piped up with, 'This is bloody ridiculous. You wait years for a white Christmas and when one finally comes you've buggered off to America.'

We all nodded in agreement, concluding that it really was bloody rude of the weather.

The BA rep continued. 'There's still the best part

of a week before Christmas, so don't get disillusioned yet. But I do understand – I want to go home too. My husband cooks a cracking turkey.'

I for one had no right to complain. I wanted to go home so I could sit on my arse on my own, my biggest decision being whether to eat cold pizza or a packet of Pop-Tarts for breakfast. Whether to watch *Pitch Perfect* for the ten millionth time or finally get round to watching *Blackfish*, like I'd told everybody I already had. But some people, including this poor woman, actually had plans. With real-life people.

OK, as Kim would say: no grumbling. It is what it is. I pulled out my phone and began to walk away from the group.

'Are you calling Elijah?' Jon stopped me.

'No, I was calling my parents, but then yeah, I might call Elijah.'

'Let's go ice-skating!' he bellowed, fists in the air.

'YES,' cried Carl, standing up behind Jon, munching into a big bag of Lay's.

'Let's go ice-skating, with Carl,' Jon said, a little less enthusiastically.

'You're going ice-skating?' said Abigail softly. 'Can I come with you? I can't really think of anything to do by myself for another day.'

'Ice-skating! What fun! Can we come? I mean, can I

come?' piped up Dee, followed by Ian with, 'Yes, and can I come too, if you're all going?'

Jon was grinning at me, and although he was definitely doing this on purpose – he seemed very anti-Elijah – ice-skating did sound very New York at Christmas, and what did I promise myself?

'Fine, sounds great. I'm just going to update my parents and then I'll call Elijah, see if he wants to join us.' I smirked and was about to turn away when I remembered. 'In the meantime, shouldn't you wait for the Virgin rep to actually confirm you two *aren't* flying today?'

'Oh yeah . . .'

I rang Mum and gave her the news that I wouldn't be home for another day. She asked me to give Anne a ring, as if I hadn't been trying, and she also updated me on Lucy (still not on a plane to Thailand: still not a happy bunny: potential to fly today, though unlikely). Then I called Elijah.

'Hello,' I said, my heart thumping.

'Hi,' he replied, yawning.

'It's Olivia.'

'The Big O. I know it's you, my British butterfly.'

I shuddered. 'The Big O' brought back memories from high school and teenage boys thinking they were funny. I ignored that part. 'So you may have already heard, but the BA rep is here at the hotel and she just confirmed we won't be flying today. Maybe tomorrow, she said, though . . . ' I paused.

'Well that sucks. Or maybe it doesn't. You all right, O?' he asked, sounding concerned. I liked when he called me 'O', just not 'The Big O'.

I edged further away from the group. 'I don't think we'll go home tomorrow. I mean already they have two days of backlog and the storms don't look like they're going to clear anytime soon. I'm not sure I'm going to get my team home for Christmas.'

'Or you?'

'Me, not so important.'

'I think you're important.'

'But I'm not going home to anything, or anyone, which is kind of the point, but I feel bad for them . . . Anyway. I don't know if you're at all interested but we're going to go ice-skating this afternoon, if you want to join us. If you want to meet up again. It's no biggie if you don't, you know, whatever, man . . . ' I trailed off and waited.

'I mean, I want to see you, but . . . ice-skating?'

'Yep. Getting my Christmas on, bitches.' Cringe.

'And you don't want to just go to a bar? I'll buy you mulled wine.'

'Nope. I can do that anywhere.' I took a deep breath. 'Ice-skating it is.'

'Ice-skating where?'

I held the phone away and called over to Jon. 'Ice-skating where?'

'Rockefeller?' Jon suggested.

Hearing him, Elijah groaned down the phone. 'Ice-skating at Rockefeller Center, oh my god. What are you turning me into?'

'Well, if you want to see me that's where I'll be.'

He chuckled. 'Bossy lady, aren't you?'

'Nope.' I smiled. 'But you live in New York all the time. I'm only here for ... well, who knows how long. And I've not shown Ms Manhattan the respect and attention she deserves so don't go thinking I'm going to let *you* boss *me* around and tell me what I can and can't do while I'm here.'

'Yes, ma'am.'

'Seriously though, if you don't want to come ice-skating that's completely fine. I understand that you're a very cool and steely musician type so why don't I meet you for dinner or a drink after skating and you can show me another little slice of your New York? If you want to?'

'Nope, I've got exactly nowhere to be, so let's do this.'

'Good. See you at Rockefeller Plaza in an hour.'

I hung up with a satisfied smile on my face. Yes, the

prospect of another afternoon in close proximity to Elijah had me feeling very satisfied indeed. Whiskey memories entered my head.

Though the BA rep was long gone, Jasmine, who had expressed no interest in joining in the ice-skating expedition, was nonetheless still loitering around the lobby after I finished my phone calls.

'Jasmine? Are you coming ice-skating?'

She sighed. 'Ice-skating? Don't you have to be, like, five?'

'Fair enough. See you here again tomorrow then, when the BA rep comes back.'

'I'll come if you want.' She shrugged.

'I'm not about to beg you.' I turned to everyone else. 'Anyone coming ice-skating, let's meet back down here in half an hour, after Jon and Carl's Virgin rep has been. OK? OK.'

Back up in my room I closed the door behind me and leant back against it, like they do on TV shows when they need to let out a good sigh. But I held it in. I wanted this. I promised myself to give Christmas a go, and I really did want to get out there and be with New York.

'Listen,' I said to myself in the mirror, pretending I was Kim, giving me a thorough talking-to. 'Nobody is asking you to be in charge any more, so stop acting like you have to be. If you don't want to hang out with these people then don't, but if you agree to it then don't you grumble, you goddamn . . . knobhead.' Ouch, tough love.

❄

We arrived at Rockefeller Center – all of us, Jasmine included – to find a queue to the ice rink snaking all the way up from the bottom level, around several railings and down along one side of the angels.

'Wow,' I murmured.

'This looks fun,' commented Jasmine, and then shut up when I gave her a cold glare to rival the ice below.

At that moment I saw Elijah striding towards me, an amused look on his face. 'I just asked one of the attendants at the front how long the queue is and if we join it now we can expect to be on the rink in, oooh, about two to three hours' time. Welcome to New York in the holidays, ladies and gentlemen. Hey, by the way,' he said to me and swooped down, greeting me with a kiss on the lips which left everyone, me included, with raised eyebrows.

'Um, so, um,' I stuttered. 'Let me explain, everybody. Elijah and I went out last night and we kissed and that's OK, because even though I'm your boss, currently, I still have . . . urges.' Oh for God's sake, *shut*

238

up, they weren't my children. Also I was not complaining – I liked kissing Elijah. Everyone would just have to get over it. 'I'm some of your bosses,' I clarified, looking at Carl (who was sniggering and eating a hot dog) and then at Jon (who was looking away, back towards the ice rink, his hands in his pocket).

'Elijah, you know Jasmine, Dee, Ian and Abigail. And this is Carl, and this is Jon. Jon? *Jon*, meet Elijah.'

Jon turned and met Elijah's eye and stuck out his hand. 'Elijah. Of the complimentary Subways fame.'

'That's me.'

'A no-strings-attached free Subway sandwich … Americans are so friendly.'

'Oh, we can be *super* friendly.'

They shook hands. I don't know how watching two men shake hands could be awkward, but it was. My bits were curling inside themselves with the awkwardness of it all. I started to sweat.

'Anyone else hot?' I squeaked.

Jasmine shook her head. 'Menopause?'

'Let's go ice skatinggggg!' I whooped with too much excitement. We looked at the queue. Er, perhaps not.

'I've got an idea,' said Elijah.

'Don't say a bar,' I warned.

'Not a bar, but we don't have to stay in this tourist trap.'

'Hey, this is Liv's favourite place in New York, buddy, and skating is what we've all got planned, OK?' said Jon.

I stared at him. I'd never seen him so ... passive aggressive. 'Hear him out, Jon,' I said.

'I was just going to suggest skating somewhere a little less ...' Elijah began.

'Touristy?' I asked, rolling my eyes at him.

He smiled at me. '... crowded. Come on, Bryant Park is like, seven blocks away. It has an ice rink, a tree, Christmas markets, all that shit. And it's all outside the New York Public Library, which may not be as tall as Rockefeller but is still pretty famous.'

I gasped. 'The New York Public Library? In the *snow*? Oh, it's going to be just like *The Day After Tomorrow*. Without the dying and things. But with the ice. But without the book burning. But with the closed airports. Let's do it!'

We all walked away from Rockefeller and as we were rounding the corner onto Fifth Avenue I took one last look behind me at the tree – I might not see it again this trip – and caught Jon's eye who was a few feet behind me.

'The *library*,' I mouthed and he smiled, his eyes having softened from the strange glares he'd been giving Elijah a few moments ago.

Jon knew all about my love of libraries. During our first conference together I'd chewed his ear off so much about *The Girl with the Dragon Tattoo* books which I'd been really into at the time, telling him that he *had* to read them, that eventually I'd marched him to the nearest library and made him sit there with me while he read chapter one and could tell me what he thought.

He had liked it. Smiley face.

We'd got into a habit for a while of always making sure we both knew where the nearest library was for every conference, in case we needed to go again, but it hadn't even crossed my mind that one of the world's most famous libraries was right here in New York City.

We strolled down Fifth Avenue. I was walking hand in hand with a man, snow falling lightly, giant window displays showing ten-foot-high pictures of models in red lipstick and tartan scarves. It all felt so surreal to me. To the average passer-by, Elijah and I probably looked like a couple on holiday. Probably like any one of those couples I'd been staring at two nights ago when Jon and I had been standing by the Rockefeller tree.

But it was just a façade. I was killing time, really, if I was honest with myself. Elijah was funny, and easy on the eyes, and generous, and a little bit arrogant in a way that strangely appealed to me, but what I liked the most about the whole situation was that it was temporary. I didn't have any expectations. This wasn't the beginning of some great love affair, it wasn't going to last, which meant he couldn't let me down. So as long as those were the rules, I was on board. I wasn't ready for anything more right now. Maybe not ever. But for now, this temporary situation where I got to kiss a handsome man whenever I liked was OK with me.

Bryant Park was a square packed with wooden Christmas market huts, a blue-lit ice rink, a big, plush, tree covered in electric blue fairy lights and the library overlooking it all. There was also much less of a queue.

It didn't take us long to get out on the ice. Once there, Jasmine whizzed off to be on her own, though Carl followed her, a surprisingly competent and graceful skater. Dee and Ian finally got to hold hands in public under the guise of helping each other, and the rest of us stayed in a group. At one point I caught Jon's eye as I whizzed past him and he jokingly flailed about like we were in Central Park again. I laughed out loud, but Elijah skated in front of me and stole my attention away with an amuse bouche of a kiss.

❄

A while later our skating session was finished, and I politely but firmly bid farewell to the others and then turned to Elijah. 'All right, mister, we made it through ice-skating, and nobody died, and you didn't get caught by your friends and kicked out of the band for being utterly uncool, so now it's over to you. What do *you* want to do tonight?'

'Well . . .' He moved closer. 'Shouldn't we make the most of our precious time together?' His eyes twinkled, a wicked grin on his stubbly face.

I shrugged. 'Mmm . . . I don't know if I like you like that yet.'

'Oh you don't?' he laughed.

'Nope. I mean, you're OK. You have a good sense of the type of food I like, and I can't stress how important that is in a man. But I don't know . . . I need a bit more convincing.'

Elijah leant in so I could feel his breath on my lips. 'How can I convince you?' he drawled, and I swear my knickers leapt up my shelangalang. But it would take a little more than a foxy accent, mate.

I pulled my head back. 'Show me more New York, Elijah style.'

He tossed his hair out of his eyes and scanned the street up and down, finally settling his gaze on something and shooting that grin across his face again. 'Come with me.' He took my hand.

We bypassed the Christmas market stalls selling

delicious-scented hot cider, and instead went into a nearby bar, where Elijah ordered us two Budweisers and opened the conversation with, 'So what's up with that Jon guy? Is he an ex?'

'What? No. No, no, no. Absolutely not. We're just friends, not exes, or anything. Nope, just friends.'

'Sorry, I didn't quite catch that – was that a "no"?'

'It was a no.'

'He seemed pissed with me.'

'Noooo, he's just antsy because he wants to get home as soon as possible, I'm sure. You know, we're now, what, six nights to Christmas Day? And I think everyone's just getting a bit worried, the closer it gets, that we might not get back.' Speaking to Elijah about Jon, specifically, felt too ... I wanted to keep the conversation neutral. About everyone. Everyone but Jon.

'They all like their Christmases at home, huh?'

'This is like a ticking bomb to them. I guess you aren't really bothered either way?' I speculated.

'Exactly. Whatever, man, I'm travelling to get *out* of New York over the holidays.' He laughed and gulped at his beer. 'Don't even get me started on New Year's Eve in this city.'

'I can't believe you'd say that,' I cried. 'I might not be wrapping the tinsel around my neck for Christmas, but the more I see of New York the more I love it.

There's something about cities, the buildings, the rain on pavements, the endless food choices. You're a lucky man. So there.'

Elijah necked his Bud. 'Consider me told. So, tell me about *your* city, London girl. If we were there, where would you be taking *me*? What's great about it?'

'Everything's great about London, but in truth I don't explore it as much as I should. I've been trying to save my money for a while.'

'Being a feminist doesn't pay well?'

I laughed. 'My job pays great, but, well, I'm trying to build up a house deposit. A few years ago I had a boyfriend and things went pretty wrong, and he was a collossal dick, and I guess I'm only just starting to realise how little I've enjoyed myself since.'

'Is that when you joined Girls of the World?'

'It was around then. I joined shortly before we split up.'

'So your boyfriend was a douche and you became uber-feminist – classic.'

'No, I didn't become a feminist because I got dumped. I'm a feminist because it would feel completely unnatural not to be. My mum has always been a human rights activist – she'll march in Pride festivals, she'll show up outside abortion clinics and yell at the people who are yelling at the women going in, she'll camp outside Westminster on behalf of refugees. She's passed that on to me. Feminism is human rights, it's nothing to do with hating men. Wait . . . don't you listen to Beyoncé?'

'Not generally . . . '

I think that was enough schooling for now. I took a drink. 'I've always believed in equality, and I like to fight for it. So you better be a feminist.'

'Oh, I love women.'

'Good. I think I have a lot to teach you.'

'You do, I'm all ears. But first, let's drink.'

❄

I was taking off my earrings back in my hotel bedroom, my emotions – and hormones – heightened from another fun and kissing-filled evening with Elijah, when I heard a noise out in the corridor. A shuffling noise that sounded like someone walking back and forth past my door, and the *rap-rap-rap-rap-rap* of knuckles sliding across the walls. There was muttering, too.

As I moved closer to the door I made out the words 'Elijah Wood' and 'Twwwwwwwat.'

I opened the door and came face to face with Jon. He was wearing PJ bottoms and a shirt that was loose and unbuttoned at the neck, with one sleeve rolled up.

He looked like someone who'd sleepwalked their way to an Oscars after-party. He looked cute. He stopped pacing when he saw me and grinned, swaying on the spot. 'Livia!'

'Jon!' I chuckled. 'Can I help you?'

'Nope.' Sigh. 'Nope, nope I don't think you can.' He sighed a second time. 'Where's *Elijaaaah*?'

'At home, I guess. Did you have a good night?'

Jon shrugged and looked up and down the corridor. 'Elijah Wood is at his home. And you are here. And I went with Carl to a very nice bar at the top of 30 Rock with views over the city, and actually, *actually*, I should have gone up there with you.'

I leant against my doorframe, amused, and a touch jealous – I would have liked to have gone there with him as well, at some point. 'Looks like you had a pretty good time with Carl. Did you wear your pyjamas?'

'Pfffffft, you're drunk,' he laughed.

'I think *you're* drunk.'

'Carl's drunk.'

'Where is Carl?'

'He's in our room. The bar was called Bar SixtyFive, because it's on floor … floor …'

'Sixty-five?' I guessed.

'Sixty-five! The views. The cocktails. You. Did you know Carl snores?'

'So I've heard. Do you want to come in?'

Jon moved over to me and leaned against the door-frame so we were close, our faces inches apart. He smiled at me, his eyelids dropping and his hair flopping over his forehead. He sighed deeply and reached for my one remaining earring. 'The question is: do you want me to come in?'

My breathing slowed and for a moment the corridor was silent except for the tiny tinkle of my earring as he played with it gently between his fingers. I remained completely still so that I didn't inadvertently find myself rubbing my cheek against his hand.

'Jon,' I said softly. 'You can have a coffee but that's it.'

'Come in for coffee?' He raised his eyebrows at me. 'I think the kids call it Netflix and chill these days.'

'Not what I'm offering,' I said gently. 'I think you really could use a coffee.'

'I want to take you on a date.'

Oh God.

Nope, shut-up, don't say that, take it back, take it baaaaack.

I stared at him and he stared at me for a moment, and I silently begged him not to say more, not to move us out of the Friend Zone. 'No you don't.' I let out a titter to break the ice. 'It's bedtime. Alone.'

He nodded and turned around, several times, unsure

which room was his. Then he looked back at me, that goofy grin back in place. 'Not tonight, bozo. But while we're here, in New York. You deserve a muthaflippin AMAZING New York City Christmas date, like Rachel Green.'

I sniggered at his reference. 'I'm already having New York Christmas dates, if that's what you want to call them, with Elijah. Maybe you could take Dani?'

'Danny Dyer?' He shook his head. 'He is a top bloke, but nope. You.'

'Dani from your work. She seemed nice.'

'You're nice.'

'But I'm busy, *with Elijah*.' I tried to be a bit firmer, a warning to Jon that he'd regret it in the morning if he crossed a line that I hadn't opened up to be crossed.

'What does Elijah know about anything? He doesn't know anything about New York dates.'

'He lives here . . . '

Jon stepped back, leaned over me and kissed the top of my head and for a moment I was engulfed by the warmth of his chest. 'If I was taking you on a date it would be something you'd really want to do. Something to make you fall in love with New York, and Christmas, and everything about the exact time and place you're in . . . not just fall in love with me.' Then he pulled back, grinned, and strode off down the corridor with a parting 'Elijah Got-No-Wood, amirite?'

I went back into my room and closed the door. Then as I removed my second earring I looked at it and thought of Jon. Was he serious? No, he was drunk. Everyone wanted to snog everyone when they were drunk. In the morning he wouldn't remember anything about it. I hoped.

20 December

5 days to Christmas

❄

I looked out of my window the following morning. The sun rose behind the Brooklyn clouds, creating a cold white light over the city. My phone was in my hand, the BBC News app open, and I already knew we wouldn't be going home today – there was no way. If anything, the snow was getting worse in the UK, and it appeared that the country had almost entirely shut down.

I wanted to shut down. I wanted my sofa and my alone-time. But I also wanted to see more of Elijah, so in that respect this was a good thing. Most of all I wanted to get everyone home to their families, but I didn't know how, I couldn't fix it. We just had to wait out the storm. Together.

I didn't want to see anyone yet, so I curled back into my hotel bed and closed my eyes, letting my thoughts drift away like snowflakes.

❄

I went down to breakfast deliberately late, prolonging my alone-time as much as possible. I showed up to the BA meeting in the lobby with a takeaway box full of bacon, which I munched at the back of the group.

Carl walked past me munching from his own box of bacon, towards the Virgin Atlantic gathering in the bar area. I stopped him. 'Hey, Carl, is Jon not with you?'

'No, he has the biggest hangover. He told me to bring him up some bacon after the meeting but I think I'm going to eat it all.' He grinned and shuffled away.

Maybe Jon won't even remember what had happened last night, I thought.

My thoughts were interrupted by the nice lady from BA entering the hotel, and we all fell silent so we could listen. My team gathered close.

'All right, I have some good news. Good news for

now, at least. But, please understand, as much as we would love to control the weather, we do not. And your safety is the most important thing for us,' she started, disclaimering the hell out of the news she was about to deliver. 'You won't be flying home today, and the snow is still heavy across Europe, I'm afraid, with no let-up in sight. However, we do have you all rebooked on a flight out on the twenty-third of December, which will arrive into the UK on Christmas Eve morning, BUT ... this is very much weather dependent, and on whether the runways can be cleared in time, and there's a chance they won't be cleared if the snow keeps falling at the rate it is now. So we're trying to get you home for Christmas but it's really just a waiting game now. I'd suggest keeping your fingers crossed for rain. Because rain will melt the snow,' she added quickly, on seeing some confused faces.

'So, we're definitely here until the twenty-third, no chance of leaving earlier than that or diverting to some- where else in Europe?' I spoke up.

'Definitely here until the twenty-third, and no chance of getting closer to the UK by other means. I'm sorry.'

'That's OK,' I said, and turned to my team. 'All right. I know you're disappointed and I know you want to get home, but at least we have more of a solid idea of what our next few days will be like now. We don't have to be here for a daily update any more. Silver linings.'

Not a single one of them said a word, all of them lost in their own thoughts and worries. I looked at each of their faces and the tiniest ripple of annoyance threaded through me, and was gone as quickly as it had come. *I want to go home too, but you don't see me whining about it*, said the thought.

I turned from them. It wasn't my job to baby them, nor could I say or do much to improve anything for them right now. I checked my phone where I had a missed call, so I moved away from the group and rang the number back.

'Olivia?' the person answered. 'It's Lara.'

'Hi, Lara, how are you?' I answered, surprised to hear from her.

'I'm good, thanks for asking. Listen, I just spoke with Scheana – you guys are still here?'

'Yep, we've been snowed out of the UK. The airline's put us up at a hotel in Brooklyn though, so really we can't complain too much.'

'Do you know when you might get to go home?'

I sighed. 'It changes every day, which isn't anyone's fault. But now they're saying the weather is just so bad the earliest we'll be flying out will be the twenty-third.'

'Right before Christmas? That's rough. I hope you manage to get on those flights.'

'Me too. New York is great, but my team are getting pretty worried about missing Christmas at home, with their families.'

'I'm sure you all are.'

Well, I wasn't. Assuming they could still get away none of my family would be in the coun—

Lucy! Lucy was supposed to fly yesterday – I wonder if she'd had any luck. I had to get off the phone with Lara and call her.

'Listen,' said Lara, breaking my thoughts. 'It's due to get a little snowier here as well over the next few days, so I'm going to head upstate today – this morning – for Christmas with my folks. Scheana and I go way back and I know she wouldn't want you guys spending Christmas in a hotel.'

'Well, we might not—'

'I know, I know, you might get home. But the reason I'm calling is to say: if you'd like to all come and stay in my apartment, consider it yours. I won't be back until New Year, I have heating, I only have two bedrooms so you guys would have to bunk in together, but it's a home, not a hotel room. The choice is yours.'

Wow, what a generous offer. 'Lara, thank you,

but it's really not necessary. This hotel is perfectly nice; we have free breakfast and dinner, so we can't complain.'

'I know, and you're British which means even if it was horrible you wouldn't complain. But just think about it and call me back within the hour if you want to stay here, and if so I'll leave my keys with my neighbour. Sound good?'

Lara rang off, but before I could allow myself to consider her offer I needed to check on my sister. I first called my flat, where she was due to stay before flying, and then called my parents' house when there was no answer.

On the seventh ring Lucy picked up with a 'Yo.'

'Lucy? You're still there. Your flight was cancelled?'

'Yeah, it sucks. Don't tell me yours is cancelled again because I am not spending Christmas alone like a fucking reject from life.'

'Thank you, honey,' I heard my mum call in the background.

'Actually it is – the British Airways rep is now saying we won't be coming home until the twenty-third, earliest.'

'Are they going to keep paying for your hotel?'

'Yes, but we just got offered an apartment – a work contact has said we could stay at her place in the

Upper East Side if we don't want to be in a hotel over Christmas. Potentially. So I'm not sure what to do.'

'Um, obviously stay in the apartment, are you mental? Believe me, my travel-challenged sister; staying in a local's house – in your case a real New Yorker's fancy-arse flat – makes for way better memories than just being cooped up in a hotel.'

'But we'd have to share rooms; we get our own space at the hotel.'

'God, you and your own space. It's Christmas, people want to be with other people, not sitting in a hotel room on their own eating endless room service noodles like a total saddo. Let people into your life, Liv. Open the door to the inn. Welcome Mary and Jo-nizzle and all the wise men and their flock.' Lucy sniggered. 'Anyway, I don't care; I want to go to Thailand.'

'You will. Keep checking back with the airline.'

'You keep checking back with the airline.'

'OK, grump-monster, put Mum on.'

With a sigh Lucy left me and Mum came on the phone instead. 'Hi, honey, how's NYC?'

'Actually, it's kind of fun. If you have to be stuck somewhere at Christmas, this is clearly the place to be.'

'Did you go to Tiffany's yet?'

'No, but that's kind of why I'm ringing.'

Mum gasped. 'Jon proposed?'

'What? No! Mum, of course he didn't bloomin' pro-
pose, we're not even going out with each other. I'm
ringing to say I'll be here a few more days. Is there any
news on your flight to Lanzarote?'

'Tenerife, and no. At the moment the website still
says it's running, but it's not for another four days yet,
so we'll see. Maybe the snow will have melted a bit
by then. Your dad and I are in holiday mode no matter
what happens.'

'It's disgusting,' said Lucy coming back on the line.
'They won't stop playing reggae music and drinking
sugar-free margaritas.'

'Dad's drinking margaritas?!'

'I know, and they go right to his head. He is literally
asleep all the time.'

'Why aren't you at my flat?'

'Your flat is depressing.'

'OK, thanks.'

Mum took control of the phone again. 'Keep in
touch, honey, and enjoy these extra days in the Big
Apple. This kind of opportunity doesn't come along
often, and you're with some lovely people.'

No sooner had we hung up than one of those lovely
people appeared in front of me.

'This is bullshit,' declared Jasmine. 'Abigail won't
stop crying.'

Behind her Abigail sniffled. 'We're not going to be home for Christmas, are we?'

'We might be—'

'*Bullshit*,' Jasmine repeated.

'*Enough, Jasmine*,' I snapped, glaring at her. 'You don't think I want to be going home too? You think I want to be stuck here with you any more than you want to be with me? But we're all in the same boat so can you please, for crying out loud, wipe that sneer off your face and act like a grown-ass *woman*.'

We don't need to evaluate whether or not I can carry off saying the phrase 'grown-ass woman', because the message had appeared to hit home regardless. Jasmine's face had frosted over like it was the runway at Heathrow itself, and she was silently glaring off to the side and refusing to meet my eye. The rest of my team were staring at me, dumbfounded. Even Abigail had stopped crying, and appeared to have the tiniest of smiles on her face.

I flared my nostrils and took a deep breath to calm myself down. I looked away and straight into the eyes of Jon, who was at the bottom of the staircase holding a coffee cup, which he raised to me in silent congratulations.

I would love a Jon hug right now, I realised. I wanted to sink into him and smell his woodsmoky coat and have him look at me with those milk chocolate eyes and for last night not to have happened. I wondered … Well, one thing at a time.

'Listen, everybody, I just had a phone call,' I said, trying to rally the troops back in. Abigail, Ian and Dee listened dutifully like teacher's pets (which I loved) and Jasmine pursed her lips and looked down at her shoes. 'As you know, I had dinner with Lara Green from Green PR the other night. She just called and made us a very kind offer in light of our current situation, which I want to talk to you about.'

My eyes flicked back to Jon, who was yawning like a sleepy pup and rubbing his eyes. Focus, Liv. 'We're definitely here for at least another three nights, so Lara very kindly said that if we didn't want to stay in the hotel she'd be more than happy for us all to stay at her apartment, which is in the Upper East Side. She only has two rooms though, and I assume a living room, so some of us might have to bunk with others. What do you think?'

'Yes,' said Abigail, before I'd barely got the question out. 'I mean, if it's OK with everyone else. I just don't want to be in a hotel any more, as nice as it is here; I want to be in a home.'

'OK,' I said. 'So that's one yes. We won't get the free food over there that we do here, remember.'

'But we'll have a kitchen. We could make Pop-Tarts?' Abigail asked with hope.

I had to smile at that, a girl after my own heart. 'Yes we could. How about the rest of you?'

Dee was struggling not to look at Ian too much, but said, 'I think it might be really nice to be back in Manhattan, right by Central Park. This hotel is lovely, it's been lovely, but if we're definitely here for a few more days we might as well make the most of New York at Christmastime.'

'All right, so Abi and Dee are in, and I'm guessing . . . yep, that's a yes from Ian. Jasmine? What are you going to do?'

'I'm going to stay here.'

'Jasmine, just come to the apartment, we're not going to leave you here on your own.'

'Uh, I'll be absolutely fine, thanks. I am a "grown-ass woman", you know.'

'Come on—'

'No, I want to stay. You guys go. I can't understand for the life of me why you'd give up a free hotel room and free meals for some tiny apartment where half of you will be sleeping on the floor, but whatever. I'll see you on the flight home.'

What should I do? She didn't need babysitting, and work was over – this was my holiday time now, even if

I was here with a bunch of people I'd never choose to spend my holidays with.

'Fine.' I nodded. 'In that case, I'll call Lara and tell her we're in. Jasmine, I'll leave you her address in case you change your mind, and I'll let the BA rep know that some of us won't be using our rooms any more. And I'll ask her to call me with any other updates. Let's meet back down here at eleven a.m.?'

My team dispersed without another word and I stood on the spot for a moment, lost in thought. Was I really about to leave one of my team behind? But this was New York City; a concrete jungle, but hardly the middle of an actual jungle. I may be in charge, but I couldn't control everything, the rational part of me told myself. At peace with my decision ... sort of ... I looked up to locate the BA rep and my breath caught. Jon. I'd forgotten he was standing there. We looked at each other and for that moment I was transported right back to last night when he was at my door.

'Morning,' he said.

'Morning. How are you feeling?'

He smiled, a little sheepishly. 'Like I've never been so pleased not to have to get onto an aircraft today. Like I need a thousand coffees. Like maybe I shouldn't have come to your hotel room last night ...?'

I wondered if he remembered everything he'd said

too. I felt myself blush, but couldn't help smiling. 'That's fine. It's always nice to have a visitor. And to be fair, you only came to hang around my corridor – I was the one who opened the door and started chatting to you.'

He nodded, noticeably a little embarrassed. 'Are you leaving the hotel?'

'Yep. The British Airways rep told us we won't fly out until the twenty-third at the earliest so we're going to stay somewhere else. What did Virgin say?'

'Same. I guess the message is coming from Heathrow centrally. So where are you going?'

'That woman I met up with for work the other night – Lara? She has an apartment in the Upper East Side, and she's heading home for Christmas this morning. She thought it would be nicer for us to not have to stay in a hotel over the holidays, and my team think so too. And my sister Lucy, evidently.'

'That's a nice offer.' He paused, staring into his coffee cup. 'When do you leave?'

'In about an hour.' Things were never this awkward between us, and there was now no doubt in my mind that he remembered perfectly well everything he said last night. But I didn't like it – he was my friend, my Jon, and I didn't want to leave things this way. 'Wait a minute!'

'What?'

'Jasmine doesn't want to come; she's going to stay here.'

'You're leaving her with me? Thanks a lot,' Jon laughed.

'No, you should come. You should come and stay at the apartment with us, it'll be so much more fun with you there – you know how rubbish I am with making people feel Christmassy. There are two bedrooms, so some people will have to share.' I blushed, realising what I'd just insinuated. 'I was thinking boys in one room, girls in the other.'

'I think . . . that sounds like a really strange, but fun, way to spend our last few days here. Maybe we could all cook a Christmas meal together?'

'Sure. My contribution will be pizza.'

'Wait, what about Carl? I can't leave Carl.'

'You don't think he'd like to befriend Jasmine?'

'I couldn't do that to him. Do you think Lara would mind one extra? Perhaps he and I could take the living room floor? If not, I'll stay here. And resent Carl for a while.'

'I'll phone her and ask her now, but I'm sure she won't mind, she's really easy-going. Oh this is going to be *fun*. Go and get packing, mister.' I went in for a quick hug but he held on and squeezed me tight and I laughed into his neck. There was my Jon hug . . .

Lara was fine with the numbers change, so an hour later, with one last glance around the lobby for Jasmine, in case she'd changed her mind, off our merry band of six went. We piled ourselves and all of our suitcases and coats and belongings and limbs into a people carrier that would take us over the Brooklyn Bridge and uptown to 74th Street.

Lara lived in a lovely neighbourhood – all delicatessens, coffee shops and boutique hotels, as well as residential buildings that had smart entranceways and long zig-zag fire escapes like on the *Friends* building. Her own apartment block was at the very end of the road, overlooking the East River, and after Lara's neighbour let us in and we all navigated up the spiral staircase with our suitcases to the apartment on the fifth floor, discussions turned to sleeping arrangements.

'The girls should just go in one room and the boys in the other,' said Abigail, to which there were nods of agreement.

'That might be a little cramped though,' Jon said. 'I don't mind sleeping on the sofa in the living room.'

'Me neither,' I added. 'I mean, instead of, not together.'

'Maybe we should take turns?' suggested Dee.

The apartment was lovely. Small, but with a spacious feel. Soft lighting, lots of cushions, and modern art paintings in shades of turquoise on the walls. The two bedrooms led off the living room – one was clearly Lara's own bedroom, which I thought the girls should take as it seemed the respectful thing to do, and one a guest bedroom. At the other end of the apartment the living room became a kitchen area, where a stack of coffees and hot chocolates had been left for us, together with a welcome note. And in pride of place by the window, 'A Christmas tree!' I cried. I was becoming weirdly fond of those.

'So, um, back to the room situation,' Ian said, clearing his throat and glancing at Dee, and everyone launched into expressing their own opinions on the situation again.

I pulled Ian aside, out of the door of the living room and into the apartment's corridor, leaving the others politely arguing about who would take the worst of the bed options. 'Ian, come on. I know. And you know I know.'

'Know what?' he gulped.

'About you and Dee, of course. I've known for a long time, and the reality is that everyone knows.'

Ian swallowed again, his Adam's apple hopping about

nervously. 'Everyone?' he asked, his voice barely above a whisper.

'Yes, you're hardly MI5 agents, it's obvious you two like each other and we've all seen the hand touches, the longing looks … Some of us have even heard the successful application to the mile-high club,' I added, raising an eyebrow.

'Oh God.'

'If you want to share a room just share a room, nobody's going to care, and at least we won't run into you in the corridor in the middle of the night sneaking off for secret trysts.'

'I'd better talk to Dee about this.'

'Do. Why don't you just come clean, admit you're seeing each other. Or bonking. Whatever this is, no one cares.'

'We're married.'

My jaw might have fallen clean off and rolled away down the corridor. They were *what*? I stood for a moment just glaring into Ian's eyeballs while he shuffled uncomfortably. Why – how – why didn't they invite me to their wedding? 'You're *MARRIED*?!'

'Shhhh.'

'What the hell do you mean you're married? To who?'

'To each other.'

'That's not possible. You don't even live together!'

Ah-ha! Liars! I knew they'd invite me to their wedding if they were really getting hitched.

'Actually we do. Dee still has her Balham house that she rents out, and we both live at my – our – place in Forest Hill.'

'But you rarely leave work at the same time or arrive together?' Wait a minute; they *were* only ever five or ten minutes out from each other … 'How long have you been married?'

'A little over a year.'

I sat down on the floor in shock and rested my back against the wall. 'Why didn't you tell anyone? We would have been happy for you. We would have wanted to get you a wedding present.' We would have come to your effing wedding whether you liked it or not.

Ian sat down next to me, his face pale and his skin clammy. More so than usual. He looked really tired all of a sudden, very much like he'd been carrying a huge secret around for a long, long time. 'This wasn't either of our first marriages, and for both of us the previous ones had ended pretty horribly. So we wanted to be cautious, and we agreed to keep it quiet while we were dating.'

He rubbed his cheeks and looked at me, searching my face for validation that what he'd done wasn't crazy. 'That way if it ended nothing would have to change, nobody would be any the wiser.' I nodded, trying to show understanding, and he kept trying to justify himself, though I'm not sure it was for my benefit alone. 'No one at work would give us pitying looks or take sides, or say we shouldn't be on projects together because it might cause problems, or maybe we shouldn't both work here at all.'

'I understand that . . .' I soothed. *The fudge I did, they were flippin'* married*?!*

'Then we got engaged, we had a very *very* quiet and private wedding ceremony, and we just didn't feel the need to change the set-up.' He was silent for a long moment, and finally added, with a sigh, 'We like to be private.'

'You did it on a plane,' I pointed out.

'That was an exception . . . Dee's taking these contraceptives which she says make her extremely horny at the moment—'

'Whoa, urgh, enough. But didn't you get sick of all the sneaking around?'

'It's only on work trips that it's even an issue. Day-to-day we're a totally normal couple; we just don't draw attention to it in the workplace. Well, we thought we didn't. What can I say, I love my wife, and I guess it shows.'

'Oh my god,' I laughed, shaking my head. 'You totally love Dee, and she totally loves you, and you're *married* – for God's sake just tell the others and share a goddamn bedroom.'

'All right.' Ian nodded, taking a deep breath. 'OK, I will – we will. I'd better just have a chat with Dee first.'

We went back into the apartment. Jon stood in the kitchen making a round of hot chocolates, talking animatedly about something to do with reindeers. 'Hey,' he said, on seeing us. 'What do you want to drink? Lara doesn't have any tea – apart from a truly disgusting-sounding herbal thing – so it's coffee, hot chocolate, or, well that's it.'

'I'll pop over to the 7-Eleven in a little while and get us some supplies. But for now a hot chocolate would be great. What are you all talking about?'

'Jon had an idea,' said Abigail, whose pink eyes were make-up free. She was tired, and worried, but putting on a brave face, and I had a feeling that Jon's idea might be something he thought would cheer her up.

'What's your idea?'

'All right. It's December the twentieth, and what would I be doing if I was at home right now? Probably eating a lot of stuff, Christmas music would be on constantly; I'd be wrapping presents, and pretty much drinking all day. Usual pre-Christmas preparations. So I was thinking, how about this afternoon we go out and do a bit of Christmas shopping, then this evening we could have a mini Christmas party. Just us, but with loads of drinks and nibbles and games, and try and forget the fact that we're not at home with our families, because being in New York at Christmas is pretty special too.'

'You wouldn't mind spending an evening in? I thought you were all about making the most of the Big Apple?'

'Are you kidding? We're in a real New York apartment! We're about as Big Apple as you get – we're basically *Friends* right now, just in the Upper East Side.'

I looked around at the six of us – Carl, by the window, munching on another big bag of Cheetos, Abigail stirring her hot chocolate and looking through Lara's bookshelf (which I'd so have to do later), and Dee and Ian, who took the moment of calm to sneak off into one of the bedrooms and have a good talk. I hoped. 'If we're like *Friends*, who's who?'

'Well, Carl is obviously Joey because he's a total ladies' man.'

'Of course.'

'The two lovebirds are Monica and Chandler.'

'Agreed.'

'Abi would be Phoebe, I guess, because she's out here learning to make it all by herself, and you know,

Phoebe used to be homeless. OK, that one's a bit tenuous.'

'And us? Gunther and Janice?' But I knew what he was going to say before he said it.

'Ross and Rachel, of course.'

Shaking my head, and shaking it off, I turned and started putting things back in their place on the kitchen counter. 'I don't think we're Ross and Rachel.'

'I know you don't. Consider us season one Ross and Rachel. All right, anyone need a hot chocolate top-up, or are you ready to hit the shops?'

Season one. When Ross is in love with Rachel, and she doesn't know it, but he's always been there.

Dee and Ian emerged from the bedroom at that moment looking nervous. 'Can I have your attention please?' asked Ian.

'Ooo, those pigeons are doing it!' laughed Carl from the window.

'Has anyone ever read any Jackie Collins?' asked Abigail. 'Lara has so many of them; I might give one a try.'

'Yes, do it, they're great,' I said.

'Everyone shut up and listen!' commanded Dee, blushing, and then, chin held high, she took her husband's hand for all to see. 'We have something to tell you . . .'

We left the apartment in a gaggle of all six of us, and for a moment I forgot that I wanted to be on my own over the holidays. As we walked down the street, Abigail quizzing Dee and Ian on everything to do with weddings and marriage and Carl listening and contributing nothing, Jon turned to me, blowing on his hands in the cold.

'Are you seeing Elijah today?'

'I asked if he wanted to come by later on for a few drinks. I mean, his travel plans have been ruined as well. Are you OK with that?'

'Sure.' Jon shrugged. 'But I get you for a few more hours, yes?'

'Yes.' I had to admit that I was a tiny bit flattered.

'When we get down to the end of Central Park I need to steal you away.'

'All right,' I agreed, intrigued.

And that he did. We stood outside the big glass cube that was the Apple store, and agreed to all split off and meet in a couple of hours back in the same spot. 'So what do you have planned?'

Jon gestured across the street. 'What do you see here?'

'The Plaza hotel.'

'Which is . . . ?'

'Massive.'

Jon laughed. 'True, and also flippin' expensive. But do you remember what film it was used in?'

'Was it the one Macaulay Culkin stays in in *Home Alone 2*?'

'It is! I knew you were a secret Christmas nerd.'

'I'm getting there – slowly but surely working my way through those Christmas Classics people go on about watching, year on year. This is cool though. Shall we have a photo in front of it?'

'Even better – let's go in.'

We spent a good half an hour wandering between the various floors and walkways and eateries within the hotel before coming to the conclusion that as nice as it was, we'd seen enough of the inside of hotels for this trip and it was time to get back out on the streets of New York to stand under some more fat snowflakes. We strolled down Fifth Avenue like we were strolling down our local village high street.

Now we were shacked up in an apartment I suddenly felt like I belonged here – this was my home. I liked the idea of being Lara – with her apartment all decorated to her personal taste, that she (presumably) owned, a short walk into an amazing city, full of life. It appealed to me, and made me feel excited and inspired, even though … even though it was a far cry from that big house in the country that was part of my game plan. I think my heart was wanting me to realise I was a city girl.

'Look at this window display.' I stopped mid-wander and moved closer to the shop we were passing, pressing my fingertips against the glass. Behind was a tiny ornate white wrought iron fence and gate protecting a miniature turquoise Christmas tree. It was like the Sylvanian Families were recreating a scene from *The Nutcracker*. In front of the Christmas tree was a little sea-glass-blue box the size of a thimble and wrapped in thin white ribbon. 'Wait …' I stepped back and looked up at the façade, reading the words engraved into the wall above the door. 'We're at Tiffany's!'

I stepped in through the door before Jon could say a word and was met with a rush of warmth, both in temperature and a feeling of golden era welcome. I removed my gloves and gazed around at the twinkling display cabinets and happy tourists (and the occasional actual shopper).

'Good afternoon.' A lovely man in a turquoise tie and a grey suit greeted us.

'This is Tiffany's!' I said by way of reply, and then turned back to Jon. 'My dad proposed to my mum right here! With this ring.' I pulled Mum's ring off my finger and held it out to show him.

'Really? Then we need a photo to send to them. Would you like us to recreate it? I could get down on one knee, and this nice gent could take the photo.'

'No,' I said quickly, afraid of the implications. But … I would like to send my parents that photo. 'OK then.'

We posed for the photo and having Jon kneeling down, holding a ring up to me, all chocolate-eyed, made me a bit light-hearted, and – oops – I nearly said yes.

'Do you know Tiffany's does a free ring-cleaning service?' said Jon, fountain of knowledge, when the nice assistant turned away to take an identical photo for some other tourists.

'How do you know that?'

'My brother only agreed to marry his fiancé once he had a Tiffany ring, and now he waltzes into Tiffany's in the Royal Exchange every time he comes up to London to claim his little slice of VIP action. You want to have yours cleaned?'

'I don't know if it really needs it, Mum hasn't worn it for years.'

'Come on, it'll be fun, you get a free drink while you wait, apparently.'

'Ooo, do you think they'll have wine?'

Jon laughed. 'Maybe.'

We stepped into a lift which had a very smart man inside whose whole job appeared to be to take people from floor to floor and be generally very suave. Like those cast members at Disneyland who work on the Hollywood Tower of Terror ride, but without the creepiness.

On the sixth floor we exited the lift into a long room beautifully laid out with cream and jade velvet lounge chairs, Christmas trees sprinkled with silver and Tiffany-blue decorations, and individual wood-panelled booths that lined the walls. We gave our names to the gracious reception lady who told us to take a seat and someone would be with us as soon as possible, and by the time we'd sunk down into some chairs by the window I'd made up my mind: 'I'm moving to New York and working at Tiffany's.'

'Oh OK. Why? That's quite a departure from what you're currently doing.'

'That's exactly why I want to do it, it's so relaxing here. I want to work in the lift.'

'Good afternoon, sir, madam, can I get you something to drink?' asked another smart gentleman carrying a silver tray.

'Can I have a red wine, by any chance?' I asked.

'Certainly, and for you, sir?'

'A coffee would be great,' said Jon.

'Of course, regular or vanilla?'

'Yum, vanilla please.'

Mmm, that sounded nice. 'Excuse me, can I have one of those too, please?'

'Instead of the wine?'

'No, as well as, please.'

Shortly after receiving our drinks, we were taken to one of the booths, where a woman shook our hands and begged us to sit down. 'Good afternoon, Ms Forest, and sir, my name is Calinda, I understand you're here to have your jewellery cleaned today with our complimentary service?'

'I have a Tiffany engagement ring,' I said proudly, holding out my mum's ring.

'Congratulations,' said Calinda, with a pleasant, genuine smile. 'To both of you.'

Jon and I locked eyes. I opened my mouth to correct her but Jon beat me to it with a bold, 'Thank you!'

'What a beautiful ring. Have you guys had the wedding yet?' smiled Calinda.

'No,' said Jon, taking my hand and holding it in his, like it was the most natural thing in the world. 'We can't quite decide on the theme, can we, sugarlips?'

'Um . . .'

'What's on the shortlist?' asked Calinda, studying my ring through a mini eyeglass.

'Well,' Jon launched into it and I just stared at him, taking in his words in amazement, 'I think what we should do is have the ceremony in England sometime in the autumn, because autumn light is always beautiful and don't you agree she'd look beautiful in it? Now, Olivia is really into books, and there's a place called Dartmoor, it's a national park, very rugged and wind-swept and hilly, in the south-west of England, and on top of one of the hills there's a tiny little stone church, and when I look at it I just think of her up there, all white-dress-billowing-in-the-wind, and imagine it to be very Heathcliffy or Poldarky or something. I'm not as well read as my fiancée, but I think it's up her street.'

'It sounds perfect,' I said, and in that moment I would have married him – it was just me and him by that church in the autumn light. Wow, Audrey Hepburn was right, there really is just something about Tiffany's. I moved an inch closer to Jon.

'That sounds like your answer,' smiled Calinda, and she popped my ring into a grey, felt-lined box and handed it to her assistant, who took it away for cleaning.

'And then,' he continued, 'the honeymoon. She likes cities, but she likes having some peace and quiet, so

I'm thinking somewhere like Hawaii, because that's a good mix, isn't it? And I don't think she's been there.' He looked at me and I shook my head. 'So maybe she could find some new books to read, about there, as well.' He sat back, satisfied.

'Wow,' said Calinda, turning to me. 'If you change your mind, honey, I'll marry him for you. So what's your idea?'

How did he come up with all of that on the spot? I wracked my brain and then blurted out the first thing that came to me. 'Family is really important to Jon, and he has a lot of them, so I think a wedding and reception at his parents' house in Cornwall would be nice. Or perhaps down on the beach. In the snow. But it doesn't snow often in England, I suppose – now is an exception. And all his nieces and nephews, and my sisters, could be part of the wedding party, and – no work colleagues?'

Jon laughed. 'No work colleagues. Except for Kim, and maybe Carl.'

'Absolutely. Kim would be my bridesmaid, along with my two sisters. But Kim would be my favourite one. OK, deal.'

'Where do you think we should honeymoon?' he asked, an amused smile playing on his lips, his arms folded in front of him.

'I'm really enjoying New York, actually. So maybe here.'

'You are?'

'Yep. It's very … Christmassy.'

'Oh my god, you two are so in love it's going to make me cry,' shone Calinda, handing back my ring, which sparkled brighter than the star atop the Rockefeller Christmas tree. 'Congratulations again, and if you do end up honeymooning in New York, be sure to come in and say hello.'

'We will,' I said, standing up and admiring my mum's ring on my hand. 'Thank you. Come on, darling.'

We rode in the elevator in silence, Jon smothering his laughter, and as soon as we were out on the street I thwacked him one with my sparkling new hand. 'You are such a—'

'Now now, don't be upset just because my idea for our wedding and honeymoon was way better. Come on, let's meet the others, get a shit-load of food and drink, and go back and play Monopoly for a few hours like a proper family at Christmastime.'

❄

'I have never seen such brazen disregard for the rules in my life. You are the biggest bank robber since Butch Cassidy, Olivia Forest!'

I gasped at Jon and held my Monopoly money to my chest. 'How dare you suggest such a thing – I earned this fair and square. It's not my fault you're the worst estate agent in New York City.'

Abigail laughed and popped another star-shaped mini-pretzel in her mouth. I was pleased to see that she'd loosened up a bit after a couple of glasses of red wine, and for once she seemed to genuinely be having fun without thoughts of her long-lost love clouding her.

Dee looked up from where she was leaning against Ian's legs. 'Guilty until proven innocent. Show us how many hundred-dollar notes you have in that pile.'

'I don't have to show you anything,' I protested. Jon lunged at me, grasping for my wad of cash and I fell back, laughing and holding it away from him as best I could, while feeling acutely aware of our close proximity right now. My laughing died down and I blushed, turning my head from him, before being saved by the bell.

'That's Elijah,' I breathed, struggling out from under Jon and walking briskly to the door without looking back.

'Oh, Elijah,' chuckled Carl. 'I forgot he was coming, did you, Jon?'

I didn't turn to see what Jon's reaction was. I think I already knew.

Elijah greeted me with a swift kiss and then looked around him with a whistle. 'Now this place is sweet. My place is like, a hundred times smaller, but small is cosy.' He grinned at me. 'Hey, what are you all doing?'

'Playing Monopoly,' answered Abigail, far braver to speak up after a couple of glasses of wine. 'You want to join in?'

'Geez, how bored are you guys? I thought you were having a party!'

'We're near the end – I'm winning,' I said, and rolled the dice … and landed straight on the 'Go to jail' square.

There was whooping all around and Jon cheered. 'Get in the slammer, you dirty thieving wench, I bloody knew it!'

'I am innocent, this is a conspiracy, you're all just jealous of my fame and wealth.' I was so not innocent; I'd been sticking my sticky fingers in the bank money for five turns of the board.

'What will you give me for my get-out-of-jail-free card?' asked Jon, and I laughed him off, embarrassed.

'I don't need your charity; I'll be fine serving my time.'

Elijah nuzzled into my neck and purred, a little loudly, 'I knew you were a bad bitch.'

I cringed and pulled away, blushing at the brief look

Dee and Abigail gave each other. I couldn't look at Jon. 'Shhh, these are my colleagues,' I hissed, sounding more annoyed than I intended to. 'Let me get you a drink.'

We put aside the Monopoly board for now and someone cranked the Christmas music up a little. Elijah was wandering about the living room and I suddenly felt uneasy. Elijah seemed great – trustworthy, kind, yummy as hell, but I didn't really know him and I felt bad about inviting him into someone else's home.

Jon caught me keeping an eye on Elijah from the kitchen, and he immediately went over to him and struck up a conversation. I tried to lip-read the conversation, praying that Jon wouldn't mention Tiffany's, because, well it would just be a bit awkward to explain, wouldn't it? Not that Elijah deserved any kind of explanation – we barely knew each other – but I'd just feel better if the two of them were separate. I was about to go on in and break them up, but Jon appeared to be *trying* to be polite, with a fixed smile and arms folded across his chest, and Elijah was smiling. Perhaps they were getting on?

A few drinks in, 'Rockin' Around the Christmas Tree' blasting from the stereo, and everyone was getting in the Christmas spirit. Dee and Ian were showing off their jive moves (they'd been taking classes together!)

in the middle of the living room, while Carl, Jon and Abigail were laughing at a handful of jokes they'd stolen from inside the box of Christmas crackers. As for me, I was just trying to keep an iota of professionalism around my colleagues when what I really wanted to do was continue with that kiss Elijah and I started last night. And the night before.

Instead we sat close, talking, laughing, looking at each other's lips. He rested his hand on my upper thigh and I couldn't think about anything else. Well, almost nothing else. I really really really really wanted to climb onto his pe—

The doorbell buzzed and I stood up quicker than a jack-in-the-box and rushed over to the door, signalling for someone to turn down the music.

'Hello?' I spoke into the intercom.

'Hey, this is Jay and Adam and Frankie, Merry Christmas!' said a male voice with a slow, Southern-drawl accent.

'Who?'

'We're here to see Elijah.'

I turned back to Elijah. 'Did you invite some people over?'

'Yeah, you said we were having a party. That's OK, right?'

I hesitated. 'I don't think it is. This isn't our

apartment; I don't think we should invite more people in, especially people I don't know.'

Elijah laughed. 'You are such a goody-goody.'

'Yep, yes I am.' I stood firm. 'How about we head somewhere else though?' Maybe somewhere away from my colleagues, and from Jon, so I didn't feel so exposed.

'Yes,' Elijah agreed, a little too emphatically. 'Finally. Let's go down to this bar near my place, it has a club attached that we can go to later. It's called X & Y. You'll like it; it's very New York, very Christmassy, all that shit.'

'Let's all go,' said Jon, standing up, not taking his eyes off Elijah.

'No, really, Jon, you guys stay and have fun.'

'I want to go clubbing,' he said, sounding really convincing.

'Yes, let's go to a bar and a club and dance!' whooped Abigail. 'I'll call Jasmine; she might want to join us ... Nope, no answer.'

I was thankful she wasn't coming, but I really should check in with her tomorrow, just to make sure she was OK.

'Helloooooooooooo,' called Jay through the intercom.

Elijah leant past me and spoke to Jay. 'Change of plan. We're coming down and going to head back to X & Y.'

'Sweet. The neighbours here think I'm trying to rob them.'

❄

So off we went, travelling on the subway downtown with Elijah and his friends, who were nice enough, and all dressed similarly to him, but seemed utterly uninterested in knowing our names.

We arrived at X, the bar-side of the complex, and went down into a basement area that was filled with loud music and plenty of liquor. It didn't feel very New York, or very Christmassy, and as hot as Elijah was I was beginning to wish he cared more about what I wanted to do, especially since I was here for such a short amount of time.

I sighed. That wasn't fair, I was being a brat. We were different people and he was just showing me his favourite places – it wasn't his fault they weren't living up to my ideals of 'real New York'.

I broke out of my mild funk when Jon brashly ordered a round of shots, which was unlike him. Perhaps this would loosen us both up? But then something else arrived to put a smile on his face . . .

'Is there one for me?' asked a female voice and we all turned. 'Hey, guys!'

It was Dani, who waved at the table, and Jon stood to embrace her and offer her his seat. Elijah's friends perked up at the addition of this unrivalled hottie, and she was immediately swamped with introductions and jokes and questions.

'Hi, Dani,' I called across the table. I didn't know Jon and she hung out outside work.

Dani faced me, big smile. 'Olivia, you look great. I know you're probably all worried about getting home, but I was so pleased when Jon said you were stuck here for a few days because then I get to see you again!'

She was so infuriatingly nice. I really liked her, so the fact I didn't welcome the sight of her was odd. I'd never been one to feel threatened by another woman just because she was attractive. Good for her! Maybe I was just getting tipsyyyyy. I reached over and gave her a huge hug as an apology for the affronted thoughts I'd had about her in my mind that she didn't know about anyway, and she laughed and hugged me back.

Jon seemed more occupied with her there, all leaning in and draping his arm on the back of her chair and smiling while she talked. I was focusing on Elijah, I really was, but I kept catching snippets of Jon and Dani's conversations.

'Have you been here before?' Jon was asking her.

'You mean, "Do I come here often?"' she teased

back, and laughed her infectious laugh, running a hand down Jon's arm. 'I've been once or twice. Thanks for the invite.'

'I'm glad you could make it; I know it was pretty last minute.'

I dragged myself back to my own present. It was good they had each other to talk to, and that they'd all but forgotten me. It meant I could pay attention to Elijah without feeling like *I* was being watched.

❄

A few drinks later and Elijah led us all down a corridor to Y, the nightclub. The club had no windows and the darkness was only tolerable because of the pools of amber light that swam like fire over sweaty arms, close kissing and a rock band that occupied a small stage at the front of this sweat fest.

Elijah leaned in and bellowed something in my ear that sounded like 'These are my buddies' but could just have easily been 'Here are my bunnies' or 'Sneeze on my nuddies'. We all moved into the dance-floor area and drifted into whatever pockets of space we could find. Dee, Ian, Carl and Abigail stayed together, rocking away like the funny drunken fools they were, and Jon danced close to Dani. They kept grinning at each other, and laughing every time one was moshed in the back and they tumbled against each other. Not that I was paying attention, of course.

The band was loud and rocky, and the noise filled my ears so entirely that I couldn't have heard Elijah even if he had been trying to talk to me. Instead we kept our eyes on each other and in the middle of the crowd our bodies, along with everyone else's, pulsed to the heady sound of the guitar.

He moved closer to me and we danced facing each other, skin and bones. I could feel my forehead perspire in the heat and it began to not matter where I was in the world: I was right here in this moment.

Elijah leant in incredibly close and we danced for a moment with our foreheads almost touching. I watched his lips, willing them on me, heat radiating from both of us. Without a word he trickled his hand down my arm, took my hand and we both exited the crowd, moving to the darker edge of the room. I looked back at Jon, I don't know why, and there he was: kissing Dani. His hands were cupping her face. She held onto his back.

Oh. Well, how could he not have been attracted to her? Look at her. I don't know why I was being so silly. Jon was my friend and I was pleased he was having fun. Really, I was. Dani was nice. And though I thought he'd had feelings for me I'd been adamant I hadn't had the same feelings for him. So now I was free to be with Elijah . . . not that I ever hadn't been.

Elijah. No more Jon. Elijah.

Still no words were exchanged but he and I moved to a position where my back was to the wall, and he covered me like a blanket, pressing against my body, which in turn pressed against the cool brickwork. We kissed, slow, fast, hard, soft, breathing each other in.

It was the middle of winter but I was on fire. I ran a hand up his back and through his hair, but he took my arms and pinned them above my head. I felt drunk. Things were blurry but perfect.

'Do you want to get out of here? I live right around the corner.'

Part of me didn't want to break the intoxicating spell of being here, in this hot, amber glow, the music guiding my mind and body, but another part of me definitely wanted to keep going, keep moving, and get out of here with him.

I caught Dee's eye and waved, and she nodded back – we understood each other. I didn't look back at Jon.

We exited the club and the cold air and wet snow hit us with surprise. I was so hot and sticky that for a moment I'd felt I could have been in a club in Cuba and had all but forgotten it was just days from Christmas, and we were in New York. The chill cooled my perspiration rapidly and silently Elijah pulled me in under his coat and we raced around the block.

Under the wing of his leather jacket I smelled his smoky aftershave and his sweat (which I know doesn't sound sexy but in that moment I was all about the animal instincts). His slim, hard body pressed against mine and my fingers could feel the ripples of his sides through his shirt. He smiled at me.

His apartment block was smaller than Lara's, dirtier, and you went in through a back alley, but I felt safe with Elijah, and when he unlocked his door I barely noticed the size or look of his place because I didn't want to keep my hands off him any longer.

We kissed and he slammed the door shut behind me, and I curled my fingers up under his hair, pushing his face deeper into mine in the dark. He pressed me against the wall again – his signature move? – and trailed his hands and his kisses down my neck and chest.

I pushed him away and turned to face the wall, leaning my hands against it. 'Undo my dress,' I instructed. He obliged, his hands pulling down the zip and then resting on my hips, and his mouth showering my back with rough kisses. I wanted this, my body needed this.

'I knew it,' he growled.

'Knew what?' I said, turning to face him and pulling the straps of my dress down, revealing my bra. He straightened up and cupped one of my breasts while leaning in for another kiss.

'That you were a dirty little whore at heart.'

Um. 'What?' I pulled my head back.

Elijah grinned and stepped in closer, pressing his body against mine. I ignored my flicker of doubt and let him kiss me again – so he liked to talk dirty? All right, mister, but on my terms. I pulled my lips away and did one of those breathy exhales in his ear like in a Britney song. 'I'm going to ride you like an escalator,' I purred. (Now, what I was going for here was 'ride you like an elevator', but at the very last second my British brain wanted to say 'lift' which is a far less sexy word, so I did a quick switcheroo and ended up at escalator).

'Oh, you want it,' Elijah said, his hands exploring, and another tiny surge of unwelcome annoyance went through me. Yes, I think we've established that, you're not some woman-whisperer who's figured out my naughty little secret.

'*You* want it,' I countered.

'Feminist, my ass, you're begging for it, you sexy little whore.'

'WHAT?' Enough. That doubt was more than a flicker now, and I pushed him away from me. 'Did you actually just call me a whore – twice – and say I wasn't a feminist because I like sex?'

Elijah's come-to-bed eyes remained and he drew back closer to me with a laugh.

'No, wait a minute – do you think women should not want, or like, sex?'

'Of course they should ...' His hands covered me again but it didn't feel sexy any more.

'But if they do, they're not feminists, is that right? They're whores?'

This time he stopped and stood back, exasperated. 'Come on, babe, you can't stand there and pretend you don't need a man when you're basically pleading with me to sleep with you.'

I pulled my dress back up and my loins turned to ice quicker than you could say 'Baby, it's cold outside'. 'What do you think a feminist is, exactly?' I demanded.

He shrugged, and suddenly in that moment, with his shirt open and his penis deflating, he looked less like a sexy, scruffy rock god and more like a naughty boy who hadn't washed for a few days. 'Someone who thinks women are better than men?'

I was lost for words, and while I tried to find them again I also gathered my things up from the floor of his titchy, crappy little apartment. 'No,' I stated. 'Nope, that isn't it at all. It's someone who believes men and women are equal, and if you were a real man, you would believe that too.' Like Jon does. The thought entered my head, unbidden. *Like Jon does.*

'I do think that . . .' he said, lamely.

'No you don't,' I sighed. 'You think a woman is a whore if she likes sex. But you don't think a man is a whore, do you? Newsflash, a sex worker is the last person who is actually likely to enjoy doing you. Thicky.'

Elijah lit a cigarette, trying to wrap his head around what was happening. I was pretty sure he'd be calling me 'crazy' to his friends tomorrow. I looked him up and down, straightened my bra, and tossed my hair back from my face. 'Well guess what, Elijah, I love sex. I love it and I'm good at it and I don't need the lights out, or for you to pretend you don't see my cellulite. I'm great at sex, but oops – you missed out.'

'Wait a minute, O, no need to be all crazy and storm out of here.'

There it was – *crazy*. 'Goodbye, Elijah. And I hope this is how you remember me: not begging for it, but walking away from you. *This* is what a feminist looks like.'

And I left the building with not even a parting Merry Christmas for him and his shocked, sulking face. It was the last time I saw him.

Back out on the street, in the dark, with plump snow-flakes falling on my head and Christmas decorations behind the glass of people's windows, I felt, oh, very alone. This is what I wanted though, wasn't it? To be alone, to have everyone go away and not bother me until I was ready? I got out my phone and called Dee's number. A tear escaped my eye and I wiped it away in anger.

'Hello?' Dee answered, shouting over music.

'It's Olivia,' I answered, trying to control my wobbling voice. 'Are you guys still at Y?'

'Liv? I can't hear you very well. We're still in Y, but we were thinking of heading home soon. Where are you? Where's Elijah?'

'I'm going to come home with you all, OK? Can you meet me outside in like . . . ' Another tear plopped out. Dammit. ' . . . in five to ten minutes?'

'Sure, see you in a mo, hun.'

I hung up and crouched on the ground, putting my head in my arms. I had to pull it together, I didn't want them all to see me like this – I'd already made a fool out of myself and crossed the professional line by hooking up with someone on a work trip. I was an idiot.

I became aware of somebody pacing back and forth past me, muttering. 'Sexy bitch, sexy bitch, hello, sexy bitch.'

Bringing my head up I looked straight into the eyes

of a man, probably in his late fifties, with stained clothing and a nervous twitch. He was chewing his cigarette and looking at me. 'Sexy bitch.'

'Go away please,' I said, firmly.

He came closer, leaning over me. 'Do you want dick?'

My heart began to pound, with fear, with frustration, with anger. '*No.*' I stood up to move away but he stood in front of me. He didn't seem so frail now; now he seemed taller than me, tougher than me.

'Want a bit of dick, sexy bitch?'

'Go away.' I tried to push past him but he pushed me back to the ground and I banged my head against the wall on the way down. The man glanced around and then bent down towards me with a look that I knew wasn't compassion or concern.

He leered closer and I felt like I wanted time to stop. A red rage was brewing in me but I just needed a moment – could someone just give me a moment to gather my thoughts?

But there were no moments, no time for reflecting or feeling sorry for myself, because I had to get myself out of my mess. I opened my mouth and bunched my fists and was about to fight back when the man suddenly hurtled to the side.

I watched him, confused, as he stumbled and fell away from me, and only when I was swept up off the ground by two strong arms did my eyes leave the man and my face bury into a familiar woodsmoke coat.

Jon held me close. I dug my face further into his chest and I didn't have the strength to look out again, but I heard shouting, felt the bump against Jon as the man clearly tried to fight back, but Jon shielded me and let his back take the force, and then we were gone, back on the main road, back to where Christmas music seeped out of restaurants and bars and the noise of people chattering drowned out the noise of my heart racing. Only then did we stop walking.

I looked up at Jon, sniffling. 'I don't need saving. I can save myself,' I said, my voice small as he put me down on the ground.

'I know you can, but that doesn't mean you always have to,' Jon said kindly, though I didn't feel I deserved it.

'Where's everyone else?'

'They carried on back to the apartment; I said I'd meet you.'

'Why?'

'When Dee said you called I figured something must be wrong. And I thought you'd maybe rather see me than a bunch of your colleagues. To save face, and all that.'

'Thank you.'

'That's OK.'

'No, but, thank you for meeting me, and for ... that ... with that guy.'

Jon pulled me in close again and we stood quietly for a bit while I stopped shaking.

After a while I pulled back. 'Where's Dani?' I asked.

'She went home.'

'Oh. I'm sorry.'

'Don't be.'

The snow was melting on my head and dripping onto my eyelashes. 'We're getting really wet.'

'I know,' he said.

'And cold. And my head hurts.'

'Do you want to get it checked, or shall I take you home?'

'No, and ... no. It was just a bump but I don't think I want to face everyone yet. I might want one more drink, to calm the nerves. Somewhere a bit quieter than Bar X?'

'All right,' said Jon. We began walking up the street, him never taking his arm out from behind me. 'I know just the place.'

❄

'You really did know just the place,' I said, sinking into a leather chair by a window, looking out over a rooftop terrace that was sprinkled with fairy lights. A candle flickered on the table between us, and gentle, quiet music was being played on a piano across the other side of the lounge. And on all the walls: books, books, books. 'How did you know about this?'

Jon hesitated. 'This ... is where I knew I always wanted to take you, if we went on a date.'

'Oh.' Oh.

'I knew as soon as I heard the name the Library Hotel that this would be somewhere you'd like, so on an evening off from the conference last Christmas I came here to check it out, came up here to the Bookmarks Bar, and thought, yep – one day I'll bring Liv here.'

I sipped my Tea S. Eliot cocktail (made with Earl Grey and vanilla-infused vodka). 'You thought about bringing me here ... last year?'

Jon nodded, watching me carefully. 'Yep. Do you want to talk about what happened tonight?'

'With Elijah? No, not really.'

'Did you fart again in front of him?'

'Worse – I sharted.'

Jon laughed and I watched him for a moment. He knew me.

I sighed. 'Arrrgghh, what was I thinking?'

'You were following what your heart wanted,' he said,

kindly, his eyes moving away from me to look down at his drink – a Tequila Mockingbird.

I think I was ignoring what my heart wanted. I'd been so obsessed with finding 'the spark' and feeling that 'instant attraction'. It was only now occurring to me that the thing that *instantly attracted* me to men, since Kevin and I had split, was their unavailability. I'm not talking married or attached men, but without fail they were always people that would never in a million years become the thing that scared me the most: A Relationship.

I'm not denying I had a great time with most of these men, for the short time they were part of my life, and they were healthy, happy choices at the time. But when they had to get back on their plane, or it was the end of the night, or I was moving on, I never once looked back and wished they'd stuck around.

'I'm not feeling entirely blue over Elijah, by the way,' I said, suddenly. 'I mean I was – I'm human and the whole thing was a bit humiliating. Never nice to realise you've made a massive mistake, is it?'

'So he was a mistake?' Jon asked, his voice soft.

'Very much. But thankfully he showed his true colours before things went too far.' I could tell Jon was concerned, and unsure about exactly what I meant, so I clarified, 'Don't worry, he didn't do anything too bad, he just doesn't understand women as much as he thinks he does. The words "whore", "begging" and "crazy" were used. He's not exactly HeForShe.' I took a gulp of my drink and waved my hand to brush this aside before Jon could get too riled on my behalf. 'Anyway, Elijah is just a fuckboy and he's gone now. Tell me about Dani. You two seemed to be hitting it off.'

Jon shrugged and looked down at his drink, and I watched his kind face fall into his thinking expression. Dani was lucky to have him.

'I don't know,' he said. 'We were both just a little merry.'

'But she went home?'

He nodded.

'Did you ask her to go?' I pried. This was so none of my business, but my filter had come off and I was too exhausted to put it back on.

'Actually, she excused herself. When I said I was going to leave the club to meet you.'

Oh, I was the worst. Dani was truly a nice girl and I cringed at the thought of her going home alone, resenting me. I really needed to figure my shit out. 'Sorry, Jon.'

'Nothing to apologise for,' he said kindly. 'Now, since we're already feeling bruised-of-heart and kind of tipsy, do you want to tell me what else you're feeling blue about, while you're at it?'

'Haha, well it is Christmas, after all, so why not?' I took a deep breath. 'I feel blue because … I've tried very hard for a long time not to need to be co-dependent, and I kind of just realised that my reasoning all stemmed back to one thing: Kevin. So in a way, I hadn't let go at all, and that makes me angry.'

'All right. Sometimes it's good to be angry. Fuck you, Kevin.'

I smiled. 'Have I ever really told you about Kevin?' Jon shook his head. I took a sip of my drink and looked out of the window for a moment. Was I really going to tell Jon everything? I took another sip. Yes, yes I was. 'Kevin and I were together for years – we met just after uni. We were even engaged for a short while. He was a bit rubbish with money, but we were happy, and com-mitted, and we were saving, slowly but surely, for our future, our family, for that house in the country.'

'Ahh, the notorious "house in the country".'

'I helped him pay off his debts, we put everything into a joint bank account, we actually had quite a healthy deposit building up for a while there. I felt completely secure, he was my other half, our families got on, our friends got on. I think you met him, once, didn't you? At post-conference drinks in London, the first year we knew each other? You probably don't remember.'

'I remember,' said Jon. 'I didn't like him very much.'

'You didn't?' I was surprised. 'Everyone liked him – he was funny and charming, and very quick to buy the rounds.'

'I remember thinking he was a bit showy, like it was all about appearing to be everyone's best friend.'

Jon's candour stung a little, but I had to admit that he was right on the mark. I wondered if Kevin's personality had been that obvious to everyone – everyone except me, that is. 'Well, I liked him. I thought I was in an absolute winner of a relationship, and I was happy and excited and, oh my god that House in the Country. It was our dream, and we were nearly there.'

'It was both of your dreams?'

'Yes,' I answered honestly. 'That's one hundred per cent what I've always wanted. It's what I *had* wanted. With him.'

Jon broke into my thoughts after I'd gone silent for a few moments. 'Come on then, hit me, let's smash this dream; what happened next?'

'Ah, now that's where he upped and left me, out of the blue. I came home one day from work and he'd moved out. He left me a note, full of apologies, full of excuses and I was just completely blindsided. It was like … he'd never cared at all. All that time and energy and years and love and he was just gone.' I let out a long, noisy sigh and shook away the tears that threatened to spill again.

Jon looked perplexed. 'But … why … '

'Why did he leave? I think "the dream" was just all too much. All the talk of the future, which he'd been completely into at the time, got on top of him and he panicked. The money was a big thing too. He could never quite crawl out of debt and he could also never quite face the fact that he really had to. So he left, and he took way more than his fair share of our house deposit with him.'

'He did *what*? That's not legal, surely? I'll kill him, and get the money back, and then we'll get you that house.'

I locked my knees in with Jon's. He was so comforting to be around. 'He's long gone, but thank you. And I couldn't get the money back because we both had ownership of the account – there's nothing at all the bank could do. I looked into whether I could take legal action but it was estimated that the fees wouldn't be that far off my half of the house deposit anyway.'

I met Jon's gaze and we stared at each other for a moment. I was drained. 'I thought I was doing everything right ever since. I wasn't crying, I wasn't wallowing in self-pity, I was building myself back up and not letting myself get attached to anyone again.'

'Saving up ever since for that house in the country?'

I couldn't help but start laughing. Was I imagining it, or did getting things off your chest make you feel like you've lost twenty pounds?

Jon's concerned smile turned into that big delighted one that I was so fond of. 'This isn't some kind of Miss Havisham thing, is it, where you'll buy the house and whack on a wedding dress and then sit waiting for him to move in for the rest of your life?'

'No. I think I've spent enough time basing life choices around him. I bet he sure as hell isn't basing much around me.'

'Then more fool him,' said Jon, and asked for a couple more drinks from the bartender. 'One more, then shall we go home? Start New York afresh tomorrow?'

I nodded. 'Thanks, Clarence.'

Part 3

Good tidings we bring to you and your kin
We wish you a Merry Christmas and a Happy New Year

21 December

4 days to Christmas

❄

I woke up, unsure if I'd actually fallen asleep at all. For a long time I just stared at a framed photo of a snow-capped mountain that was hanging on the wall. Next to me, Abigail slept peacefully; the deep slumber of some-one who had had too much wine and was exhausted by all the worrying they'd been doing.

Eventually I reached for my phone and checked the time, shielding the light under the duvet cover. Three twenty-five in the morning. My body felt uncomfort-able – aching, stiff, protective of itself.

As silently as I could manage I stepped from the

bed and collected my discarded slipper socks from the floor. I told myself I wanted a drink from the kitchen, but actually, I knew I was just finding an excuse to be near Jon.

I walked into the kitchenette, calmed by the sound of Carl's snoring coming from the sofa bed, like a purr in the dead of night. I stood for a moment, listening, focusing on the noise, and trying to get out of my own head. It was as I was pouring a small glass of water that I heard a whispered, 'Hey.'

I squinted into the dark to see Jon sitting up in his lilo bed on the floor. 'Hi,' I whispered.

'Can't sleep?'

'No. Did I wake you?'

'No. Do you want to come and lie with me?'

Lie with someone? I hadn't wanted that for a long time. I'd wanted distance or I'd wanted passion, but closeness ... 'Yeah,' I whispered, and put down the glass.

Even in the small apartment his bed seemed a great distance, and I felt clumsy and on-show picking my way towards him, but I didn't mind feeling vulnerable in front of him – he didn't make me feel ashamed about my vulnerabilities. I reached him and he held open his duvet for me to climb inside.

Jon's body was warm – I could tell before I even

touched him. He placed the duvet over me and lay beside me for a moment with us both staring up at the ceiling. And then I made a decision.

I rolled onto my side and reached for Jon's hand, pulling him over me so we spooned, his breath on my neck, his heavy arm resting across mine, and our legs entwined. I snuggled back into him, the consequences of my actions no more than a tiny pinprick of a thought to worry about in the morning. Our breathing slowed and synced, and I finally felt calmer.

Only I still couldn't sleep, and I lay there with my eyes open, thinking, thinking about all the things I didn't usually give myself time to think about.

After a while Jon whispered in my ear, 'Are you still awake?'

'Yeah,' I whispered back.

'Do you want to talk?'

'No, I'm talked out, but thanks.' But I did feel the need to blast a bit of cold air through my head. 'Do you want to go on the roof?'

'I know it's been a shitty night, but I don't think you should kill yourself,' he said, wrapping an arm around me tighter.

I wriggled out from under him. 'Lara mentioned it in the note; you can go up on the roof and look out over the city. You wanna come?'

He climbed out after me and handed me one of his large hoodies to put on over my PJs, which I was grateful for the minute we left the warmth of the apartment.

'It wasn't entirely a shitty night,' I said, as we climbed the stairs to the roof door. 'I had a nice date with you.'

As soon as I said it I regretted it – I was on dangerous ground here, and until I knew what I wanted I had to stop saying things like that. It would be so easy to like Jon in the way he seemed to like me. And I knew I could feel it – a small ember in me that burned for him. But I didn't want to play with his heart, Britney-style.

We stepped on to the rooftop and it took our breath away. You could see it all from here: the Empire State Building, 30 Rock, the One World Trade Center ... If it wasn't so nose-numbingly freezing I would have happily slept up here. The snowflakes the size of ten-pence pieces would've been an issue too.

'The snow's getting harder here now,' I commented. 'The US will close its airports next. I love this city.' I huffed out, my breath plumbing into a frosty cloud in front of me.

'You do strike me as a city girl. And yet you want to move out to the country?'

'It was always in the plan, but now ... I guess I've been thinking about what we were talking about back at the Library Hotel. I've been so angry at Kevin for so many years – and I don't know if I'll ever stop being angry at him, really. I know you should forgive and forget but how do you do that when someone you truly believe cares about you takes everything you've dreamed about and runs away with it? Not just the money, but that was my life. And I've been trying so hard to build it all back up again that I've barely had time to think about whether I still want what I thought I wanted. Maybe my plan should change.'

'Do you think it's changing now?'

'I think I'm changing now. I wanted to prove I was unbreakable, that I could claw my way back to financial freedom and get that house, and that nobody could stop me. I don't quit anything, so quitting this idea is hard.'

A cold wind whipped my face and I stared hard at the city, willing the new dream to break through.

'It's OK to quit a dream that was never yours in the first place – it was yours *and Kevin's*. What you need to not quit on is yourself. Building yourself and *your* dreams back up.'

He was saying the words that were already floating inside my head, that had always been there really but had been pushed back behind this wall, this intense focus. 'I don't want to move out to the country. I like my life and my job and my friends and I like living in London, so maybe I should just shut up and actually *live* in London. I know I want my own place, that I can paint how I want, and I can hang pictures where I want, and I can have a pet if I want. So, I've decided …' I paused. What was I thinking? Just say it, Liv. 'I've decided that maybe rather than spending the next four years trying to save for that house in the country for my non-existent family and my arsehole of an ex-boyfriend, that maybe I should buy a flat, just for me, now, in the place I actually want to live in.'

'That's some big decision-making. And you one-eightied all because of our talk over a couple of Manhattans?'

'No. It's a tiny thought that's popped into my head a couple of times this past week. Being in New York is inspiring, and it reminded me how much I love being just what you said – a city girl. I'm sure one day I might live in the country and love that too, but for now, I don't want to move away. I want to be able to go out and buy a weird snack at eleven p.m. if I feel hungry. I want to be able to go to the theatre on the spur of the moment. I want to walk to Kim's house whenever I want, whether she likes it or not. So up yours, Kevin, I might not forget what you did but I can forget about the life we planned together, and live my own life instead.'

'Bravo! Up yours, Kevin, you douchebag!'

'Yeah!' I laughed, my eyes running over the

skyscrapers, glittering in the night sky. 'How about you? Had any epiphanies on this holiday?'

'No.' He chuckled, keeping his eyes forward, and my heart sank a little. As much as I was scared about him admitting any feelings to me, I still felt conflicted about whether I wanted him to have them or not. 'Well, unless you count that I've realised that Carl might be my best friend. Did you know he's quite funny? Especially on a night out.'

I shook my head, laughing. 'I had no idea.'

'Any other epiphanies I had happened long ago for me.'

'Dani?' I hated myself for asking.

'What? No, not Dani.'

'She's a lovely person. Nice hair. Have you two had something going on for a while?'

Jon looked at me, really looked at me. 'No,' he said.

I could kiss him. Right now I could kiss him and I was pretty sure he'd want me to. But . . . if I did it would change everything between us, and I was still a little woozy, and my skin still had Elijah's touch and Elijah's kisses on it. It just didn't feel like the right moment. Would it ever be the right moment? I didn't know, but I knew I shouldn't decide now.

'It's getting a bit cold,' I murmured.

'OK,' he replied, nodding with understanding. We

went back inside, and though a part of me wanted nothing more than to climb back under the covers with him, I bid him goodnight at the bedroom door, and closed it behind me.

※

'Good morning,' I said, rolling over to see Abigail awake, sitting up in bed, texting.

'Hi,' she said. 'I have a really big hangover. I threw up in the bin.'

'What kind of a bin is it?'

'Just a plastic one.'

'That's OK then, it'll wash out. Boyfriend OK?'

She sighed. 'Yeah. He says he just wants me to come home now.'

'I bet he does.'

'I also texted Jasmine, just to check in.' Abigail rubbed her face and yawned. I felt a pang – I really should have been the one checking in with Jasmine. 'I asked if she wanted to come over, but she said no.'

I felt petty and unsure what to say, so I changed the subject. 'Do you want a cup of tea? Or coffee?'

'Can I have a really really strong coffee, and a new head, please?'

I got out of bed and looked at myself in the mirror

before I opened the door. I looked a bit bedraggled. But bugger it.

'Good morn—' Where were Jon and Carl? I padded over to the kettle, flicked it on, and then went to the window. The snow had thickened overnight and New York was looking more like a scene from *Serendipity* than ever. At this rate Britain would thaw out and we'd get snowbound in New York instead. I grabbed an extra jumper of Jon's that was lying on the sofa bed and finished making the coffees, delivering one to Abigail, who had fallen asleep again with her phone in her hand.

I was about to flop down and watch some American morning TV and pretend I couldn't hear Dee and Ian doing it in the guest room when I heard a noise at the front door, like a small scratch.

Opening it, I was faced with an extra-large red retriever, who looked up at me with big soulful eyes and a singular 'woof'.

'Well, hi,' I said, sitting down on the step and facing the dog. 'Who are you?'

He gave me his paw.

'Thank you. Do you live in this apartment block? What do you do for a living?'

He blinked at me, and I heard a small giggle from above. I looked up, and a tumble of curly hair hid a face that was peeping down at me. 'He doesn't have a job!' the curly hair cried.

'Oh you don't?' I addressed the dog. 'Well how do you afford to go to the hairdresser's and get this lovely red dye put in?'

'That's his real fur colour!' exclaimed the little girl from under the hair. She ran down the spiral staircase two at a time from the floor above. 'His name is Chewy, and he's a really bad dog, because he knows how to open our door so he keeps coming downstairs to visit our neighbours. Were you making coffee?'

'I was . . . would you like one?'

'No, I'm six and a half! But Chewy loves the smell of coffee – I bet he was scratching at your door, huh?'

'He was.'

'Are you staying with Lara? I thought she went home to her mummy and daddy upstate?'

Chewy settled down in front of me, his big tummy wide open for a rub. 'She did, but my friends and I are staying in her home because we can't go back to our homes in England at the moment, because it's too snowy and the airports are shut.'

'Airports don't shut in the snow!'

'British ones do – we don't have snow very often, not like here, so we don't have all the equipment to deal with it.'

'So you're all from England? Can I meet everyone?' The little girl had wide eyes and she peered past me into the apartment.

'They're asleep at the moment, but maybe later.' The last thing I needed was a little girl witnessing Dee and Ian Cirque-du-Soleiling around the bedroom in the buff. 'I'm Olivia.'

'I'm Steph. Did you know that Sir Walter Raleigh was an English explorer who sailed to America back in 1578?'

Oh my god, she was this kind of a girl. *My* kind of a girl. 'I did know that – you like history?'

'Kind of,' said Steph, playing with Chewy's ears. 'I like exploring. I have this book that I borrowed from my school library all about explorers and how they went to all these new places and collected things to bring home, and there are old maps that show what the world used to look like. But you know what?'

'What?'

'Even though there are now people all over the place, even at Costco on Christmas Day, Mom says, I think there's still more to explore.'

'Oh, there's plenty more. And just because other people have been to places doesn't mean you can't explore them too. And some people go and explore space – there's lots of that to discover.'

Steph nodded, grinning. 'My grandfather says I should marry an explorer because I'll get free holidays for life.'

'You know what would be even cooler?'

'What?'

'If *you* grew up to be the explorer. Have you heard of Ellen MacArthur?'

Steph and Chewy thought for a moment. 'No.'

'She sailed all the way around the world on her own, faster than anyone else ever has.'

'Wow.'

'I know.'

Steph stood up. 'OK, I have to take Chewy out to make peepee. I'm going to take him down by the East River today, in case Ellen MacArthur's going by.'

I waved her goodbye and took a gulp of my coffee, remaining outside the apartment on the step. I took out my phone and firstly tried Anne again – no answer – so I left her a voicemail to say we were still here but hoping to leave the day before Christmas Eve, and then I called Kim.

'We are *such* twins – I was just going to call you!' Kim answered. 'Are you still in New York? How's Elijahhhhh? Did you get the D yet?'

'I am still in New York, Elijah is … gone … D and all, thank the lord. And I have a problem.'

'What?'

'I think I might like Jon.'

Kim squealed down the line. '*Steve, Liv said she thinks she likes Jon!*'

'No, don't tell Steve.'

'Steve wants to speak to you.'

'No . . .'

'Hi, Liv.'

'Hi, Steve.'

'You have to go for it with Jon. I really need you to stop being the gooseberry in Kim and I's rela— Ouch! I'm kidding! Liv, he sounds so nice, and I need another guy friend to hang out with, so if you like him can you just go for it?'

'But I don't need to be with someone to be happy.'

Steve laughed. 'Of course you don't. But are you going to deliberately *not* be with someone who makes you happy, just to try and prove a point?'

Kim came back on the line. 'So how did this happen? I need to know everything. Have you kissed?'

'No, no, we're not there yet. I've just been doing some soul-searching. Letting myself think things through properly. A Christmas present to myself, as it were.'

'And you just decided you liked him?'

'It's more that . . . I stopped being such a big fat

brick wall, and now I can see a bit clearer. I've been Berlin-walled.'

At that point I heard voices and looked down over the spiral staircase to see Jon and Carl, hair wet from the falling snow, and clothes damp like they'd been for a morning run. Urgh, if we even had to run to the bathroom it would probably make any of the rest of us throw up this morning.

'Kim, I have to go.'

'What, no wait, what are you going to do about him?'

'Love you, call you later, bye.'

'Liv—'

'Hi,' I greeted the men as they got to the top of the stairs. Carl, a broken man, simply waved at me, pink-faced, and collapsed through the door.

'Hey, you,' said Jon, a huge grin on his face. His arms glistened with sweat and his damp T-shirt clung to his torso and showed every outline. I struggled to keep my focus on his face.

'Hi back. You went jogging? In the snow?'

'Yep, round Central Park. It was beautiful; so many dogs, and the snow is thick, and still falling. It's a brand new day,' he said with meaning.

'But ... you could barely stand up when we walked through there the other day, because of all the ice. How did you run through it?'

'Carl and I had to hold hands from time to time,' he said, and we walked back into the apartment. 'We are so BFFs now.'

'Can I get you a drink?'

'A coffee would be great.' Jon pulled off his T-shirt, revealing a surprisingly toned chest. 'I'm just going to jump in the shower.'

OK, he was definitely being provocative, and though I hated myself for it, as I poured him a cup of the hazelnut roast I was picturing him there in the shower, the water dripping from his hair, his body warming in the heat ...

I needed a shower of my own. Later. Without Jon.

I left his coffee on the side and disappeared back into the bedroom, where I lay next to Abigail and blamed it all on the alcohol.

❄

An hour or so later I had a plan. A plan in my head, clothes on, a brush through my hair, and my parka at the ready. I walked out of the bedroom door and into the living room. Jon was on the phone. He motioned for me to come forward.

'Mum, I'm going to put Liv on,' he said, and handed the phone to me.

'What? Why?' I blustered, caught off guard.

'I'm gagging for a wee, back in a mo,' he whispered, and shot off, leaving me holding the phone.

'Hello?' I said nervously.

'Oliviaaaaaaaa! It's so nice to finally talk to you; Jon says you two have been having a lovely time in New York, snowy, he says, can't be as snowy as here though, do you think you'll be home for Christmas, my love? Are you on the same flight as Jon? We're all here, you know, his whole family, luckily we all live fairly close by, say hello, everyone!'

'*Hello!*' came a chorus down the phone.

'Hello,' I replied, confused about which part of all that I should be answering. 'Jon's just popped for a wee.'

'Ooo, that naughty little bugger, I've told him before to spend a penny before he phones us, he always has to cut our talks short because he needs to urinate, I tell you one thing though, Liv, he's just like his dad in that respect, did you know that . . .'

Jon's mum kept chattering and I smiled, realising he probably used the needing-to-wee excuse as an excuse. Finally he returned, said goodbye to them all, and I had him to myself.

'I have a plan for today, if you want to hang out together,' I said. Confidently.

'You have a plan? Aren't I supposed to be showing you a New York Christmas?'

'You've done so much already, and this isn't anything amazing, like the things you've shown me, but I think we should do it.'

'Then I'm in.'

'OK. Get your coat.' *You've pulled*.

❄

We emerged from the 34th Street subway station into a New York blizzard. Snow covered the ground and whipped around us, stinging our cheeks and making us blink at a million miles a minute.

I took Jon's hand and raced with him towards the illuminated word that graced the front of the building in giant, three-storey letters: *Believe*. We were at Macy's.

We pushed through the revolving door and the department store was every bit as special as *Miracle on 34th Street* had led me to believe it would be. Stretched in front of us were counter after counter of handbags under spotlights, jewellery displayed behind sparkling glass, and cosmetics of every colour under the sun. Garlands of plush green and white fairy lights covered the ceilings, fans blew warm air out, giant baubles containing intricate miniature scenes of Santa and reindeers hung from the roof and 'It's the Most Wonderful Time of the Year' rang out loudly from the speakers, accompanied by the cha-ching of cash registers. If John Lewis had a baby with Buddy the Elf, Macy's would be the result.

'Have you seen *Miracle on 34th Street*?' I asked Jon.

'Of course.'

'This is the store! The real store that it's based on! *On Thirty-Fourth Street!*'

'Does that mean the real Santa is here?'

'Maybe.' I looked around me and then back up at Jon. 'I don't know what we're going to do here; it just seemed like a place you should come. Do you need to do any Christmas shopping?'

Jon laughed, and shook his wet hair onto me. 'Let's just have a wander around.' He took my hand, and I didn't resist.

There were people everywhere: shoppers, tourists, those just sheltering from the snow outside. We walked around the store and everywhere you looked the word *Believe* was dangling from the ceiling, written across walls and shopping bags, emblazoned above our heads across sparkling garlands.

Christmas. Did I believe yet? I was beginning to . . .

We found ourselves in the Christmas department, where rows upon rows of multicoloured baubles and decorations and candle-holders and fairy lights twinkled under the spotlights of the store. I picked up a little tree ornament in the shape of the Empire State Building, with that word again – *Believe* – written across it. I needed that. I wanted to always be reminded of New York at this time of year when I needed to believe in Christmas, in love, in myself.

'You look like you're having your own miracle here on Thirty-Fourth Street,' Jon commented, coming to stand beside me.

'Maybe not a miracle, but I do feel like I'm changing. Not too much, but I feel a bit more open than I was before. Does that make sense?'

'Open to what?'

I looked up at him. 'I'm not a hundred per cent sure yet. I'm nervous.'

At that point, I shit you not, Santa Claus walked past. Granted, he was probably the store Santa going for a quick loo break, but according to the movie the Macy's Santa is the *real* Santa.

'Look up, kids,' he said to us, with a wink and a pat of his belly.

Jon and I broke our gaze with each other and looked up. Mistletoe. There were small bunches of it hanging from candy-cane hooks from the ceiling in various places around the Christmas department, so it wasn't entirely a miracle, but it was there, right above us.

'Mistletoe,' said Jon, looking back at me, a look of both amusement and a touch of nerves on his face. He grew serious and his eyes softened, and for a moment the music seemed to die down, the other shoppers faded away, and it was just him and me, under some mistletoe on 34th Street. I clutched my ornament; *Believe*.

I stepped the tiniest of steps closer to him, never having felt this nervous about being near to Jon before. He rested his hands on my hips, pulling me in just a tiny bit more. I put my own hands on his arms and there was no turning back. Our faces drew close and moments before our lips touched he hesitated, smiled, a new smile I hadn't seen before – soft and personal – and then he kissed me.

It was the lightest of kisses and lasted no more than a couple of seconds, but it felt more real than anything I'd had with Elijah. In that moment it was just how I'd imagined it: I felt his hair on my forehead, his warm nose against my still cold nose, his lips – Jon's lips on mine – which were firm but sweet.

I think I could believe again now.

We pulled apart, both of us blushing a little, both of us ignoring the magnitude of what had just happened given that we were in such a public place.

'Um, so, I'm just going to buy this,' I croaked. 'Do you want anything?'

'I'm good,' he smiled.

We paid, held hands again, and made our way back through the crowds slowly, and out again onto the street which was fast becoming a white-out in the snow.

'Shall we walk a little way, before we get on the subway?' I suggested. 'I could do with a little air.'

'Sure.'

We began crunching our way up Avenue of the Americas, watching our steps carefully, the snow coming up over our shoes. 'So *this* is what a real, traditional Christmas looks like,' I said.

'How does it compare to your winter sun holidays? Or hanging out in your flat, for that matter?'

'At the moment, it's pretty good.' I smiled. 'Very cold though.'

'It's so cold, the temperature's dropped since yesterday, I'm shaking under my coat.'

'Me too.' My foot slid a little underneath me and I gripped hold of Jon. 'Whose idea was it to walk? Do you know how far it is to the next metro station?'

'There's one on Forty-Second Street, so we're about six blocks away. How's that?'

'That's fine.' I brushed a massive snowflake out of my eye, probably smudging half my mascara while I was at it. Chuff me, it was cold. Then I noticed we were walking past a tourist shop. I dragged Jon inside and grabbed two of the nearest sweatshirts. 'Six blocks is fine, but we need another layer or we're going to freeze to death. So these are on me. Do you want New York Knicks or NYPD?'

'I'll take the Knicks,' he said, grinning.

I paid for the sweaters and we pulled them on over our other clothes, then put our jackets back on over the top. Exiting the shop, Jon took my hand again, smiled, and said, 'I like you. You're fun.'

❄

We'd made it back to the apartment later in the day and hadn't ventured back out since. I'd avoided talking to Jon about what had happened between us any more because I didn't quite know what to say, and what I wanted. I needed just a little time to think, first, and having all these other people around the whole time made it easy to avoid making any decisions too soon.

There was a buzz at the door and Abigail got up to answer it. An American woman's voice said, 'Hi, can I speak to Olivia Forest please?'

I frowned at Abigail in confusion. Who could that be? I slipped out of the flat, made my way down the spiral staircase and opened the door to the apartment complex. There, enormous Eskimo hood pulled up and standing in the thick snow, looking every bit the snow angel, was Dani.

'Hi,' she greeted me, big smile, and my mind sped about wondering what she wanted, what she'd heard, was she in love with Jon, did I have any sign of Jon's kiss on me?

'Hi, do ... do you want come in?'

'No, thank you, I can't stay because I think the snow's getting worse; I was just at a café on Madison a few blocks down and I wanted to come and see you.'

'OK, well, nice to see you. You look great. I like your coat, is it ... warm?' Shut up, Olivia.

'Thanks, I like your sweater, you look cute.'

I looked down at my NYPD jumper and couldn't help but smile.

'Listen,' Dani continued. 'I just wanted to apologise for last night, for kissing Jon. I hope there's no bad feelings between us, because I think you're such a great and interesting girl.'

She was apologising to *me*? 'Wait, I'm not sure what you mean. It's OK that you kissed Jon.'

'No it's not. I know you were with that guy last night, but I'm guessing things didn't end well because as soon as your friends came over to me and Jon to say you were waiting outside and sounded upset, I knew Jon wanted to be there for you. I didn't mean to get in the way.'

'You didn't get in the way; he obviously likes you, Dani.'

'No he doesn't,' she laughed softly. 'His face lights up when he talks about you, it always has. I think he just picked me last night because he was lonely.'

'I'm sorry,' I whispered. She was so lovely, and she hadn't deserved to be tangled up in the mess I'd created. I really was sorry.

'Don't be, I get it. I was feeling a little lonely as well, and Jon's a great guy. But will you believe me when I say it didn't mean anything – for either of us? One mistletoe kiss after a few drinks doesn't override years of Jon's Christmas wishes.'

'You are literally the perfect woman,' I said, leaning in for a hug, which Dani warmly reciprocated.

'And you are *his* perfect woman. Can you go get him already?'

22 December

3 days to Christmas

❄

'Hello?'

'Hello, may I speak with Olivia Forest please?'

'Yep, that's me.'

'Oh hello. Lovely. This is Amanda, your British Airways rep; we met at the Brooklyn Marriott the other day.'

'Yes, hello.' I edged away from everyone else, who were all standing around the window watching the blizzard blow sideways across the street outside. We were definitely getting the brunt of the storm that had hit Europe now, but did that mean it was clearing the other end? I went and stood in the kitchen, about to find out.

This was it – she was either calling to confirm our flights for tomorrow, meaning everyone would be home for Christmas, or she was going to give us bad news again. 'Do you have some news?'

'Yes,' she said, hesitantly. 'Good and bad. The good thing is that the forecast is looking like it's going to start clearing, which is marvellous, so we'll be able to start clearing runways at Heathrow and around the UK and get some planes back in European airspace as soon as possible ... but that won't begin happening until the day after tomorrow at the earliest.'

I spoke quietly into the phone. 'So, we won't be flying home tomorrow?' *Shit*.

'I'm afraid not. I've managed to secure five seats for you and your party on the nine forty-five p.m. flight from JFK to Heathrow on Boxing Day.'

'After Christmas ... there's nothing earlier, not even for some of the seats?'

'No, I'm afraid not. The snow will still be falling tomorrow, and the clearing will begin, fingers crossed, on Christmas Eve. We also have a large backlog of passengers waiting to go home, and we have to prioritise families, elderly travellers or those with medical or assistance needs, and single travellers.'

'I understand. Would it make any difference, do you think, if we tried another airline, or flew into another airport?'

'I don't think it would, to be honest with you. We're all in the same boat . . . or plane . . . here.'

'OK, thank you. I'm sorry you're going to miss out on your husband's turkey.'

Amanda laughed, softly. 'Thank you, that's kind of you to remember. I am sorry your party won't be home for Christmas – if there was anything I could do . . .'

'Not your fault at all, thanks for looking after us all. Right, I'd better tell the others.'

'Oh, I've already informed the member of your party who stayed at the hotel, Miss . . . Jasmine Stone. I hope you don't mind. We called a short meeting in the lobby as soon as we heard this morning, with everyone who was in the hotel at the time. Better to get these things out in the open as soon as possible, like a plaster being ripped off. And I've been calling around breaking the bad news left, right and centre ever since.'

'Absolutely. OK, thanks. Merry Christmas, Amanda.'

'Merry Christmas, Ms Forest.'

I hung up and faced the room, where Dee and Abigail were in front of the mirror trying on each other's woolly hats, and the boys were googling how to make mulled wine from scratch, in case we needed to pick up any ingredients while we were out. The plan was to bundle up and take a walk to Central Park, and then pick up some things ready for a night in.

'Everyone,' I said, commanding attention. They turned to me with smiles that I was about to wipe from their faces like snow from a windscreen. 'Specifically, Girls of the World employees. That was BA . . .'

❄

The atmosphere in the room was sombre. Abigail was staring out of the window, phone to her ear, trying to call her boyfriend, Dee and Ian were sitting side by side on the sofa, not sure what to say. Jon had gone to call Virgin to see if the news was any different, but we suspected it would be the same, and Carl was sadly munching his way through a packet of cookies.

'I can't reach him,' huffed Abigail, eyes pink. 'I just want to go home and see him and now I can't even talk to him.'

'You'll get through, maybe he's just in the shower,' soothed Dee.

'But even if I do, what difference does it make? Christmas is ruined.'

'You've spent Christmases apart before, haven't you?'

'Yes, but through choice. Our *choice* this year was to

336

be together, and we had it all planned out, and instead I'm basically stuck at work.'

My eyebrows raised. I'd never seen Abigail get shirty before; it was strangely interesting to see a bit of spark under all that shyness, and occasional drippiness.

'It's all right for you,' she continued. 'You're here with your husband, and Liv's got Jon . . .' *Um* . . . 'And all I've got is Carl.'

'Hey,' said Carl, crumbs floating out of his mouth.

'Sorry.'

'All right, Abi, I know this is far from ideal,' I said, reluctantly putting the stop to what could have been quite an interesting argument, but Ian interrupted me.

'We are lucky to be here with each other, especially now you all know about us so we can be out in the open, but we wanted to be home too. We had my mother coming to stay with us for Christmas, and I don't know how many Christmases she has left. Now she'll be on her own, so I'll be sad as well, if you don't mind.'

'And you'd be lucky to be stuck here with Carl,' said Jon coming back into the room. 'Same story with Virgin – we'll be leaving sometime after Boxing Day.'

'And I'm not "with" Jon,' I said, without looking at him.

Tears spilled over Abi's eyes again. 'Fine, I'm sorry, I just—'

Knock knock knock.

We all looked at the door, and eventually Jon backed out of the room to go and open it, and that's when we heard a familiar voice.

'Hi. Some kid let me into the building. Can you take my case?' Jasmine walked into the living room. Jon, looking bewildered, followed her in, pulling her suitcase behind him. 'Merry Christmas,' she addressed us. 'It's fucking horrible out there. Can I join you, please?' She held out a large frozen turkey; a peace offering.

Abigail, Dee and Ian rushed over to give her hugs, and the ice maiden's face even cracked into a smile until she locked eyes with me. 'I don't want to spend Christmas alone, OK?'

'OK,' I said. What else could I say? 'Does anyone want a drink?'

There was a chorus of yeses and I popped open the port like I'd been hosting Christmas my whole life. I was mid pouring tumblers for everyone (OK, I didn't a hundred per cent know what I was doing with the port) when Jasmine came over to me, and plonked the turkey down in the sink.

'I might be a bitch, but I know how to make a good Christmas dinner, so maybe I can make it up to everyone a little bit.'

'You're not a bitch,' I said, my eyes firmly on the ruby liquid.

'You're not a good liar,' Jasmine said, taking a glass and gulping it down.

'OK,' I said, keeping my voice down, so the rest of the room didn't have to hear us. 'I don't like the word bitch, so I don't use it lightly, but you have been kind of a bitch, so what's changed?'

'Nothing. I just ... it's not that I don't like any of you, so I decided I'd rather be here, squashed in this tiny, quite cool, apartment with company than in that hotel on my own over Christmas. Where everyone is depressed and angry about not going home.'

'You've walked right into a similar scene here, I'm afraid. But come on, you clearly don't like me. What have I done that's pissed you off? Do you want my job? Did you want Scheana to put you in charge of the trip?'

'No, for God's sake, I am not trying to be you,' Jasmine stropped, then took a deep breath. 'It's not *you*, it's just that you remind me of my sister.'

'Right,' I said, confused. 'I didn't know you had a sister. In what way do I remind you of her?'

'I have two sisters—'

'Me too!'

'Which child are you?'

'Middle, you?'

'Youngest. And my sister – both of them, actually – are just infuriating.'

Hmph. I gulped my port. 'Thanks.'

'To be honest, they've always been kind of bitches, and I've always been a bitch because I've wanted them to like me, and I know that kind of thing is exactly what we're always preaching to young women not to be like – don't follow the crowd, be your own person, be nice, blah blah blah – and although I agree with everything we're saying it feels like every day I'm pouring salt in my own wound because I know I'm the opposite. I know I'm not as good a person as that. As the girls we deal with. As you lot.'

'Jasmine—'

'Shut up a minute, I need to explain myself. My older sisters are in these big high-flying law jobs, and both of them look at what I do and keep saying how I need a real job, and that what I do isn't important.'

I gasped. 'It *is* important!'

'I know that, that's why I've stayed! Anyway, they're always trying to be "helpful" and set up job interviews for me, but it always feels like they're just saying who I am isn't good enough.'

'But why do I remind you of them?' I said, a little bit hurt. 'I've never said that to you.'

'Because you're always so perfect, always the star of

Girls of the World, and I can never be as good at my job as you are.'

'Why not? I'm not holding you back just because I'm good at my job.'

'I know you're not. I just get frustrated. I feel like I'm always competing, whether I'm at home or at work, with my older sisters. You're basically my work older sister. Favourite child. The one I should aspire to be like.'

'I don't want you to aspire to be like me, it's better to aspire to be like you,' I said, though I couldn't help but feel smug AF right now.

'I don't want to aspire to be you either, or like my sisters, I just always feel like I'm expected to.'

'Well,' I refilled her port, 'I think you should get over it and stop worrying about what other people think. Be yourself, just preferably a slightly less stroppy version of yourself.'

Jasmine nodded, a small smile on her face. 'All right then.'

'So you and your sisters aren't close?' I asked.

'We used to be. At school we only hung out with each other. We all wore brown lipstick and matching choker necklaces, and smoked on the playing fields. We were such twats.'

'I hung out with my sisters too, though I was kind of making them hang out with me. They ate lunch with me, and one time I got them to perform with me in the school concert, but then they refused to hang out with me after that.'

'What did you make them do?'

'An interpretive dance based on the holocaust. I choreographed it myself. It was *not* a crowd-pleaser.'

Jasmine chuckled. 'I performed with my sisters at the school concert as well – we did the B*Witched routine from "C'est La Vie".'

'That sounds like it would have gone down better.'

'It did, but then we would have threatened to chin anyone that didn't like it.' She smiled and shook her head.

I picked up the remaining ports to hand them out. Jasmine and I would never have been friends at school, and I don't think we'd ever be friends today, but at least maybe we could understand each other a little better. 'I feel like I've learned more about you in the past three minutes than I have the past three years working together.' We walked back in to the living room, where Abigail was back texting, Dee and Ian were leaning into each other on the sofa and Jon and Carl were chatting by the window.

Jasmine came to a halt and looked at Dee and Ian. 'Wait, what? Why are you two holding hands? Are you together?'

'They're married!' said Abigail.

'What the *hell*? I wasn't even invited? I was only in Brooklyn, for God's sake!'

'No,' said Dee. 'We've been married for nearly a year. Now, we've all decided to take a trip to Central Park to see what it looks like in all this snow, so I'll tell you all about it on the way. Did you really not know?'

Jasmine shook her head. 'Jesus, maybe I am self-absorbed.' She winked at me and my first instinct was to look at Jon, eyebrows raised, who mirrored my expression.

❄

We were wearing so many clothes by the time we all left the apartment that we looked like a gang of Michelin men walking down the street. Abigail had wanted to stay home and keep trying her boyfriend, but we convinced her that getting pounded by a snowstorm would totally stop her mulling over her problems.

My top layer, the one just under my coat, was my NYPD sweater, and Jon's was his Knicks sweater. We were thinking of each other, even if that's all it was at the moment.

'I've never seen this much snow,' commented Carl, as we passed a café that had left its tables outside, now covered with discs of foot-high white powder.

'Me neither,' said Jon up ahead, who suddenly stooped, picked up a handful of snow and turned to hurl it into Carl's face. We all gasped, Carl the loudest, before he wiped his eyes, burst out laughing and began chasing Jon down the street, the two of them doing high-knees as they ran to pick themselves through the snow.

And that is how the Girls of the World vs. HeForShe Snowball Fight of the Century began. We turned Central Park into our very own paintball-like course, and nobody came out of it dry or warm (including a runner, who Abigail accidently lobbed a snowball at, mistaking her for Dee).

I had fun. We all had fun. We were so far away from what any of us defined as a traditional Christmas – far from our homes, far from our families, not far enough from our workmates. But actually in that moment, wet and cold and under the shadows of New York's skyscrapers, I realised I'd never felt so festive. And I wondered; could we enjoy a Christmas all together?

23 December

2 days to Christmas

❄

I woke up early on the day we had been due to fly home and did what I had done every morning, first thing: pick up my phone to check my weather app. I had a text on my screen from my mum asking me to call as soon as I woke up, so I climbed out of bed, careful not to disturb Abigail next to me or Jasmine on the floor, and crept out of the apartment to sit on the stairs.

'Hi, Mum,' I said when she answered, speaking softly to avoid waking anyone in the other homes.

'Livvy, thanks for calling. How are you doing? Having fun in New York?'

'Yep, though everyone's a bit down in the dumps about not going home for Christmas; is everything OK?'

'This is where it comes in quite handy being part of our family, I expect – you're used to being all over the place at this time of year so you're probably not bothered at all.'

I wouldn't have said that ... 'They say they're going to be able to start clearing the UK runways from tomorrow, so unless the snow comes back I think I'll see you the day after Boxing Day. I'm thinking I might just come home, rather than stay in my flat.'

'I don't think we'll be there, love – we fly to Tenerife tomorrow.'

'Surely your flight's cancelled? We were told airports would literally *start* the process of getting back to normal tomorrow?'

'It's showing as going at the moment. That's why I wanted to speak to you, actually. Your dad and I are going to head up towards London after lunch, get the journey out of the way so we don't need to worry about it any more, and then we'll be right there by the airport.'

'What if they then cancel the flight?'

'If they do, they do! Would you mind if we stayed at your flat tonight, with the Coyhamptons?'

'But isn't the weather still bad today at home? The snow's not due to stop until tomorrow.'

'That's why we want to get the drive done today – we know it'll be a bit trafficky, but much better to do that now and not be sitting in a traffic jam tomorrow worrying about missing the flight.'

'But I thought the roads were closed, I thought people were abandoning cars.'

'Your dad's bought a new satnav, I'm sure we'll find a perfectly good route. So is it OK if we stay in your flat?'

'Um . . . ' I pulled up an image of my flat in my mind. 'Can you go in first and move the clothes horse full of my underwear into the bedroom? And I know I left a few dishes unwashed, but I thought I was only going to be gone a few days.'

'Will do, thanks, honey. We'd better dash but have a nice day today and I'll call you before our flight tomorrow.'

'Mum, I really don't think you should go out on the roads today. Is Lucy with you?'

'She's in the bath being a total misery guts about missing Thailand. Absolutely refusing to come to Tenerife with us instead. Give her a call later, will you, love? Try and snap her out of it?'

'OK. But if the roads look bad just turn around, all right? Is your phone charged?'

'We will, and yes of course it is.'

'Do you have your insulin?' Mum was diabetic, and I was a worry-wart.

'Yes, love. Who's the mother here?'

'Let me know when you get to my flat, OK?'

'All right, honey, speak to you later.'

'Bye, Mum.' I hung up feeling nervous, wondering if I should have done more to stop them. Maybe if I found some scary-sounding news stories about road conditions I'd have some good solid facts to put a stop to this.

A wet nose pushed into my ear and I jumped.

'Chewy,' giggled Stephanie, pulling the retriever back. 'Hi, Livia.'

'Hi, Steph, you're up early.'

'When Chewy's got to go, he's gotta go. He's just like us,' she said, wise beyond her years. 'You look sad.'

'I just spoke with my parents and they're about to go on a car journey I don't think they should take, because it's really snowy in England, still.'

'I've been in a car in the snow before, it's not that bad.'

'But in England we're not as used to it, and I'm worried they'll get stuck.'

'Are your parents stupid?'

I laughed. 'No more than anyone is, really, and we all make stupid decisions when we really want something to work out.'

'I think you just need to trust them. They are the grown-ups, after all.' Chewy woofed and Stephanie patted him on the head. 'Shhh, you'll wake up everyone. Again. I have to take Chewy outside now, are you going to be OK?'

I smiled at this funny little six-year-old. 'I'll be fine, thanks for making me feel better.'

'You're welcome. See ya.'

I sat on the step a moment longer, worry still gnawing at me. My parents would be fine, I'm sure. But knowing how cold the weather was here, and that this was what the UK had been going through, I knew I wouldn't want to be stuck in it with only a car door between me and the freeze.

❄

I walked back inside to find, to my surprise, that everyone else was up. Jon was comforting Abigail while Dee made a round of coffees. The others were sitting around chewing their fingernails, not sure how to help.

'What's going on?' I asked.

Abigail held her phone up. 'I still can't get hold of my boyfriend. It's been two days now.'

'Well, more like one day,' I murmured.

'We're *always* in contact – we never go to sleep without

texting or calling to say goodnight, or wake up without saying good morning. We tell each other everything, and now he won't answer his phone, he's not replying to my email, or Facebook messages, or tweets, he's not appearing on the Find My Friends app. Nothing.'

'Could you call his parents?' Jon suggested.

'I don't have their number, and I've emailed them but I don't think they check it very often. What if he's stuck in the snow somewhere? What if he's in trouble? What if he's finished with me and snogging someone else under the mistletoe?'

Jon and I inadvertently glanced at each other and then quickly looked away.

'I'm sure it's none of those things,' I said, pulling the conversation away from snogging. 'Just keep trying him and try not to let it stress you out. It's only Wednesday morning, and you last heard from him, what, yesterday lunchtime? Sometime before the BA call? That's not too long. Maybe he just had a night out with friends and is suffering from a hangover? Sometimes people forget to call.'

'Especially when they're lying next to some other girl, or they're *dead*,' she wailed.

'OK, we need to get out of this funk,' I said decisively, ever the boss. 'What does everybody want for Christmas?'

Abigail looked up. 'What?'

'I'm going out and buying you all Christmas presents, because Christmas is *not* going to be ruined, but also, I don't know you all that well and I can't deal with the stress of finding six secret santa presents.'

'We don't need anything, Liv,' said Dee.

Ian turned on the news. 'Besides, everything's closed – the roads, the subways, the shops are bound to be.'

'No they're not, this is New York City. Something will be open. I'm going to have a shower, wrap up warm, and go out. So you all have a think about what you want. Also, Jasmine, the turkey you bought really needs to be eaten, I don't think it'll last until Christmas Day, so I'll buy the rest of the trimmings today and then let's have a Christmas Eve feast tomorrow, yes? Good.'

I marched off towards the shower before anyone could argue with me. This was for me, not them. I had to keep busy today otherwise I'd turn into Abigail, checking my phone every five minutes. Once I knew my parents were at my flat then I'd be fine, but for now . . .

❄

When I emerged from the shower, Jasmine was sitting on the bed in our room. 'I'm going to come with you,' she said.

'You are?'

'Don't look too excited. I have everyone's wish lists, and I'm quite good in the snow – I did a season in Whistler when I was at university. Besides, you can't go out there on your own, nobody will know if you die.'

She was so soothing. 'Thank you. I'm thinking we try Bloomingdale's first. We're going to have to walk it, but it's only fourteen blocks down and a couple over, and if anywhere has its doors open today it'll be Bloomingdale's. Also, if they're open, we'll grab a Starbucks en route to stay warm. Do you have enough layers on?'

'I do.'

'Even though you only brought enough perfectly planned outfits to last you the days of the conference?' I raised an eyebrow at her and she smirked.

'I picked up a couple of extra things over the last few days. You still have my skirt, by the way.'

'I know, I was going to wash it and give it back.'

'Have it; it suited you more than me.'

❄

Bloomingdale's was open – the only shop in the area that was, but it was all we needed. We revelled in the hot blast of air as we walked through the door, and sales assistants were keen to chat to us about how it was looking out there and how we had travelled to Bloomingdale's.

'All right, let's see the list,' I said, taking it from Jasmine. I read it over and felt a wave of fondness. Everyone had asked for such small, token things – stuff that I doubted were really on their Christmas lists but that they knew would be inexpensive and easy to buy. Dee and Abigail had both asked for candles, Ian wanted a New York Christmas decoration, Carl wanted some cookies and Jon wanted 'a second-hand copy of *The Interpretation of Murder*'. Even Jasmine said she only wanted a candle too. We were done within twenty minutes.

'I've just got something to get quickly,' she said. 'Meet you back by the Kate Spade handbags in fifteen?'

That was perfect with me, because I was itching to check in with Mum and Dad.

I called Mum's mobile and on the eighth ring, after what I presumed was a fair amount of 'Where's that bloody phone?' and 'What do you press to answer the bloody thing?', Mum came on the line.

'Mum? How's the journey going?'

'Hello, darling, it's um ...'

'Where are you?'

'Well, we haven't got very far yet. The M4 was closed so we've come down on the A36 and are somewhere north of Salisbury.'

'How long have you been on the road now? Since just after we spoke?'

'About two . . . two and a half hours perhaps.'

'And you're only just north of Salisbury? What's happening?'

'We're stuck in a bit of a traffic jam at the moment.'

I looked at my watch. It was past three in the afternoon at home. 'It'll be getting dark soon, Mum, it's not worth it. Can you find somewhere to turn around and just head home?'

'No, darling, it'll be fine. We'll only have to do this all again tomorrow if we don't carry on now. Besides, the snow's died right down here. Compared to what it has been, anyway . . .'

'But are the roads still bad? Can you see nothing but snow from where you are?'

'. . . Maybe. Listen, we'll give it another half an hour and then think about alternative options, OK?'

'Half an hour max, Mum.'

'Yes, boss.'

I hung up and thought about my parents, sitting there in their car in the cold, and nerves chewed away at me. I would be calling them back in exactly half an hour and I'd be ready for an argument if that's what it took to make them see sense.

I found Jasmine and we bundled ourselves back up

ready to face the blizzard again. 'All right, we need to make one stop on the way home at that 7-Eleven on Sixty-Ninth Street for some veggies, bacon ... do you know if they have gravy in America?'

'We'll have a look,' said Jasmine. I still couldn't believe I was hanging out with Jasmine – Kim would laugh her head off when I told her. 'Are you OK?' she asked.

I shook my head and stared through the doors of Bloomingdale's into the snowstorm beyond. 'Just ... I think all that out there is still going on in Britain as well. And my parents, in their wisdom, have decided to take a little road trip. Come on; let's get home as soon as possible.'

❄

Back in the apartment, the others had done their best to create some Christmas serenity. Jon was pouring snacks into bowls and brewing some mulled wine on the hob, Carl had found a crackling log fire video loop on Netflix that played Christmas classics music over the top of it, Dee had cranked up the heating so we could pretend the fire was real and Ian was reading through the instructions of the Game of Life to see if we could turn it into a game for seven players.

Abigail was still staring out of the window.

'No luck with the boyfriend?' I asked Jon, dumping the food shopping onto the counter.

'Nope.' Jon shook his head. Then he smiled at me and held out a wooden spoon filled with mulled wine. 'Here, try this.'

I tasted it. 'Mmm, just what I need. Did you find any spices?'

'Just cinnamon and ginger, so then I put in a bit of sugar as well.' He paused for a moment. 'Listen, Liv, can we talk at some point?'

'At some point,' I said, feeling awful for shutting him down. 'Really we can, but right now I'm having a bit of … a parent crisis and I need to go and try to sort something out.'

Jon frowned in concern. 'Is there anything I can do?'

'You can pour me some mulled wine when it's ready. I'll tell you all about it when it's sorted.'

He nodded, and before I could walk away, he gave my hand a small squeeze. A gesture that, even though he didn't know it, made me more nervous than calm. I just needed to focus on one big thing at a time.

I closed the door to the bedroom and called Mum again.

'Time's up,' I said forcefully. 'What's the current situation?'

'Well, we turned around,' said Mum.

'Oh good, I really think that's the right thing to do.'

'We had to – I forgot my insulin.'

'*Mu-um*. At least you've remembered it now. How long do you think it'll be before you get home?'

My mum paused for a little too long. 'That's the problem. We're stuck.'

'Stuck how?' I felt like throwing up. 'In the snow? In a traffic jam?'

'Both. There are quite a few cars around, but we're all in the same boat. The snow is burying the tyres and so . . . we're stuck here.'

'For how long?' I asked quietly, as if she'd know the answer.

'I don't know. Someone has called the emergency services, apparently, your dad spoke to a couple of other drivers out here, but they don't know when they'll get to us. We're not even on a road with a hard shoulder, it's just two lanes.'

'Are you warm?'

'We have all our holiday clothes—'

'—like kaftans and shorts?'

'It's better than nothing, so we've layered up, and we've got the beach towels wrapped around us. We just have to wait it out, I guess.'

'Without your insulin.' My heart was thudding. My parents needed to get home, get somewhere warm, get some insulin for Mum.

'Don't worry about us, sweetie,' said Mum. 'We'll be fine.'

'OK. I'm going to keep calling back. Do you have lots of charge on your phone? Put the car heater on if need be, no need to save the battery.'

'Yes, plenty of phone charge.'

'All right, I'm going to hang up now so it stays that way. Take care, Mum.'

'And you, sweetheart.'

I hung up and immediately called Lucy.

'Mum and Dad are stuck and Mum doesn't have her insulin,' I said, before Lucy had even had a chance to say hello.

'I thought she took it?' said Lucy.

'No, she forgot it. They're north of Salisbury, that's about fifty minutes from you on a good day, but it took them over two hours to get there. They say there are emergency vehicles coming but you need to be on standby to go and try to get them if needs be.'

'It's getting dark,' said Lucy in a small voice.

'I know. I'm going to call them again in another half an hour and if there's no news you need to get out on the road.'

'Wait, Liv, I can't drive!'

'Yes you can, you passed your test first time.'

'Third time, and I haven't driven since.'

'Well, now's your day. Which car did Dad take?'

'The Ka.'

'Oh for God's sake.'

'Liv, I can't drive his estate, it's huge. And it's snowing.'

I took a deep breath, running through everything that had to be done. 'Yes you can, if you need to, you can. I want you ready to leave when I call back in half an hour. Go and put Mum's insulin in the car, wrap it in something so it doesn't get too cold. Pack lots of food and water, and find some thermos flasks from under the sink and fill them with tea. Wear lots of layers yourself, and take extra blankets, maybe a filled hot water bottle or two if you can find any. Um . . . a torch, spare batteries, a phone cable – that one that you can plug into the cigarette lighter. Are you taking this down?'

'Yes. You're overreacting though – if Mum said the emergency people are coming anyway then you just need to chill. It'll be OK.'

'Please, Lucy, humour me and get this stuff ready. I'm too far away to help, so this is on you. Please.'

Reluctantly (but I know Lucy, and despite her sulky exterior I knew her reluctance was really down to nerves and worry), Lucy agreed to do as I'd asked. And once I'd hung up with her I thought, why not, I'll try Anne again.

Lo and behold, she answered!

'Heyyy, sister sister, Merry Christmas! Still in the Big Apple, freezing your balls off?'

It was so nice to hear my big sister's voice, and without meaning to my voice wobbled on answering her. 'Anne, Mum and Dad are in trouble ...'

❄

After talking with Anne, where she basically told me to snap out of it and of course everyone would be OK (it seems the older the sister the wiser she thinks she is), I emerged from the bedroom. I'd call Mum back in about ten minutes, but right now I needed that mulled wine.

When I walked in everyone stopped talking at the sight of my pink eyes. Even Abigail put down her phone. Jon jumped up and led me towards the sofa, slipping a wine in one of my hands and his own hand in the other.

I filled them in, and for once *they* were the ones full of answers and advice and soothing words.

'They're all going to be fine, Olivia,' said Abigail, sounding surprisingly level-headed. 'Your parents aren't stupid, they'll be completely fine.'

'And if Lucy can navigate herself around the world she'll cope with a short car trip in the snow, no problem,' Jon added, still holding my hand.

'England is small,' stated Carl, through a mouthful of Cheetos.

I nodded. 'Um ... good point, Carl?'

'I mean,' he pointed an orange-dusted finger at me, 'it's not like if you were to get stuck in the snow in the middle of Vermont. Where you might not see anyone for days and so you'd probably freeze to death and just ... die ... ' He cleared his throat. 'England is small. Your parents won't be stuck for long. They won't be too far from anywhere and someone will come by really soon.'

I realised something. When I moaned about always having to be the voice of reason for other people, I never *actually* minded, because when it came down to it I never wanted any of them to feel lost or sad or worried. And they were doing the same for me now, without me even asking.

My comfort was short-lived, and before long the ten

minutes was up and I downed my wine, heading off to call Mum back.

There was no change. No sign of any emergency vehicles. And I could tell by their voices that they were getting worried now. So I called Lucy once again.

'You don't think we should wait a little longer, for the RAC or whoever to turn up?' she asked.

'No,' I said firmly. 'Listen to me, Lucy. You need to step up here; you're the only one of us at home. And Anne agrees with me—'

'I know, she called me, like, ten minutes ago, and told me to go and shovel them out.'

'Well ... actually a shovel is a good thing to take. Grab one of those from the garage as well. But listen, you can do this; you need to do this. Just think of the heroic tales you can tell around the campfire on your next backpacking trip to Byron Bay.'

'But ... I might just get stuck in the snow too.'

I tried to soften my voice. She didn't need me getting riled up. 'I know, and we'll cross that bridge when we come to it – together. But at least you and the insulin, and Mum and Dad, will be closer to each other.'

I heard Lucy gulp. 'OK. I'll leave now.'

'Keep in touch with me; I'm right here at the end of the phone. Good luck, Lucy.'

It was a nail-biting few hours but Jon stayed by my side the whole time, and everybody else was very calm and quiet during the Game of Life, speaking in the type of voices one might use in a spa.

Nobody really wanted to play, but it was a good distraction for both Abigail and me. Jon let me be on his team, and even whispered that he didn't mind if I cheated at this game, if that's what I wanted to do.

Lucy was making slow progress, but progress none-theless. She was on a different road to the one Mum and Dad had taken which meant she still had a way to go but at least she wouldn't be stuck in the same traffic jam. Mum and Dad were still doing OK. Dad was turning on the engine and letting the heater blast in bursts, and Mum wasn't yet feeling the symptoms of high blood glucose.

It was a waiting game. When Ian stood up and wandered off for a wee break I too stretched my limbs and meandered to the kitchen to generally fiddle about. Jon followed me.

'How are you doing?' he asked.

'I want to go home. I want to be with my family. Why have I always been so blasé about spending time with them? I'm so sorry you're missing Christmas with yours.'

'That doesn't matter, and you're going to be home with your family soon. Everything's going to be absolutely fine.'

'Seven hours they've been out there now. They must be so cold. I told them not to go out on the roads.'

'I know you did.'

'When will people realise that I'm always right?' I gave a wry smile.

Suddenly my phone rang and I leapt for it – it was Lucy.

'Hey!' she said.

'What's up, what's going on, what time is it, how are you doing?'

'I'm doing well, we're all doing well. Mum and Dad have been picked up by an ambulance and they've given her some insulin, and they're bringing them to meet me.'

'They're OK? You're all OK?' Relief whooshed through my body and my colleagues – my friends – all cheered and the chatter instantly became much louder and happier. I smiled and moved into the bedroom.

'Everyone's fine. It's seven forty-five here and I'm parked up in a pub car park near Warminster – gotta love that half the roads are closed off and ungritted, but a pub car park is as clear as if it hasn't even been snowing. Fuck it's cold. I'm going to wait inside the pub in a moment but there's not much signal so I wanted to call you first.'

'And you'll be able to get home? The road you came in on wasn't too bad?'

'Nothing I couldn't handle,' Lucy said proudly, and rightly so.

'I'm so proud of you, Lucy.'

'I basically just saved Mum and Dad's lives. You owe me.'

I didn't point out that the ambulance people played a slightly more key role in that. 'You've done brilliantly. You didn't smoke in Dad's estate, though, did you?'

'Gotta go, I'll text you when we get home, byeeeeeee!'

I put down my phone and felt the weight of the world tumble from my shoulders. I picked up my *Believe* ornament from the bedside table, running my fingers over it and holding it tightly. When my family finally got together come January, I wasn't sure I'd ever let them go again.

※

I was sleepy come the early evening, tired out from – well – everything. We were all lazing about watching *It's a Wonderful Life* on the TV, and I was nestled against

Jon like it was the most natural thing in the world, when there was a small knock on the door.

'I'll get it,' I said, uncurling from under Jon's arm and making my way across the apartment. I opened the door, and there was Steph. 'Well, hello!'

'Hi, Olivia,' she said, walking past me straight into the apartment. Jon paused the TV. 'Hi, everyone, my name is Steph and I'm friends with Olivia. Are you the explorers from England? Did you guys know that the snow's stopped? The weather lady says it's going to be blue sky all day tomorrow, and they think the roads and trains will be back up running. That's good news, huh?'

Carl nodded silently and offered her the bag of Lay's he was holding.

Steph took a seat on the sofa in between Dee and Ian, and plonked the large book she was carrying down on her lap. 'No thank you. Olivia, did your mommy and daddy get where they needed to in their car?'

'Yes, well, they turned around and went home. It was a bit tricky for them for a while, my sister had to go out and rescue them.'

'You have a sister? Is she an explorer too?'

'Oh yes, far more than I am, she just got back from South America.'

'Wow. I brought my book to show you, the one I was telling you about. It doesn't have any maps of space though, and I was thinking about what you said, and now I'm thinking that maybe I want to be a space explorer.'

'An astronaut?'

'Yeah. Maybe. I need to look into it before I completely decide, but right now I think it would be really cool.'

'That *would* be really cool,' said Jasmine, and Steph nodded, pleased that the grown-ups agreed with her.

I had an idea. 'Steph, does your mummy let you go up on the roof?'

'Yeah, all the time.'

'And you said the snow's stopped?'

'Yeah . . .'

'Do you want to go and look for stars?'

'We can't, there's too much light pollution,' said the kid, all brains.

I beckoned for her to follow. 'But they're still out there, believe me. Go and check with your mum and then I think we should go on an adventure of our own.'

❄

It was still bitterly cold outside, but Steph was right – the snow had stopped. We'd bundled her up in Jon's Knicks jumper and my parka, and she and I huddled together up on the roof with New York City watching over us.

I had my phone open on an app that tells you where all the stars are in relation to where you're standing and the direction you're looking right now. So although Steph was right, and the billions of New York lights gave the night sky a dark amber glow, I could tell her that, 'Right above the Empire State Building right now is Orion's Belt. You can't see it, but it's there.'

She was fascinated, and spent a long time twirling the app back and forth and staring between it and the night sky, until her mum called up the stairs that it was time for her to go to bed. She thanked me and scarpered, and when I turned around, there was Jon.

'Hi,' I said. 'How long have you been standing there?'

'Not long, I didn't mean to creep up on you, but I didn't want to interrupt.'

I laughed. 'Steph is a very cool girl.'

Jon nodded and walked towards me, his hands in his pockets. The night breeze tickled my face and my breathing slowed as he came to a stop in front of me, his eyes soft, his face serious. *Was this it?*

'I didn't think the snow was ever going to stop—'

'I'm in love with you,' Jon interrupted.

Everything stopped. I'd been wanting this to

happen, in a very teenage crush-y way, since Macy's, if not before. But now it had, I couldn't handle it.

He was in love with me.

But when did this happen? He couldn't be in love with me – in love was too much, too real; it was a commitment road that I didn't think I could handle going down again. I exhaled, my words catching in my throat.

'I'm in love with you,' he repeated. 'And I need to know if you feel the same way. Because I think you do.'

'I'm scared,' I breathed, stammering with indecision.

'I know. But too scared, or just scared enough?'

'I don't know.' My voice was shaking and I didn't want to say these words, but I just couldn't comprehend giving my life over to someone else again, and getting hurt again. 'I don't know.'

'You don't know about me?' He looked so vulnerable out here in the dark. His beautiful eyes searched mine.

'I don't know about us.' It was out of my mouth and in the air, and it hung between us.

He stood silently for a while, kicking at the ground, not looking at me any more. 'Might you know? At some point? Is it just a matter of time?'

I didn't answer him, it was like my voice had been taken away from me as punishment for breaking his heart.

'I know I can't *make* you feel the same, but if it's just

that you aren't sure yet maybe I could do something to help you . . . decide.'

I reached a hand out. 'I think you're the best person in the world, but I'm just not sure I'm . . .'

' . . . in love with me.' He took my hand before it touched him, and he held it at his side. It hurt me that too much contact would hurt him. 'I had to tell you. You deserve to know if someone loves you.' He then smiled gently and turned to walk away.

I was going to say 'ready'. I'm just not sure I'm ready.

Stop him, stop him, stop him, my heart chanted, but my head kept my mouth closed. It was better this way. We were better off just being friends.

Christmas Eve

❄

By Christmas Eve early morning I knew one thing: that I didn't know anything. I'd been twisting and turning all night, my mind full of 'what if's and my heart full of nervous thumping and excitable little flutters.

When my brain asked me for the thousandth time that night, *What do you want, Olivia, for crying out loud?*, I sat up in the dark and stomped (quietly) out of the bedroom. I needed to call my life coach: Kim.

I made my way through the dark apartment without allowing myself a glance at where Jon was sleeping, and stepped onto the landing outside.

'What the chuff?' Kim answered on the second ring. 'It's the middle of the ni— Oh, wait a minute, it's seven a.m. Everything OK, Liv? Steve grunts a hello.'

'Sorry,' I apologised. 'Sorry to Steve as well. I just kind of needed to run something by you.'

'Go for it.'

'Do you think I should be with Jon?'

'Wait ... what?' Kim made some shuffling sounds and I heard her ask Steve to go out and get her a cappuccino. A moment later she came back on the line. *What?*

'Jon. Do you, honestly, knowing me and knowing everything, think he and I should be together?'

'So you meant it the other day, the hunky Elijah really is gone, and you're still thinking about Jon? What happened there?'

'Elijah's well out of the picture.' I filled her in on the whole sorry tale.

Kim listened without a word, just a few empathetic murmurs here and there, peppered with noises of indignation at Elijah's behaviour. Eventually she said, 'Good riddance to Elijah, you did exactly the right thing. Jon is a total yum-fest though, isn't he? Even I'm a little bit in love with him.'

He was such a good guy, and retelling the events of last night not only made me comprehend that even more, but I also found myself feeling unable to keep the smile from my face because this guy seemed to like – *love* – me. WTF? LOL.

'So now you're thinking you might have told him the wrong thing?' Kim prompted. 'And you do like him after all?'

'That's the problem, I don't know. I think it could be really good with him.'

'Ohmygod, this is so exciting,' Kim breathed down the phone. 'But?'

'But it's a big step.'

'Neil Armstrong made a big step. Getting a boyfriend isn't a big step. Stop sweating it and go and have fun.'

I laughed. I knew she knew it was indeed a big step for me, but I do dwell, and I do overthink ... unless I don't want to think about something and then I block it all out. Kim was giving me the type of talk we give to girls stressing about their exams, by taking away the 'big and scary' element.

'So what are you going to do?' she asked.

Ummm ... 'I'm ... wait, did you say it was seven a.m.? I'm going to put the turkey in the oven, that's what I'm going to do.'

'And then?! Don't you run out on me, Olivia.'

'And then ... I don't know.'

'Yes, you do.'

'Bye!'

We hung up and I collected my wits before entering the apartment. And by 'collected my wits' I mean 'pulled my PJs out of my bottom and checked my buttons were done up across my boobs'.

Was she right, did I know? I knew this: Jon made me happy, and I wanted to make him happy, and I wanted to kiss him again as soon as possible.

So should I kiss him? Just walk in there and kiss him? But I already let him down so what if he didn't let me near him? Well I was never going to find out out here, staring at the front door. Come on, Olivia, be brave. Get yours.

I was revved up, but when I stepped inside and into the living room, I saw that it had come to life since I'd been gone. Jasmine was already up and playing kitchen goddess, and Dee and Ian were pottering around tidying up empty mugs and glasses from the night before. Carl was sitting up on the sofa bed and rubbing his eyes, and Jon was still snoozing on the floor.

'Hello,' I said, side-eyeing everyone. I hadn't quite expected to see them all. I folded my arms over my chest, a little too aware of being braless in front of my colleagues.

'Merry Christmas!' grinned Jasmine, and I recoiled a little, unintentionally, from her chirpy mood. *Why can't you all go away? I need to snog Jon.*

I crept over and knelt next to Jon, who looked delicious with his hair a mess and the duvet pulled up over his shoulder. Nerves hit me; would he be angry with me today? Or hurt? Had I missed my chance with him?

'Olivia, guess what?' boomed Dee, appearing behind me with some dirty wine glasses and a piece of tinsel around her neck. God damn you, Dee. I stood up and faced her.

'What?'

'It's Christmas Eve!'

… 'Yep!' I was very pleased they were getting in the spirit, I was thrilled nobody seemed too blue about not going home, but could they all just stop being such a bunch of knobheads for two minutes?

I looked back at Jon, and suddenly he peeped open an eye, gazed at me for just a moment, and then smiled, and I knew everything would be OK. Then he made a 'shhhh' motion with his finger over his lips, and pretended to go back to sleep again.

I did know, Kim had been right. I wanted to be with Jon. I couldn't tell if it was love yet; the whole concept of love was a forgotten mystery to me, but everything would be OK. And we had all of Christmas to talk about our feelings; I could wait, I was pretty good at that by now.

'Jasmine, this looks incredible,' I said, as she put the centrepiece – the turkey – on the coffee table in front of us all. We couldn't all fit around Lara's dining table, so we were creating a food spread on that and the coffee table instead, and we'd then happily eat off our laps. But even so, as someone who'd only ever had Christmas dinner mass-made at a Christmas party, or served in a hotel restaurant with steel drums playing in the background, this was the best and most traditional Christmas dinner I'd ever had.

'Everybody, before we get started, I just wanted to say that I know you'd all rather be home with your families right now, and, Abi, I know you're still worrying about your boyfriend but at least his parents replied to your email and said he was fine, and I know I didn't want to be still staring at any of your faces this far into the Christmas holidays, but here's to you guys, my makeshift Christmas family, for making an old Grinch believe.'

We chinked glasses and were about to tuck in when my phone rang.

'Hello,' I answered, intending to tell the caller I'd ring them back.

'Ms Forest? This is Amanda from British Airways.'

'Oh, hi, Amanda,' I said, and everyone fell silent, watching me.

'Ms Forest, I have an update for you and your party,'

said Amanda, sounding rushed. 'Heathrow is back up and running and they're putting all possible planes in the air today to try and clear the backlog of passengers. If you want them, I have four seats held for your party in a flight leaving in three hours' time.'

'For four of us?' I looked around the table at the expectant eyes on me.

'Yes, which I know isn't ideal as there are five of you, but that's all I could manage. At least those people would be home in the early hours on Christmas Day. They'd be home for Christmas. But I do need to know now if you want to take the seats, and those people will need to leave for the airport ASAP. What would you like to do?'

I wanted one of those seats. I wanted to go home and have the traditional family Christmas now that my parents and Lucy would be around. But one look at everyone's expectant faces and I knew I couldn't do it to them. I put down my fork. 'Yes, we'll take them.'

'Great, under what names?'

I looked at each of my colleagues in turn as I said their names, and they all turned to each other, wondering what was going on.

'All right,' said Amanda. 'That's all confirmed for those four. I'll call you if anything else opens up for you; otherwise you're still on that flight on Boxing Day.'

I hung up.

'What's going on?' asked Abigail.

'The roads are back open, right?' They nodded. 'OK. I'm going to call an Uber and you four need to pack up your things *right now*; you're going home for Christmas.'

'Wait, what?' said Jasmine. 'We're going home?'

'Yes, but the flight is in less than three hours so you need to get to JFK super-quickly.'

Dee stopped mid-stand-up. 'You're not coming?'

I shook my head. 'No, there's no space on the flight for me. But that's fine, don't think about it, and don't any of you even dare to try and swap with me; it's all confirmed. Now, *go*.'

The four of them scuttled off, grabbing discarded socks, chargers, glasses, cables that they'd left around on the way. I turned back to Carl and Jon. 'Tuck in, gents, looks like the three of us are sharing now.'

'So what's the story back in the UK?' asked Carl, midway through a turkey leg.

'Europe is open again, and flights are back on. I guess they're staggering them because of airspace and the airlines are rushing to make sure everyone is as full as possible. So it's just us for Christmas.'

'I am such a third wheel,' Carl sighed, and Jon and I locked eyes.

I checked my phone. 'The Uber will be here in ten minutes, people.'

'We haven't done presents,' said Abigail, hurrying back into the living room.

'Let's do them now,' I said, hauling them out from under the tree. No time for dilly-dallying.

Everyone gathered together and tore into their gifts; small, token gifts, but ones they vowed to love and cherish. And then Jasmine brought out one for me. 'We all chipped in. It was Jon's idea.'

'For me?' I asked, and looked at Jon for a moment, before remembering we were in a huge rush. I ripped open the paper and what was inside made me laugh out loud. 'A Christmas jumper, and some earmuffs!' And then something else fell out– a tiny sprig of mistletoe.

Jon leaned over to kiss my cheek and I breathed him in. He whispered in my ear, 'Just in case you need reminding of the miracle on Thirty-Fourth Street.'

I opened my mouth – now was the moment – but his phone rang.

'Hello?' he said, and listened, walking away from us for a moment and then beckoning me over.

'You have about six minutes, people,' I said before making my way to him. He held the phone from his ear and covered the mouthpiece.

'It's Virgin. They can take Carl and me this afternoon as well.'

No. But yes, for him, good for him. 'You ... you have to go for it.'

He looked pained. 'I can't leave you alone for Christmas.'

I didn't have time to think about the weight of this, so I babbled, 'No, it doesn't matter about me; I'm the Grinch, I'm Harry and Marv, I'm Mr Potter, I'm Ebenezer Scrooge. I don't have chestnuts roasting on open fires, or stockings hung by the chimney with care. I don't have any presents waiting for me at home to be opened on Christmas Day, I don't even have a whole family waiting for me at home. For Christmas Day. And that's OK. It's totally OK. But these people do, and they want to be home, and New York is, actually, way better than I could ever have dreamed of, but it isn't home. And you need to go home. Your whole family is waiting, Jon. You should go.'

I could tell he was torn, and I couldn't ask him to stay because he didn't know how I felt. What were my words yesterday? *I don't know about us.* Why would he stay when he thought I felt like that?

'Carl, call a second Uber and get packing, we're going to go to the airport too,' he shouted out, his voice strained. He searched my eyes one more time. 'You think I should go?'

'Yes.' Of course he should. My feelings didn't matter.

'You'll be OK on your own?'

'It's what I wanted this whole time.' I plastered a smile on my face.

'Yes, please, we'll take the seats,' he said into the receiver and hung up. We stood in silence for a moment.

He was leaving. This afternoon. Now. It felt like time had been ripped away from us, and I'd never been so annoyed at myself for not paying attention to my feelings earlier.

There were too many people around, watching us out of the corner of their eyes, interrupting us with questions, and so he placed a hand on my back and led me quickly outside and around the corner of the building, where suddenly, in the middle of Manhattan, we were completely alone. We stood on a patch of snow-frosted grass with my back against the cold wall and Jon standing in front of me. He was looking down at me, intensely, searching my face, and my right hand involuntarily reached out and fiddled with the arm of his jumper, all of me craving contact with him before it was too late.

'I'm not asking you to stay,' I whispered, my breath clouding in the air.

'But is this what you want?' he asked, moving closer still, and I wanted it so much. All of me wanted to kiss him, wanted him not to leave. My other hand touched the soft material of his other arm, and I gently pulled on his sleeves, pulling his arms towards me.

He put one hand on my waist, which made my breath catch in my throat, and his other hand pressed against the wall by my head. I was trapped, and yes, it was exactly what I wanted.

'Do you?' I whispered.

'You know I do.' His face was close to mine, his hair, damp and tousled in the cold air, hung over his forehead. His milk chocolate eyes were warm and familiar. I couldn't believe I'd thought that wasn't chemistry, that familiarity was a bad thing for so long, because when they looked at me now nothing had ever felt so right.

'Kiss m—' Before I could finish his lips were on mine and I felt everything at once: the warmth and hunger of his mouth, his body pressing against me, heavy and perfect, the crunchy snow beneath my feet as my legs wobbled with nerves and happiness. I felt his damp hair on my own forehead, I felt the material of his soft jumper cover me and brush against my neck as his hands moved upwards and cupped my face.

My own hands couldn't move from his sides – I needed to steady myself somehow. He was everything I'd ever wanted and all of me was screaming 'It's about time!' at my silly, stubborn mind.

His thumb brushed my forehead as the kisses slowed down and he pulled away slightly, at which point I arched my body away from the wall, desperate for this not to end.

He smiled, still stroking my cheek with his thumb. 'Have a very Merry Christmas, George Bailey,' he said.

'What? Nope.' I launched at him, wrapping my arms around his neck this time and kissing him, willing him not to leave me. This time his arms circled me completely and I was in a Jon cocoon that I didn't want to climb out of.

'Olivia?' Ian's voice called suddenly and we broke apart. 'Jon? The cars are here.'

'I'm not going without you,' Jon said.

'Yes you are.' I pulled him out from behind the building. 'Go and be with your family, you have to have that proper Christmas for me, and you can tell them I'm your girlfriend and that I'll be down to visit as soon as I can when I get back.'

The next sixty seconds were a blur as I watched my team exit the apartment block with suitcases and then run back in for forgotten coats and shoes. Jon left me and ran upstairs for his own holdall, and Ian was taking charge by yelling at everyone to make sure they had their passports.

'I'll bring back anything else you forget,' I called to them as they piled in the cars.

Jon was the last to climb in, and I had to push him inside the car door. He grabbed my hand before the door closed and to the whoops of everyone else in the car, including the driver, he pulled me close and kissed me one last time.

The car pulled away and I stayed on the street for a few minutes until the cold began to set in. I was alone. I had Jon in my life now, which made me immeasurably happy, but right now I was alone, and it felt very quiet.

I missed them.

'Excuse me,' said a voice, interrupting my lonely thoughts. I looked up from staring at the snowy pavement and into the spectacled eyes of a young man, I'd say early twenties, with a wheelie duffel bag and rather grubby clothes. 'Do you know which apartment belongs to Lara Green?'

I took a large breath, trying to focus on this boy with a British accent, and not everything that just happened. 'Yes, but she's not here at the moment,' I answered. 'Is there anything I can help you with?'

'I'm here to see someone staying in her home over Christmas, a girl called Abigail. I'm Ross – her boyfriend.'

'You're "my boyfriend"?'

'Pardon? No, Abi's boyfriend.'

'No, that's what I mean – all I've heard about for days is "my boyfriend" this and "my boyfriend" that. So your name is Ross?'

He was obviously chuffed she'd been talking about him. 'Yes! Are you one of her colleagues?'

'I'm her boss ... sort of ... I'm Olivia.'

'Oh, hello.' He stuck out his hand. 'Nice to meet you. Sorry I'm a bit of a mess, I had a hell of a trip getting over here, I can tell you.'

'Wait a minute,' I said, ignoring his hand and reaching for my phone. I called Abigail. 'Abi, how far have you got?'

'Not far, is everything OK?'

'You've forgotten something really important; can you swing back around? I'll have it here waiting for you.'

'What is it—'

I hung up and beamed at Ross. 'So how exactly did you get here, considering none of us can get home?'

'It's taken me two long days,' he laughed, stifling a yawn. 'On the twenty-second I heard the flights wouldn't be running on the twenty-third as planned, and I knew Abi wouldn't make it home for Christmas. So let's see. First I took a Brittany Ferries to Santander, then I took a coach all the way to Madrid, that took a fair while, then I flew from Madrid to Dubai, from

Dubai to Miami, took the train up as far as New Jersey, where I arrived yesterday evening, and then had to wait until the roads were back open before I could get on another coach to Manhattan. I'm a bit smelly now.'

I was stunned. 'You did all that just to see her for Christmas?'

'That, and to do this.' He dug into his pocket and pulled out a ring box.

'Oh my god. She is going to say yes on the spot. Though you should know that she's pretty mad that she couldn't get hold of you for two days.'

'I know, I felt so bad. My phone battery died and the first place I could charge it was at the motel in New Jersey last night, but I didn't want to give away the surprise so I kept that friend finder app off.'

At that moment, the Uber carrying Abigail, Dee and Ian swung back onto 74th Street, and before it had even come to a stop Abigail was jumping out and running at Ross, eyes streaming, shouting a strange garble of 'How are you here? What's going on? I love you so much!'

I allowed them ten seconds of smooch time before pushing them back towards the cab. 'He'll explain everything on the way to the airport, don't miss your flight.'

'We can't leave now, he just got here,' flustered Abigail. 'I'm not leaving without you, Ross.'

'Maybe we should stay, and have Christmas here.'

'Decide what you're doing in the car, go,' I encouraged.

'Olivia, we'll stay, you take my place on the flight.'

'There's no time – I'm not at all packed, and I can't leave the apartment like this, with half a turkey carcass sitting on Lara's coffee table.'

'But, but—'

'Abi, go, and if you get to the airport and don't want to get on the flight then give it to someone else; I'm sure there'll be people there on standby who are hoping to go home.'

'Are you sure?' Abigail asked, between Ross kisses.

'Yes, go, nice to meet you, Ross, Merry Christmas, everyone.'

❄

And just like that, they were all gone again, and I was back to being alone. I went back up to the apartment and stood, surveying the modern city-equivalent to the *Mary Celeste*. Carl's turkey leg sat half eaten on the counter, an untouched bowl of roast potatoes was becoming cold, a sock, fallen from someone's bag during the dash, lay in the middle of the hall, and every single one of them had left their toothbrushes in the bathroom.

I stepped over and around the mess, the place seeming very quiet. I put the fireplace on the TV, took my ornament from my bedroom and hung it pride of place on Lara's Christmas tree. Perhaps I should change into my pyjamas, like I'd been wanting to do all week. I could do what I wanted now. But . . . the sun was shining, it was Christmas Eve, and I was in one of the best places in the world to be in at this time of year. I wanted to go out and spend Christmas with New York City.

I was staring out of the window, formulating a plan, when I heard a song, softly at first, coming from the landing outside the door to the apartment. I strained my ears to listen . . . It was a carol singer!

'*Good King Wenceslas looked out, on the feast of Stephen, when the snow lay round about, deep and crisp and even.*'
I opened the door without thinking, and there he was.

'You came back,' I breathed.

'I forgot my toothbrush.'

'Are you staying?'

'I never left.' Jon stepped inside the apartment. 'I just went down the street to make a call to Virgin, and to buy this carton of eggnog. I bet you've never had eggnog, have you?'

I shook my head, bewildered. 'But you took your bag?'

He dropped it on the hall floor. 'That was for dramatic effect. Worked, didn't it?'

'But you have to go home, you'll miss Christmas. You love Christmas, and your family want you there.'

He wrapped his big arms around me and wouldn't stop smiling. 'I have four brothers and sisters, and seven nieces and nephews – nobody in my house is going to be lonely this Christmas. But I only have one you, and spending Christmas with you means my Christmas wish is coming true.'

Jon kissed me, and I didn't protest any more, not with any part of me. He pulled back, briefly. 'And tomorrow, if this is OK with you, we're booked into the Plaza for Christmas lunch—'

'Like proper New Yorkers! How the hell did you get us in there?'

'Well, we have to have "lunch" at three forty-five in the afternoon, because it was such a last-minute booking, and we could be seated in the housekeeping closet for all I know. *Also*, I bought you a present. I picked this up a few days ago, but I didn't know if I'd get the chance to give it to you this year.'

He pulled out a box of pale turquoise wrapped in white ribbon. About the size of a ring box. Whoooooooooa, I didn't know about this, this seemed like way too big a leap into the adult world. I opened it with shaking hands to reveal . . .

A tiny silver charm in the shape of a Christmas tree,

covered in dots of Tiffany blue. It was perfect, and exactly what I never knew I wanted.

'Did you think it was a ring?' Jon asked, pulling me close and not letting me go. 'Haha. No, crazy, we only just got together. But one day I'll marry you, when you're ready. A guy only gets one Christmas wish at a time.'

* Christmas Day *

❄

Jon and I walked hand in hand through Central Park, the snow glittering under the bright sun and sky. It felt good. Not just to be with Jon, but to feel like me again. Not someone who was afraid of relationships, who'd grown apart from their family, who was always chasing a plan rather than listening to what I actually wanted, *now*, and who craved being alone. Not any more. I felt stronger now I was more exposed.

I looked at Jon, something I found myself doing every few minutes since he'd come back, like I was checking he was really there. This time he caught me.

'What are you thinking?' he asked, squeezing my hand.

That sometimes you might not get fire straight away, but actually that spark just needs a bit of stoking, but of course I didn't say that. I'm not a total crazy. 'That it turns out I'm *not* always right about everything, and Kim is not going to let me live this down. Thank you for making me *believe*.'

He shook his head. 'This was all you. You said to me a week ago that you wished you'd had time to give Christmas a go. *You* wanted this. It's not about me or anyone else "fixing" you, or telling you that you have to be in a relationship to be happy at Christmas. And you and I are a happy, unexpected outcome of a path you chose to follow to let people back in. Christmas was your catalyst, New York was your method, and connecting with people was your conclusion.'

'And my new boyfriend is my very own wise man.'

'That is true,' he laughed, and pulled me into his coat with him.

My phone rang and I looked at the screen. 'It's Anne!' This was a nice surprise. 'Hi!'

'Jack *Frost* it's cold here!' said Anne's abrupt voice down the line.

'In Miami?'

'In New York. Brrrrrrr, what the *hell* were you thinking getting stranded here, did Mum and Dad's winter sun holidays teach you nothing about how warm Christmas should traditionally be?'

'You're in New York! Where?' I stopped Jon and me in our tracks.

'Grand Central Station, or outside Grand Central Station, more accurately. If you tell me you've just got on a flight I'm going to curl up in this snow and just die.'

I stood up taller, as if Anne might be able to see me better. 'No, I'm here, staying in an apartment in the Upper East Side.'

'Oh, OK, Bethenny Frankel, let me just sling on my Louboutins and pick up my teacup dog and I'll head right over.'

'You came to New York?' I grinned up at Jon, who brushed my hair from my face with affection. My big sister came to New York, for me.

'I'm not going to let my little sister spend Christmas alone, am I?'

'I'm not quite *alone* ...'

'Are all your workmates still there? They don't count, they're not family.'

'Actually, most of them just got flights out, now it's just me and Jon.'

'*Jon* Jon? The one Mum's always saying is obviously your Mr Right?'

'Mum's never met him!'

'Maybe not but we can read you like a book.'

I grabbed Jon's hand and we started speed-walking in the direction of the skyscrapers. 'Wait right there, we're just in Central Park, I'll see you really soon.'

'Do you mind?' I asked Jon, without stopping. 'Do you mind that she's here? You and I are only just alone, but I haven't seen her for so long. And she's my family.'

'Of course I don't mind!' said Jon. 'You know I love a big, traditional family Christmas; this is as good a start as any!'

New York is a place you never have enough time in. I knew that now, and I wouldn't dwell on the fact that I hadn't made it home to my TV, or even that I hadn't had the big family Christmas this year.

The Christmases of my childhood were still Christmases, even though they weren't traditional, but I couldn't pinpoint exactly when we'd stopped thinking it was important to be together. I was determined to make that change. Next Christmas, my family were not going to know what hit them. Hint: it would likely be a party popper in their FACES.

I was grateful to my family and how they raised me, to my sisters for being the strong women they were. I was grateful to this beautiful city, and this lovely, familiar, but new man, for helping me see that there is magic in the air at this time of year, drifting in the sky with the snowflakes.

Most of all I was grateful to myself, because I felt open, and alive, and unchained to my past for the first time in years. Thank Christmas for that.

22 January

4 weeks after Christmas

❄

Send help: we're *still* in New York.

Kidding! I'm happy to report that everybody else arrived home safely on Christmas morning, and apparently had a blissfully traffic-free zoom around the M25 as they headed to their respective destinations. Even Ross and Abigail made it back on the day, just, with her staying by his side and travelling home via a few other countries en route. By the time Jon and I returned in the early hours of 27 December, the snow had all but melted, leaving slush by the roads and a thin white powdering on England's highest peaks.

My New York Christmas was merry, bright, and more fun than I'd ever comprehended it could be. Jon, Anne and I spent the big day getting fully into the spirit. After our festive 'lunch' I even had a go on one of the Salvation Army's bells. And I didn't miss my sofa for a second!

Well, that's not quite true. Boxing Day was spent doing Christmas my way: we flopped on the sofa and stared at the TV in companionable silence. But by the late afternoon I was itching to get back out there, and Jon and I spent a fab evening in matching blue hoodies watching the Knicks game at Madison Square Gardens.

We'd said goodbye to Anne the morning of Boxing Day at Grand Central Station. She was missing her sunshine and shorts, and wanted to enjoy it while she could before coming back to England for her two-week visit at the end of January. And now here we were, the evening she was due to fly in. Jon and I were in a shabby-chic gastro-pub in West London to celebrate Abigail and Ross's engagement drinks, and in a little while we'd be moseying to Heathrow to pick up my big sister.

As for my little sister, she'd reluctantly put Thailand on the back burner following an unexpected Christmas with the parents. But she'd told us, in no uncertain terms, that as soon as Anne left she was off, and we shouldn't expect to see her again until next Christmas. When maybe she could be persuaded to come home again . . .

I was listening to Abigail give a speech about her husband-to-be when Jon returned to my side with a fresh glass of champeroo for me. Could he be any more perfect?

'Listen to her,' I whispered. 'She's so much more confident now when she's back in her comfort zone.'

'I think she's more confident after you pushed her out of it, in New York,' he replied, taking a long drink of his Coke. Jon was designated driver tonight, so Anne and I could catch up in the back of the car on the way home. He grinned that big grin, which is only for me, and looking at him I can't believe I never realised how much I loved this guy. Look at that face! I could just squash it and kiss it and stroke his hair and then squash his face again. 'What are you thinking?' he asked.

'I was thinking she's going to make quite a public speaker one day,' I lied, turning back to Abigail.

Jon slipped a big, warm hand into mine just as Kim appeared, still looking bronzed and relaxed from her adventure in the Caribbean.

'Those two are too cute, I'm going to have to vom my head off,' she said.

I looked around the room. Dee and Ian, fully out of

the closet as a married couple, were making up for lost time and subjecting the rest of us to as many PDAs as possible, barely stopping for the speeches. Jasmine was there, *smiling*. Actually, she's been making a big effort lately. We both had. She's been trying hard to stop acting like a petulant little sister, and I'm trying hard to not treat her like one.

Scheana was, at the risk of sounding clichéd, glowing. She looked a million dollars with her tiny baby bump, and after the success of Lara Green PR, and New York in general, she'd had a quiet word in my ear one day at the office. She was going to need someone to be her maternity cover, and she could think of nobody better suited than ME. ME.

Jon plucked a glass of champagne off a passing tray and passed it to Kim. She accepted it, and then excused herself, saying, 'Just going to the loo.'

'Do you want me to hold your glass?' I broke away from Jon and followed her.

'No no, that's OK.' She kept walking, not looking back at me.

'Kim?' Never one to shy from following someone else into a bathroom, I stayed at Kim's heels right up until the cubicle door, when she double checked nobody else was in the room and then faced me.

'Look. Don't ask questions, but I'm just going to

chuck most of this champagne away and top it up with water.'

'Why—' I gasped. 'Are you *with child*?'

Kim rolled her eyes and looked around again, lest anybody had sneaked in through the window. 'Yes. Probably. I mean, yes, but only by a few weeks so I don't want anyone to know yet, and you know what it's like when you have a soft drink at a work event and suddenly you shoot to the top of some secret who's-preggers office poll.'

I burst out crying, which was a bit over the top but the two champers I'd quaffed already was giving me *all* the feels. 'We're having a baby,' I choked, patting Kim's still-flat stomach.

She laughed, and on came her waterworks, and as we hugged, crying, in that slightly grotty pub bathroom, a sea of memories of us doing just this at different stages of our lives swam by. That time we were both too pissed and kissed each other to impress some boys and then felt like horrible anti-feminists. That time Kim got engaged to Steve and she was crying with happiness, and I was pretending that was why I was crying too. That time I split up with Kevin and she took me on an all-night bender. And all those other times where you're on a night out and can't help but have a quick wee and a cry with your best buddy for no reason.

I pulled back, sniffling. 'Did this happen in Antigua?'

'I think so.'

'See, if you'd come to New York you'd still be able to drink champagne.'

She wiped her eyes, a light, happy smile coming through the tears, and picked up her champagne flute again, moving towards the sink. 'I know. And now, infuriatingly, I have to spend the next seven to eight months drinking bloody orange juice at every major celebration.'

'Well, don't waste it.' I took the glass from her and knocked the fizz back. 'What? I'm getting in the fake-Christmas spirit!'

'What time do you leave for the airport?'

I checked my watch. 'Oh, very soon actually. I can't believe my whole family is going to be together again, it feels like it's been so long. They have no idea what's going to hit them, my flat is decorated head-to-toe. It looks like the Christmas department in Macy's.'

'Good for you! A month later than the rest of the world, but you got there in the end.'

'Next Christmas I'm not missing out. I'm going to make sure we're all together, all of us. Everyone. My family, Jon's family, your family.' I patted her belly again. 'I'm so happy for you and Steve, and me, having a baby . . .'

'I'm so happy for you,' Kim said.

'Why?'

'Because you had a merry Christmas. And I have a feeling that this year's Kim and Olivia Christmas Twosome Party might have more than one candle on a plate and 'Let It Go' on loop. And you might even have something better than that crap Christmas tree.'

'Hey! My Christmas tree is perfect, and it's coming out every year.'

Kim laughed. 'I still can't quite believe it.'

'What?'

'That you now *believe* in Christmas. It's a Christmas miracle!'

It may be close to a year away, a year of big changes for all of us, but next Christmas couldn't come soon enough. I was already itching to go back to New York in December, leading the Girls of the World trip once again, returning to my Central Park, to my Empire State, to my 30 Rock, to my mistletoe on 34th Street.

The End
(Merry Christmas!)

Acknowledgements

Firstly, I'd like to thank the 2010 snowfall that created a whopping great white Christmas over the UK, meaning I was stuck in New York with a rapidly out-dating tourist visa. Without those snowflakes, this story idea may never have been born.

I'd like to send a thanks and a mistletoey snog to all the Little Brownies, especially Manpreet With The Good Hair, Clara, Jennie, Marina, Rachel, Ella, Bekki and Liz.

Sleigh-riding over to Hardman & Swainson for a big thank you to Hannah, and a big WELCOME to baby Nell! And a lot of love and mince pies to be handed around to her wonderful, supportive, hilarious crew of authors, Fergie's Angels, who I'm very lucky to be a part of.

As always, lashings of festive cheer to the book cheerleaders in my life; my friends and family, not limited to but including: Phil, Mum, Dad, Paul, Laura, Beth, Rosie, Mary, David, Robin, Jude, Eleanor, Peter, Kath, Liam, Katie, Ross, Corey, Emma, SJ, Sarah, Al, Ellie, Bethany, Nancy, Karen, Linda, Hannah and EX5.

Thank you to those who gave generously to Husband Phil who ran the 2016 London Marathon in aid of Children With Cancer: Rob & Sarah, Hannah CQ, David & Mary, my mum and dad, Paul & Laura, Robin and the gang, Ross & Katie, Ellie, Emma, Sarah, Mark, Isabella & Freddie, SJ, Linda, SarahLouise and Liz.

Special thank you and mention to Lara Pollard-Jones, who won a character named after her in a raffle to raise money for Parkinson's UK, and to SarahLouise Tallack who has dedicated her heart and soul to fundraising for this charity. It's an absolute pleasure to have you both be involved in my book, ladies.

And a big big big, stocking-full of thanks and love to YOU, for reading my book and spending a little bit of your Christmas with me. Happy Holidays and Mistletoe Kisses to all of you *xxx*

If you loved
Mistletoe on 34th Street
read on for an extract from
Catch Me If You Cannes

Part 1

Once upon a time Jess accidently stole a superyacht from Cannes marina, but we'll get to that . . .

Jess was awoken by her best friend punching her in the back of the head.

'*Get off me please, I have a knife and I will kill you to death!*' she shrieked, rolling over and remembering in the nick of time that she was three bunks up. In the opposite bed, Bryony lay face-down, fast asleep, a long arm stretched across the gap between them like a rope bridge with her clenched fist on Jess's pillow. Jess exhaled in relief and pushed her friend's hand off her bed.

Bryony lifted her head, her face painted the colour 'grump'. 'Jess, I love how bubbly you are at any God-given hour, but could you keep it down a bit? I *just* got to sleep.'

'If you're going to sleep-punch me I'll fight back, you know.'

'You're a lover, not a fighter,' Bryony yawned.

'Where's everyone else?' Jess rubbed the back of her head and peered over the side of the bunk at the empty beds below.

'The Scot with the earrings declared at two a.m. that he couldn't sleep, and that they should all go to the bar instead. I haven't seen them since. Did you say you have a knife?'

'I thought you were a robber. I was just warning you that I'd kill the hell out of you if you tried anything.'

Bryony raised an eyebrow. 'You couldn't kill a robber.'

'I could, I'm feisty. I do boxercise. And Zumba, if that's relevant.'

'You said "please".'

'Huh?'

'You definitely said, "Get off me *please*". Even when you think you're being attacked your manners are impeccable. Anyway, you don't have a knife with you. Did you mean your plastic spork?'

'If you'd been a robber you wouldn't have known that.' Jess sat up as best she could when the ceiling was less than two feet above her bunk, pulled on her glasses and cracked open the curtain, letting bright Riviera sunshine flood into their compartment of the sleeper train. 'Wow!'

'Urrrrgggghhhh, what time is it?' Bryony pulled the covers over her head, exposing her feet, which dangled off the end of the bunk anyway.

'Nearly seven.' Outside the window, glittery turquoise sea whizzed past. White sails shook like elegant swans waking up, while yachts the size of houses gleamed lazily in the early-morning sun.

A beam of happiness and hope pushed its way across Jess's face. It was happening, and this was exactly what she needed: two weeks of fun somewhere different, somewhere out of her comfort zone. She reached over and yanked the blanket off Bryony. '*Look.*'

Bryony scrunched her eyes closed. 'It's beautiful.'

'Bryony, *look*! We're in the South of France, the Côte d'Azur.' She pulled down the window as far as it would go and pushed her face up to the gap, breathing in the Mediterranean air. '*Bonjour la France!*' she yelped into the breeze.

Chuckling, Bryony pulled her back inside. 'Okay, Édith Piaf, I'm awake. Let's go and get you a croissant and me some strong coffee before we arrive.'

Jess couldn't drag her gaze away from the window as she and Bryony sat in the restaurant car munching their way through a basket of flaketastic croissants. The sea was a never-ending turquoise ribbon, and every thirty seconds Jess would point out yet another beachside eatery she wanted to try.

'We're still half an hour from Cannes,' said Bryony. 'I'm sure there will be plenty to eat there. Now answer the question; I need to know the protocol should this happen.'

'It'll happen, I can feel it. So if Mr DiCaprio makes eyes at me across the marina and says, "*My love, come to my yacht,*" I will warble, "I'LL NEVER LET GO" and you'll know I want you to skedaddle.'

'And you'll do the same if Zac Efron invites me for a Cannes-Cannes-Cannes? Only my code word will be "*Cougar Town*".' Bryony stuffed in another croissant.

'Sounds perfect. But George is off limits – he's a married man now. I shall be content to be just friends with him, and perhaps be the recipient of a good-natured Clooney prank.' Jess's phone buzzed with a text message. 'It's Mrs Evans. She says "Havv a NICE tIME swetie" – she's just learnt texting.'

'From you?'

'Yep.' Mrs Evans was one of her regulars at the café, ninety years young and obsessed with gadgets.

'How will those villagers cope without you for the next fortnight?' Bryony smirked.

Excitement fizzed like popping candy in Jess's chest. 'They'll be fine. I can't wait to be in Cannes. Sunshine, red carpets, rosé wine, celebs everywhere … Thanks again for letting me tag along.'

'My pleasure. Any time you want to muscle your way on to one of my trips suits me fine – this would be my idea of hell without my short-stack. Besides, when we spoke about it you were a right grump. You were practically *me*.'

The unlikely friendship of Jess and Bryony had begun the day after Bryony moved to Cornwall and joined Jess's secondary school in year nine. The personality and height differences back then were even more pronounced than they were now: Jess was the tiniest girl in their year, while Bryony towered above most of the boys, her chunky canvas high heels adding to the effect. Bryony didn't speak to anyone on her first day, just stared straight ahead among a sea of whispering teenagers. Jess had felt for this serious new girl, so made her a welcome pack of Rimmel Heather Shimmer lipstick, some Impulse O2 body spray, a copy of *Bliss* magazine and a homemade map of the school that showed which toilets to avoid and the best places to sit in certain classrooms. Bryony, who'd felt trapped in a lonely, awkward body, painfully and angrily aware that – at the time – she was the only black girl in the year, that hers was one of the only black families in the village, instantly felt a fondness for this funny, petite ray of sunshine.

They were as different then as they were now, with Bryony honing her sharp mind on crime and mystery books as she grew up to become a fiercely intelligent journalist – though not the type she yearned to be, yet – whose heroines were *Scandal*'s Olivia Pope and C. J. Cregg from *The West Wing*. Meanwhile, Jess had clung on to her *Sweet Valley* novels until the bitter end, before moving on to feel-good fiction and travel writing, all the best of which now lined the bookshelves of her very own café; she ran a homely, happy place that was like having everyone in the village come into her living room for a cuppa.

They bonded that first school lunchtime, over the pages of that *Bliss* magazine, and although life took them along different paths after school, they still got together as often as possible.

One rain-soaked Saturday evening back in April, Bryony had been visiting for the first time in weeks, and she dropped the following over a bottle of their favourite wine ...

'Guess what? I'm being sent to the Cannes Film Festival.' Bryony reluctantly worked for *Sleb*, a highly disrespected gossip magazine with a readership of close to zero and morals at about the same level.

Jess, uncharacteristically not in the best of moods, had dragged herself back to the present, forcing herself to engage in the conversation. She had to make the most of Bryony while she was here, feeling low and lost wasn't an option. She knocked back some more wine. 'Shut the *fridge* up – really?'

Bryony shrugged. 'Apparently *Sleb* needs me there. To see, in the words of the ever-eloquent, never-misogynistic Mitch, "Which stars are shagging each other and get the skinny on who's actually a fat chick.'"

'Urgh, he makes my skin crawl and I've never even met him. What a penis.'

'There's literally no point in me even going; he'll Photoshop fat onto everyone anyway, regardless of what I say . . . I know, I know, I shouldn't complain: a magazine job is bloody hard to come by and a free trip to the South of France isn't exactly the crappest thing in the world. But one day, Meems, *one day*, *Sleb* will magically turn into *Marie Claire* and he'll actually take me up on one of the current affairs features I keep begging him to publish.'

'Exactly.' Jess swirled her wine, racking her brain for something more insightful to say, but she was all over the place.

'So how's everything with y—'

'Maybe I could come?' Jess said, desperately interrupting Bryony. But as soon as the words were out of her mouth it was as if a pinprick of light had formed behind her eyes. *Maybe I could go to Cannes.*

'What?'

'Can I come?' The pinprick grew larger, the light seeping in like a sunrise. She sat up straighter. Jess's one true love had always been Marilyn Monroe, to the point that Bryony even started calling her 'Meems' years ago. From the safety of her little seaside village, through reality TV and old films, Jess dreamed of what it would be like to go to golden Hollywood and live like a movie star.

'Can you come? To Cannes? *You?*'

Jess nodded and gulped some more wine, colour coming to her cheeks and a non-faked hint of happiness coming back through. *Hello again, old friend.* Maybe it was the alcohol, maybe it was the tail end of the shittiest week she'd ever had, or maybe it was that this was the live-a-little-more chance she'd been looking for, but she really wanted to go with Bryony. Jess didn't hate a lot of things, but people who moped and moaned without doing anything about it was one of them, and she realised she was being exactly that sort of person. Her words tumbled out: 'I won't get in the way, and I'll pay for my half, of course. Yes, it's time for me to get out there and explore the world. Starting with the country closest to us.'

'Are you okay?' Bryony looked at her carefully, the transformation of her friend from hunched, wine-gulping misery-guts back to her bouncy, excitable self not going unnoticed.

'I'm fine, I'm really fine. This is good; we're still youngish and should take advantage of not having any responsibilities, right?'

'Um, right?'

'Besides, Bry, I'm a bit worried you'll throw yourself under a yacht out of sheer career frustration if you go by yourself.'

'This'll be pretty different from a relaxing package holiday—'

'I know, but that's what I like about it. It'll be completely different. It'll be busy and glitzy, and all over the place there'll be people richer and fancier than us. But you have to experience how the other half lives when you can, huh?'

Bryony nodded and went to pour herself another glass of wine but the bottle dripped out nothing more than a few crimson dregs. She peered at Jess, who waited with bated breath.

'Pleeeeease.'

'You'll keep me sane?' Bryony asked.

'Trust me, you'll be keeping *me* sane. Now let's get you some more wine, you've drunk the lot,' Jess countered with a real smile.

Join the fun online with
Lisa Dickenson

🐦 @LisaWritesStuff

[f] /LisaWritesStuff

www.lisadickenson.com